T0277151

Your Love
Is Not
Good

JOHANNA HEDVA

SHEFFIELD – LONDON – NEW YORK

This edition published in 2023 by And Other Stories
Sheffield – London – New York
www.andotherstories.org

9 8 7 6 5 4 3 2 1

ISBN: 9781913505660
eBook ISBN: 9781913505677

Editor: Jeremy M. Davies; Copy-editor: Larissa Melo Pienkowski; Proofreader:
Bryan Karetnyk; Cover design: Tom Etherington; Cover photograph: Whitney
Hubbs; Author photograph: Ian Byers-Gamber; Typeset in Albertan Pro and
Syntax by Tetragon, London. Printed and bound by CPI Limited, Croydon, UK.

And Other Stories gratefully acknowledge that our work is supported using public
funding by Arts Council England.

To my family, blood and spirit—
all ghosts are queer.

"That horror, was that love?"
—Clarice Lispector

SILHOUETTE

*the dark shape and outline of someone or something visible
in restricted light against a brighter background.*

Love stories lose their middles after a while, the stuff in
between the edges and turns. The beginning remains, as does
the end, like the damage that lingers, those remain vivid. There
are some pivot points that stick, small breakages, honesties
that sting, blurted cruelties that can retain their clarity, distorted in the moment but looking, upon later reflection, like
the dramatic keystone holding the whole thing up, warnings
that should have been heeded, red flags, symptoms, and then
there are the contingencies that skid. Beyond those, the days
that accumulate, the sex that happens and happens or doesn't
happen, the comforts and modest raptures, the small deci-
sions collaboratively made about what to eat, what to watch,
where to go—that is a vast, imprecise flatness.

PENTIMENTO

the revealing of (part of) a painting beneath another painted
over it at a later time: if the overpainting is not thick enough,
ghostly figures will appear in the final image.

I have been in a fistfight with another girl only once. I was thirteen and she was fourteen. I don't remember her name. She asked me if I'd ever been finger-fucked. I said, "Yeah," she said, "By who?" I said, "A boy named Hunter," and she said, "You lie." Then she told the other girls at school about it, and the next few days were unbearable. Finally, I saw her in the hallway and my face heated. I shouted something severe, not really made of words, and ran at her. In my head, I saw a slow-motion blow that crushes a nose, neck snapping back, but ours was a raw mess of clawed fingers and red cheeks and feet that stayed planted. Blood, none. I had too much saliva in my mouth, so I spit it on the floor, my best move.

I've been punched in the face by a grown woman, a lot, but I didn't reciprocate, it was by my mother, that was long ago.

PIETÀ

a representation of the Holy Mother with the dead Christ across her knees.

Her voice hissed through my sleep one morning and I opened my eyes to see her face, huge and an inch from mine. The sky behind her was pale, dawn. It was summer. I didn't have school, or perhaps this was before I was in school. "Quick, come on," my mother whispered. "Get up, hurry." She pulled back the blankets and pulled my arms toward her, putting them around her neck like jewelry. Her eyes were round, black marbles, and she smelled strange, sharp, like burning plastic. We fumbled for my clothes. I said something. She hushed me, finger to her lips, then she called me *darling* and kissed my mouth. She never kissed me, never called me darling. She tasted of tinfoil, and my lips stung, then went numb. She brought her dog, Nyx, a large, silver-and-black German Shepherd. The three of us rode for several hours in my mother's car, a 1974 Pinto station wagon the color of mustard, which she'd named Auntie Gethsemane the Gold.

My mother's name was—is?—Marina.

Marina smoked chains of cigarettes and sometimes sang along to blasts of radio, then she'd flick the volume knob and we'd ride in silence. She'd laugh or shout, and when I asked her what she meant, she shushed me by flapping her hand in my face. We reached a beach far from Los Angeles. It was still morning. A layer of fog has softened the scene in my memory. I remember watching Marina and Nyx walk ahead of me down the gray coast. Marina started to blend in, her blue vanishing, Nyx a smudge of black. I sat in the sand. They came back when the sun had burned away the haze. For the afternoon, I watched Marina build a figure in the sand, piling handfuls to form a body, it became the body of a woman trying to claw out of the earth. Marina laid strings of slimy, brown-green kelp across the head for hair and stuck gnarled pieces of driftwood into the lumps that were the hands, making hooked fingers that twisted upward. Nyx and I were hot under the sun. There was no shade, the sound of the waves unmitigated, crashing, all there was. No one spoke, but I remember Marina saying a few things under her breath, now lost. The sun began to set. The sky was fiery pink, and Marina's eyes went back to clear. We drove home and I fell asleep in the car. She pried me from my comfort and carried me into the dark house. As she put me to bed, she said, "You did good work today. You're going to be a great artist."

Now I pay my dominatrix to whip me as she taunts me with this: "Are you going to be a great artist?" I come best and hardest when she laughs at me for saying yes.

TROMPE-L'ŒIL

literally "deceives the eye," appearance of reality achieved by use of minute, often-trivial details or other effects in painting; a visual illusion used to trick the eye into perceiving a painted detail as a three-dimensional object.

With Zinat, I remember everything, and I remember everything about our time together because, though it was my first experience of love, after, of course, my mother, it wasn't actually love. It was something more like a comminution, a defining disintegration, it produced a truth, fundamental to survival, the fact of how easily and reliably the body, or any small thing inflicted by the aim of another thing, can be ground down to nothing. This is love, and this is not love.

Her name was Zinat Fatemah Asgari.

Zinat A was what she called herself. First day of class, professor stumbling over her name, she interrupted, "Call me Zinat A." *Zee-knot Ah.* The professor chuckled, "Well, okay then," and he called her *Zee-gnat Ey.*

When he got to my name, he also mangled me, the Eastern European first name from my mother's mother's mother and my Korean father's last name, neither of which he even tried to get right.

I had just begun my second year of art school. Zinat was in the sculpture class we were required to take as sophomores. The professor who taught it had done so for a hundred years. His name was something sturdy and manly and easy to say, like Jack Potts or Joe Dodge or Bob Mudd. He was tall and Superman-shaped, with a gray bun and beard, in his sixties, and he only ever wore a white T-shirt tucked into jeans and a belt the same color as his tan work boots. He said things like, "It's art if it tells the truth," and, "Duchamp was more of a genius than Picasso." He'd hold up thick fingers to count off the great artists of the twentieth century: Pollock, de Kooning, Warhol, Johns, Serra, man, man, man. He'd been an art star in the 1980s, solo shows at the Whitney, whatever. He'd tell the class, unendingly, "New York—New York or Florence—*that's* where you gotta go if you wanna be a real artist." This was in the twenty-first century in Los Angeles.

On the first day of Jack Potts's class, I stared at Zinat the entire time. She seemed older than everyone else, and she smelled intoxicating, I would later learn it was a musk perfume. Her body was long, rail-thin, and boyish, no curves of any kind, as though someone had drawn two parallel lines to silhouette her shape, and when she moved, she sort of floated and flopped, half ballerina, half newborn horse. I had never seen someone wear a face like hers, the expression a mask of boredom and intelligence. Her eyes were large and black, edged with thick lines that swept off the sides and lowered into sharpened points near her nose. Her hair was so black and shiny it resembled wet tar, and looked just as heavy. As I looked at her clothes, each day a new dress, which I studied every time I saw her, I began to understand that they were all handmade, not badly fitted the way my mother's had been but custom-tailored for her, elegant, simple dresses of plain but fine cotton, silk, or voile that looked like expensive nightgowns, with a line of stitches down each side and long sleeves. They stopped above her ankles, enough fabric to swirl around her when she walked but narrow through the torso and waist. Each dress was hand-painted in fuchsia, saffron, acid-yellow, cerulean, absinthe green, talon-like flowers, large eyes furred with eyelashes, scraggly looking suns grouped like barnacles, long forked tongues the color of a red stoplight, though some dresses were only patterns, wobbly polka dots and irregular stripes, and others were spans of tableaux with bent nude figures, sleeping, praying, fucking. Some had writing on them, strokes of Farsi that I couldn't understand, the curves and dots exquisite in broad, black paint. Her shoes were also homemade, chunks of heavy canvas sewn together and wrapped in strips of grosgrain ribbon that trailed behind her in many colors. A maypole. She never wore a bra, and her small, triangular breasts were, to my eyes, relentlessly perfect. A single opaque orb the color of milk and the size of a marble hung from an invisible fishing line around her neck. It rested in the hollow there, like a growth of bone poking through the skin. Later, when I saw her naked, it was still there. I never saw her without it, her own moon.

Within weeks of the new semester, she started hanging out with the group of cool boys. There were about four or five of them, one mixed-race, the rest white, all of them with tattoos of barcodes or words in all-capital letters, paint-spattered jeans, T-shirts of naked pinup girls, logos from the 1990s, money to buy drugs on a regular basis, shitty cars with good stereos. I've heard that some of them have had bits of careers since then, but mostly they've disappeared into graphic design jobs, branding, posting pictures of themselves with their more successful friends. They made large, arrogant sculptures out of expensive materials that had to be manhandled, metal, neon, so much plexiglass. Against the rules, they installed their work in the hallways, blocked the doors to the building, wrapped campus trees in Saran wrap and duct tape, and when they received a notice from the school of a fine and disciplinary action, they posted this next to the work as its title.

They were Jack Potts's boys. He gave them good grades, even though they never went to class, and he made them tutors to the sculpture studio, giving them keys for all-hours access. Zinat soon became one of them and, by extension, a Potts boy. He allowed her to work in the studio instead of going to class, making her own work rather than the assignments. She'd appear in class only for her own critiques, to present mystifying objects that looked like the stuff decorating her dresses but in loopy, shiny 3D, tubes and masses and coils made of stainless steels and resins, rare materials bent to her use.

She had a massive black dog that never left her side. Without a leash or collar, he walked beside her in the hallways and rested at her feet while she worked. He was sleek and graceful and immense, lion-sized with a proud, knowing face, the kind of dog you imagine will save you from a house fire. He reminded me of Nyx before she was crippled. If someone came near Zinat, he raised his head and fixed his eyes in defensive alarm. Once I was working in the studio on an assignment where we had to make a sphere out of cardboard, and I listened to her conversation with some of the boys. She had a deep voice, like a man's. "Yesterday I came into my room and there was blood everywhere—everywhere! 'Gohar Taj!' I shouted, but I knew he was hiding under the bed. There he was, one of my bloody pads in his mouth, blood all over his face, and he was *chewing* and *licking* and, just like"—she wagged her tongue, drooling—"*loving* it. *Loving. It.*"

The boys made sounds of disgust.

"No, no," she said. "Haven't you ever had coq au vin?"

Thinking of using Zinat as a model prickled my scalp, that someone looking at my paintings of her would see my bald desire, a record of my sucking inspiration out of her body. This was my first taste of such a thing, and the prickly heat pushed around my ears and behind my eyes and went into my stomach enough that I finally did it.

I found Zinat's email on the list of sculpture tutors in Potts's office. I wrote something timid and overly sweet, the way I used to write to my muses then—*If you don't want to or are busy I totally understand no matter what thanks anyway.* Now I write with a vagueness that protects me, at least on the surface. I know how to wrap up my words indeterminately so they have a sheen of mystery, that my work is so very important and this invitation for them to participate in it is an extension of my graciousness, but beneath it all, I'm still petitioning, so familiar it feels genetically coded, my mother tongue.

She responded in lowercase, no punctuation, not even words:

19

funfun / have
u n i
coooo
kiss
z

Zinat and I were never in a relationship the way relationships
tend to be defined. We were not a couple, not girlfriends—at
least, Zinat would have never said we were. We were, though,
together: naked in each other's rooms as we got dressed for
parties, openings, school, drunk and high, tired and hungry,
we slept in each other's beds after we'd talked until very late
and fell asleep like children at slumber parties, we left notes,
bits of twigs, pieces of cloth under the windshield wipers
of each other's cars, we brought each other gifts of flowers,
books, pages of articles, shells, we knew each other's dreams
because we told them to each other, and we shared with each
other the secret opinions that made us bitches, the wicked-
ness we felt for "them," the other women in our program who
we felt made women artists look bad, the girls who painted
sad-eyed self-portraits of their skinny bodies with sharp
elbows and knock-knees and called themselves the muses
of Egon Schiele, whose eyes frightened and mouths closed
when Zinat or I talked during critique about feminism and
political lesbianism and how the clitoris has twice as many
nerve endings than the penis.

And we especially hated those art boys who Zinat regarded
as her foolish servants, who stank of their plexiglass and
hangovers, who spoke the loudest and the longest in critiques,
proud of their complicated and unintelligible sentences with

references to Deleuze or Badiou or whoever, who all said we made "angry" art, art that was "too insular" and therefore "pretentious," or "too bodily" and therefore "emotional," or "too emotional" and therefore "just therapy." They accused us of being lesbians but framed their accusations as a rhetorical question, "Well, aren't you?" as if it were a polite gesture on their part, to reveal to us our error in judgment, so we'd sloppily grope each other's breasts in response and feel pleased with ourselves for our performance of transgression.

How cliché of me, I know. It's perhaps the most universal story for a queer girl, to fall into the hole of a straight girl and not be able to get out.

We'd meet in dark, quiet bars that had candles on the tables and languish in gossip and insults. Zinat drank sangria, I Baileys with one ice cube, this was our earliest ritual, indulging our eccentricity. The first time we met was for a drink, to talk about her modeling for me, so I could explain her purpose to my work, which was what she called it, "I want to know my purpose to your work," and I was born into something when she said that. She chose the bar, which had no name or sign, just an address and a closed door. She arrived in a long beige trench coat that hugged her lithe waist, and it was the first time I'd seen a sophisticated, womanly garment being worn by someone my age. We were all scraping by on student loans and here was Zinat, wearing something that must have cost more than rent. In that instant, I noticed my obliviousness to my own body, to the fact that I'd always slouched, kept my hair flat, long, and plain, like my white mother's thin mane, wearing thrift-store dresses two or three sizes too large for me, the silhouette another thing I'd inherited from my mother. At the sight of Zinat in her fine coat, and, when she took off the coat, her smart tits unembarrassed through the thin fabric of her dress, the dark circles of her nipples showing through, and the sight of her ordering her drink, barely looking at the waiter while I gave him my politest regard, and his eyes fastened on to her and not me, I saw the power of the artist for the first time. It was a power different than my mother's—who, yes, was a painter, like me. But my mother was monstrous. Her power seized attention with its tumult, the hysterical woman artist channeling some supernatural vision, a pretty banal archetype. But Zinat's power was magnetic. It put something together instead of blasting it apart. It was a performance she was in control of, it wasn't a mask she wore but rather a kind of glamorous mask she slipped over the face of whoever was watching her. It gave her dominion over what *she* saw. She could transform what she was looking at into what she wanted to see.

Of course, this power came from money. Zinat had it, had always had it, and I didn't. Even though Zinat was Iranian and did not remotely pass as white, she acted like a white girl, not just unaware of race, class, and how she was read or not read but bountiful and extravagant with all the freedom afforded to her, with how the entire world belonged to her. If a stranger stared at her on the street, it must only be because she was mesmerizing, not because she was a brown woman dressed in bizarre clothes. If people desired her, she simply accepted it as the natural order, of course you desire me, of course you can't stop looking. Without hesitation, she conflated this with her art, of course you can't stop looking at it, of course you want it, and this conflation didn't bother her because her art and her self *were* the same thing.

Now, twelve, thirteen?, years later, I know I've learned to practice a version of such confident ownership, although mine is a performance I worked on by watching Zinat use hers. At first, I felt jealous that Zinat's uniqueness seemed to come from her like a kind of ubiquity, as if the well of her was more beatified than mine by birthright, and I hunched over at the fact that I'd had to work so hard to cultivate mine over the years, but now I see that for artists, it doesn't matter how your self comes to be constructed, nor out of what materials, because the distinction between authenticity and performance is meaningless. All that matters is if it accomplishes what it needs to, what you want it to, that it looks good, that it feels right, and this conclusion itself becomes part of your authority to demonstrate that you are unbothered by questions of provenance, by something as false as veracity. It's a trick of perspective, of depth. Like a painting—a two-dimensional surface that, when looked at, becomes three-dimensional, a whole world with its own laws of physics, and you feel as though you could reach into it and walk around in its rooms.

That evening in the bar, on our first date, is that what it was?, I learned that Zinat was born in Frankfurt to parents who'd left Iran because of the Revolution, then raised in Vienna, Athens, Paris, and London. Four years ago, her parents had moved to Ojai to join a kind of cult for group therapy, where everyone gathered in the woods and unleashed their ugliest emotions on each other. The group was made up of wealthy people who didn't need to work, who bought avocado ranches or wineries and hired Mexican laborers to run them at minimum wage while hosting yoga retreats and seminars on enlightened consciousness. Zinat had gone to a few of these seminars before becoming bored, and none of her brothers, she had four of them, all older, wanted to keep going either, so they all moved out. Within a few months of being part of the cult, their parents became different people, shrieking at Zinat and her brothers over the phone and sending long letters in the mail. They called the police, saying their children had been kidnapped, and soon her brothers started, one by one, to move to different cities, back to London and Paris. Zinat's escape had been to apply to art school in Los Angeles.

When she received her acceptance letter and moved to LA, she didn't tell her parents because she'd decided to stop talking to them, though of course her entire life continued to be sustained by the money they put into her account every month. She bought Gohar Taj for herself as a symbol of her new life and gave him the name that meant "crown jewel." The culture of her parents considered dogs to be unclean, she told me, but she'd always wanted one, she'd been jealous of her friends at school in London, who came from families that had five Corgis galloping across the grounds of their country estates. At that point, on our first night in the bar, she hadn't seen or talked to her family in almost two years, and when I heard this, my attachment to her was cemented, for I hadn't talked with my mother in more than a year, and it was raw in me still, a hole that hadn't closed. I blurted it out, the first time I'd told anyone, and I could feel that my face was earnest and my voice squeaky as I said, "Me too!" It was like she'd thrown a rope out and invited me to tie myself to her. I grabbed her hand, but she only nodded curtly, good for you.

Having her as a model in the small bedroom of my dorm, standing or seated or supine, posed or not, it didn't matter, as I bent over my canvas, mixing colors to match her bronze skin, was the most exhilarating experience. Often, she yawned, smoked, and talked without stopping as I painted, Taj napping on the floor, occasionally snoring, he made his way into many of the paintings, her royal guard. I will never forget the night she came over, stripped, and spread her legs to show me the white string of her tampon hanging out of the solid mass of black hair and proclaimed, "The universe is in the cunt."

She talked without shame of her own vanity, how famous she wanted to be. "When they write the book on twenty-first-century artists, they'll start with me, of course." She talked about how art was the only way humans could create beauty, which meant it was the only way we could get close to the purpose of life, and that women were especially good at it, positioned intrinsically, because we alone could create from our bodies without needing any additional materials. We make *people*, she'd say. We *are* God. I'd feel the weight of my uterus then, an object inside of me that felt like an error, and my mother's, the door in her that I went through that never afterward closed, was making the right word for what my mother had done to me?

When we first met, Zinat was in a Francesca Woodman phase, taking black-and-white self-portraits in the nude, pieces of her limbs, torso, and shadow wedged into corners of a refined but decrepit house.

"Whose house is that?" I asked.

"My family's."

"I thought you didn't talk to them."

"I don't," she said, huffing through her nostrils.

She lived in a large, dirty house by the lake in Echo Park with a few of the art boys. The dishes calcified in the sink, and once the smell got bad enough, usually every couple of months, Zinat paid for a maid to come. She had the largest bedroom upstairs, with its own bathroom and a little balcony that held two folding chairs. She'd painted the room amaranth and the walls would thrum like blood, the rule of the room was fevered, like we were inside the belly of the beast. We'd lie around, smoke, and get high, too hot to move. She'd persuade me to undress without ever asking, slipping a strap off my shoulder, tugging at my T-shirt. "It's so *hot* in LA," she'd say. Her clothes would disappear from her body with a weird wizardry, often I'd look up from the book I was reading to see her sprawled naked exactly where she'd always been, as if I'd blinked her clothes off with the magic of my want. The first time it happened, there was a huge clap of it, like I'd been slapped across the mouth with the fact that I'd desired her, an absolute, crushing desire, all of the things I'd noticed about her, memorized about her, I knew the shape of her nose, her habit of licking her bottom lip while rolling her cigarettes, her smell, that smell, how many times I'd not been able to drag my eyes away.

It gave way to an ache that was mine in a way nothing had ever belonged to me before, because it was not a thing I felt, not nameable or easy like I have a crush, I desire this, but a fact of how my world had dilated, required to grow monumental to fit all of her in it, even though now I have to admit that, no, that feeling of expansiveness is one of the tricks of desire, because my world had, in fact, shrunk. At the time, I'd never thought it could be like this, and now it was and I was in it. I didn't know myself and I did, I knew something but I didn't want to know it, and I knew I wanted to know. It signaled an innovation: new information about who I was and where I should go because of that: It was her: It was me.

One night, very late, we lay on her bed side by side, thickly stoned, and spoke to the ceiling. After a pause in the conversation, her voice lowered. "Have you ever masturbated when you were stoned?"

"What?"

She rolled onto her side, and I could feel her face close to mine. "Have you ever jacked off when you were high?"

"No," I said. I'd never been stoned alone before.

"Turn off the light," she said.

I did. The bed moved, and she was climbing onto her hands and knees. My heart thumped in my head. I put my hand down my underwear but felt nothing, neither on my fingertips nor my clit, it was all numb. Zinat's breath started to wet my forehead. I heard the click of saliva in her mouth. I tried to move my hand, but it felt paralyzed, so I didn't move it, just kept it there like a little rock. She breathed harder and faster and I could hear that her mouth was open, her throat sucking on the air. Then I heard a click of wetness from another part of her, and I was washed in heat, I was sewn to the bed. She made a small noise, a whine, and pushed her head down against my chest, her hair swarming my face, squashing my breath into my mouth, and then she bit me.

27

She kept teasing me like this and I'd hope for it, wait and need and wait. She didn't do it often. She'd drape an arm around my shoulders and roll my nipple between her fingers and she'd look into my eyes while doing it, then she'd sigh distractedly, release me, hard, and go to her phone. At parties, she'd want to make out if she got drunk enough, but only for a few minutes, and it was nothing, a dry mouth bumping against mine. She'd pull her face back from kissing me and her expression would be one of blank disappointment, as if she'd opened a takeout container to find that the food had started to turn. For me, though, these moments were huge and cinematic, as though I was watching a movie of us as star-crossed lovers, the scenes gaping with longing, and the melodrama of it, my asinine craving, started to define everything about me.

There was an evening in the bloody light of her room when I thought I had the courage to tell her that I'd been making a world for us. We were getting ready to go somewhere. She was trying on different dresses, watching herself in the mirror. There was loud music coming out of her laptop, a woman's voice singing to a man about how he makes her feel as though she is alone in the universe but in a good way. I came up behind her and joined her in the mirror. I looked at us, her thinness to my lumps, her straight, tiny shoulders to my large, bowed ones, her skin dark against the yellowed milk of mine. I wanted her, sure, but I realized something new then. A great trouble. Perverse, malefic, I saw our edges, how sharp Zinat's were and how soft mine were, how my body's outline was a many-fingered hand reaching for her, medusa jellyfish, I knew her smell, how she used her mouth, I'd been watching, looking, and it wasn't only that I knew these things about her and that I wanted them, but I wanted them to be mine. There was no difference between wanting to fuck her and wanting to be her. It would've meant the end of us. She would have found me pathetic, and fuck, the neon red blazed, I *was* pathetic. All I wanted to do before her was kneel.

She must have felt me looking at her with this stupid yearning because she removed herself from the mirror quickly and went away, starting to talk about how sweetly pretty I was, how I was like a child-woman, that's what she called me, "child-woman," saying I was erotic because I was innocent. "You behave as though you've never been spanked," she said, "which of course makes you seem begging to be spanked." She huffed her fire-breathing laugh and took off the dress she was wearing. She crushed it into a ball and threw it at me. It fell weightless to the floor, the flattened lumps and strands of jellyfish washed up onshore.

Naked, she came across the room and put a hand firmly on my sternum. She pushed me toward her bed. "Sit down," she said, her voice hard, like she was giving an order to Taj.

I sat down.

"Lie down," she said and pushed my sternum again.

I lay down. She reached her hand toward my head and pulled it back by tugging my hair, and I could smell her.

"I know what you want," she said and straddled me, bent legs on either side, tits hanging in my face. She took one of them with her hand gingerly. "This is what you want, isn't it."

She'd found me. There was nothing to say.

She held herself for a moment, then stood brusquely as if nothing had happened and walked across the room. She picked up her tobacco and rolled a cigarette in silence, moving toward her balcony.

In the doorway, she stopped and turned around, as if she'd remembered something. Her face had a different expression now. I was still flat on the bed, pushed into the cushions.

"You never say no to me," she said in a careful voice. "Do you know that? You only ever agree. Anything I want. You never say no."

She went out on her balcony and smoked, naked in the hot night, her cigarette a little red heart burning near her face. I watched her. I felt loved.

John William Godward, a neoclassicist who painted gauzy women in flowing robes, committed suicide in 1922, leaving a note that said the world was not big enough for both him and Picasso.

In October of our third year of art school, Zinat found me after class, her face twitching with excitement. I'd never seen her look like that, bare with feeling. She was going to have a solo show, "My first solo show!" It was going to be in a curator's house. "Which curator?" I asked. An independent curator, "Very *important*," she said, "Where?" "In his house. I just said that." "His *house*?" "Never *mind*." She was impatient with me. "I'm having a solo show! Be happy for me! You *must* come to the opening, the show is about *you*! You're my muse!"

She said those words. It was about me. I was her muse.

She took me to buy something to wear. For her show. So I would look the part, belong there. We went to a boutique that had a fluffy, white shearling rug in the center of it and an enormous chandelier hanging from the ceiling. The clothes were hundreds and hundreds of dollars, dry-clean only, all in educated color combinations, plum with butter yellow, teal with puce.

I had my first credit card in my wallet, I could feel it smoldering in there. I'd never used it before. It was a student card with a credit line of two hundred and fifty dollars. It was so much money, it made me dumb. I'd decided on the way there to spend the entire amount on whatever Zinat picked out for me.

Zinat brought Taj into the boutique without hesitation, which made the face of the saleswoman twitch, then crease into a smile. "What a magnificent animal!" she exclaimed.

Zinat ignored this, dipped her hands in the clothes, texted on her phone, pointed at pieces she thought were good for me. She took half a dozen dresses off the rack and handed them to the saleswoman without looking at them.

"Do you want to try these on?"

"No, I'll take them," Zinat said. "I bleach them and paint over them with my own images."

The saleswoman made a face as though her foot had been stepped on. "Very well."

I could tell Zinat was gratified at this response, her face haughty as she made more piles. I floated around, voiceless, dizzy with the wealth around me. I had a vision that I was a rat, sniffing for a crack in the wall.

Zinat picked out a simple silk blouse that looked like a man's pajama shirt. It was aquamarine with the pattern of a willow tree sprayed over it in vermilion. "This," she said, holding it up to me. "It goes with your eyes." The blouse was five hundred dollars. "Where are the trousers?" Zinat called without turning her head, and the saleswoman brought them. Zinat said that she would buy both pieces for me. "It's not my money." She shrugged.

I insisted I pay half for the blouse, my little student credit card offered like a stack of pennies dropped into a hole. I wouldn't be able to pay it off for several years, not until I was my own artist with my own gallery, money, career, which would happen, but I didn't know that at the time, I had no idea how I could pay off such a sum. With interest, the total would end up being more than seven hundred dollars. But what I knew then was only that I wanted what I wanted and that it hurt, which means it made sense to me that I would have to pay, so I did. I still have those two pieces. I only wore them once.

The house of the important independent curator was in Los Feliz. His living room, where the show was installed, was as large as a gymnasium with ceilings nearly twenty feet up, the walls so immense and white that they seemed like panels of light. I'd never seen so many people at an opening before, the crowd was thick and I couldn't see whatever was hanging on the walls, but I started to feel glittery with anticipation of what Zinat might have made about me, of me.

She came through the crowd like Moses. I watched how she looked at everything, her eyes frolicking at herself, though her face was still set in its marmoreal mask. She was wearing an electric-pink coat with voluminous shoulders, though I saw the hem of one of her regular dresses peeking out by her feet.

I thought of all her proclamations of fame and success, her determination that was also casual, of course I'll be famous, but also, I want it so bad. I tried to congratulate her, I think I said, "It's starting, Zee, you're on your way!"

But she turned to me, her eyes serious. "Please do me a favor." She gripped my shoulder. "Watch Taj tonight. He will be nervous if he can't see me, but if he is with you, he will be calm. He knows you. Please keep him close."

"Okay," I said, and then she was gone, swallowed back into her evening. The crowd closed around me, I couldn't find Taj, how was I supposed to watch him in this place? He didn't have a leash, he was the size of a man. We'd have to sit outside, I decided, we'd smoke alone, wait for her, keep a vigil. But I wanted to see the art first, I wanted to see me.

When I got close enough, I saw that the pieces on the walls were composed of cut paper and photographs collaged into circular shapes of bright primary colors. They were distinctly Zinat, they looked like her sculptures and dresses, but, I saw then, it was easy, they were not very good. They looked naïve, whimsical, too symmetrical. It is difficult to say where the boundary to kitsch is, but Zinat had passed through. The bluntness of it sat on my chest, an ugly little creature squatting on my sternum. I felt embarrassed for Zinat. But also for me.

I watched the crowd, did they know the show was about me? I came to one that formed a face or a shape that inferred a face. There was nothing between me and the work, I was a narrow dirt path beneath her beautiful shoes, but it was not me. It was of Zinat, a self-portrait made of cut-up photographs. I stared at its pieces. I could make out a familiar texture, an uneven, earthy surface I'd seen before.

It was from one of my paintings. It was a photograph of one of my paintings.

Were they all made from my paintings? The label next to it gave its title—my name, then a colon, then *The Lovers*.

A lie.

Why did she think she was great? I tasted something gross. I went around the room again, looking, all of them made from my work, looking again, but they didn't look like my paintings cut to pieces, they were just photos of dirt. It gives you everything else, but does wealth also allow you the freedom to make bad art?

I lurched out of the room and found myself in a less crowded hallway, scraps of conversation snapping in my ears, "feminist," "heavy-handed," "visceral." More than once, "visceral," which was the art world's way of saying it was made by someone who is not a white man. I remember distinctly hearing a guy say, "Zee-gnat Ey, the new self-appointed guru." I found the bar and drained a plastic cup of sugary wine, then another. I looked around, I touched my hair, I breathed with comfort that it was still there.

I noticed that no one was looking at me, no one was looking at me, no one. I thought of my mother, her dark house, her aloneness, the paintings she'd labored over, how she made so much that was never seen by anyone, except herself and me. We were seen, we saw. What is an artist. It was her world, then mine, willed into existence through the sheer force of her aim. What she wanted became what I wanted.

That's how it works: what is yours first belonged to someone else.

I hid in the bathroom, splashed water on my face, went upstairs. I found a dim room, a relief after those huge panels of light. I slipped through clusters of people, but I closed my ears to what they were saying. My head was underwater. Did I let this happen? Was it my fault? I was trying to get to something to lean on, then I heard a voice, Zinat's voice, coming from the room next door. It was raised, sharp, a chant of spitting sounds and flashes of yelling. The room was like this one, murky people and sunken furniture, I wished I could find one of its walls, but they were far away. I moved toward her, the voice, and found her spread on a sofa. There were two or three men around her, crowded like onlookers to a crash. When I got close enough, I heard her saying names of women, St. Catherine of Siena, Simone Weil, Karen Carpenter, and then her own name, "Zinat Fatemah Asgari!" which she yelled much louder than the rest, and I assumed she was delivering another one of her lectures on overlooked women and how we would one day be famous. Then I saw light come from her face. It undid all my certainties about her. I pushed the men away and knelt. She wasn't looking at any of us and her face was still the smooth stone, but there was water pouring down it, "Then they took me to the hospital *again*, the fourth time! I was so sick of it by then, I was in a trance, I somnambu . . . somnambu . . . oh, what is the *word*, I was in a trance! But at last I dove into my body with *extraordinary* accuracy, you see, and I lived—*lived*—so sweet it was to *be* like that, in silence, the silence *erupted* from *within* me, I created it, me, from nothing! Listen, listen now," she reached out to grab someone, my hand darted up and caught her arm at the same time that the men leaned backward, like they were too close to a fire that had started to take. A wave of nervous chuckling passed through them. "Whoa, now," one of them said. Then Zinat hissed, "*Listen*," and tugged my arm and pulled me into her lap, "I was surrounded by *light*." Her eyes were starry, with the look that drunk people get where they look confused and angry about being confused. One of the men gave a snide laugh and said, "Fuck, this chick is *fucked*," and the rest of them laughed, loose and loud, relieved to have an explanation. For at least an hour I stayed with her, clenching her arm as it waved around, all my weight on her lap, keeping her prone on the sofa, while beneath us the city had gathered to look at her bad work that wanted so earnestly to be great. I noticed that her shoes had fallen off and her big pink coat was gone and there was a wine stain on the front of her dress, huge and brown. It was immeasurably sad to see, one of those beautiful hand-painted dresses ruined, her feet bare without their maypole ribbons, oh, where was Taj? She kept speaking in the same monotonous, hissing chant, it floated in and out of my ears, I didn't know what she was talking about. She talked about her body "quaking," she talked about "the protest of appetite," I flattened my hand on her chest and felt the thudding of her blood. In between words, she made gurgling noises of suffering. Finally, she leaned over, pushing me out of the way, and vomited a flood of red onto the floor. The wine stench hit as she grabbed at my face and said, "I didn't eat today, not one thing, it's coming back, the silence! The light!" And I finally understood, I understood, and then she shrank right there, she became a girl wilted into her illness, as my mother, too, had withered, bent beneath the icy-black ghost that sat in her brain and sang to her, just to her, the hymn of how she is not who she wants to be.

At some point, she stopped making noise and seemed to fall asleep. By then, the room was empty, except for the two of us. I peeled myself off her and went to wash my hands. They were flecked with vomit and wet with her sweat, then I saw there was a brown stain on my own blouse. I felt exhausted at this, crushed. I went downstairs. The crowd down there had thinned but not by as much as I wished.

I looked at the work Zinat had made, the vanity and pride of it, and I thought of her pushing her manicured fingers down her throat.

Zinat—whose name is no longer Zinat Fatemah Asgari but Zoe Benedict.

I've seen her picture on the social media pages of fashion magazines, at an opening, at a benefit in the Hamptons. Her hand-painted dresses have been replaced by designer gowns. She holds her young blond children in her arms, holds the hand of her white British husband, an art collector and philanthropist whose name is everywhere, they have a foundation together. In the captions, she is listed as his wife, never an artist on her own, and she grins, something I never saw her do in the years I knew her. Her smile is happy, safely happy, still sure of its value.

I tilted away from the wall and started to walk through the crowd, looking for her dog. The house was huge. Taj was nowhere. There was another room next to the room with her work. It was somehow as large as the gallery room, and I was lost. The walls of this room were bare, but it had dozens of people in it, where had they all come from? I leaned against a wall that had materialized, mercifully, and rested my head against it and felt empty. The faces of the crowd were smudges of gray, brown, dirty white. Where was Taj?

Then I heard a scream, a full-throated woman's scream, like in a horror movie. It came from outside. It made everything become a movie. We didn't want that so late into the evening, we all turned lazily. When the scream repeated itself, we had to allow the room's composure to cave in. We listed toward the front door, dribbled onto the lawn. Even more like a movie, the screams came one after the other now. "Jesus, *what*?" a woman said. Someone stumbled drunkenly at a ninety-degree angle to a flutter of chortling. The drunk person laughed the loudest.

And then it was Zinat, kneeling in the driveway in a halo from a car's headlights at her back. How did she get down here? She was viciously awake, her eyes wild with fury. A man was leaning over her, the bottom half of her was black. She was howling, the climax of the movie, but wrong, it was wrong, too shredded, someone laughed at it. She bent over the black in her lap, wrapped her arms around it, pulled it toward her. It was her crown jewel lying still, sprawled in the road. He was too heavy for her to lift, but she still tugged at him. A voice behind me calmly said, "Is that her dog or something?" and there were murmurs in the crowd. I saw the man leaning over her, frantic. "It just jumped in front of the car! I couldn't see it! It's night! No one would've seen this thing!"

Zinat kept making her dirty, violent noises, rocking the big dark body back and forth. I pushed through the crowd, called

38

her name. She jerked her head up, and the serpent let its tail fall from its mouth. The end. Her eyes landed on me, and she lifted her arm and quaked a finger. Her hand was shining with blood. I tried to speak, to apologize, but I only felt a fast, slimy rush of humiliation spread across my face. She said one word next, it sounded like an egg getting cracked, I didn't know what to do but to turn around and go away from it, her serrated voice shooting it like an arrow, I felt it land in my back, the last word she ever said to me: "You—"

CHIAROSCURO

the management of light and shade in a picture; from Italian, "bright dark."

Since I was a child, whenever I close my eyes to sleep or feel myself falling into it, emptying out as though rehearsing how to be finally dead, I have the vision that I'm being followed by a massive, opaque, black cube, thirty feet by thirty feet by thirty feet, that hovers behind my head, attached to me by an invisible force, never more than a centimeter apart from my body, swiveling like a dance partner as I turn my face, so that, though I never see it, I know it's there, following me, guarding, and watching me wherever I go, and it is soundless, which gives it a dignified, dreadful authority, like the eye of God. At some point, perhaps when I started to need one, I accepted that this was my guide. This dark cube. A monumental, light-less mass, the color and shine of obsidian, who knows what storms inside, its surface calm, a soft touch at the base of my skull. I feel right when I think of it.

ULTRAMARINE BLUE

literally "beyond the sea," a deep blue pigment made by grinding lapis lazuli into a powder; for centuries the pigment was primarily used in depictions of the Virgin Mary because it was the most coveted and expensive in Europe; during the Renaissance, contracts between artists and their patrons would stipulate how much ultramarine was to be used in the painting ("at least five broad florins an ounce for the robe of the Virgin").

I despise my mother and haven't spoken to her in fifteen years, and yet I am her duplicate. I carry around her face, so those fifteen years hardly feel motherless, it's as though I see her every day. My entire childhood, she could never shut up about it, our likeness, telling me, "You're just like me!" Not only that I looked *like* her, but *was.*

Despise isn't the right word. I don't know the right word.

When I was very young, there were many things about my mother that seduced me. In my memory, she glows blue. When she speaks, blue smoke falls out of her mouth. She leaves swipes of blue on the chairs she sits in. Her bedroom had only blue things in it: blue bed, blue furniture, dozens of photographs of the ocean tacked to the walls, and a blue rug in the center of the floor, oval-shaped, like a little pool. I'd step around the edge of the rug, scuttling close to the thrill

41

of falling in. All of her jewelry was the scattered green-blue of agate, which she wore in large chunks wrapped in copper wire, she made it herself, using needle-nose pliers and a hammer. She of course wore only blue clothes.

In my memory, she's taken me to the pool to teach me to swim at five years old. She keeps her hands underneath me as I float and flail. She twists me around her. Reflections from the water streak her face. Then there's a luminous bruise spread across her back and thighs, crawling up her rib cage, a blast of octopus ink black in the clear turquoise of the chlorinated pool water. "What's that?" I am frightened. "What's what?" she says. "You are all blue, Mommy!" I point at her. She laughs and lifts a wet finger, pointing back. "So are you, baby."

Her eyes were the blue of sea glass and small. Her hair was thin and dark, the color of mud, with frayed ends a few shades lighter, the weathered, middle-aged-looking hair of white women. I wish I'd inherited my father's hair, black, thick, coarse, Korean, and fabulous, but that's not how family curses work. I got my mother's.

When I was thirteen, I began to sneak her clothes, the handmade dresses and the jewelry. I'd cover them with my own baggy pants and sweatshirts as I left the house, then unveil myself after I turned the corner. I loved how I felt with the dresses dragging on the floor, heaving around me in waves, bubbles at once aqueous and impermeable. Once the principal took me into his office and whined that I needed to learn that his school wasn't a fashion show, and I triumphed at how distant his sad, small life was from ours. Then, when I was sixteen, I spilled wine on one at a party, the best one, the one carefully dyed in multiple baths so that it looked hyaline, I'd watched her do it, it took her weeks to make, and I couldn't get the stain out. That's how she caught me. I put it back in her closet with the mark, where it hung for ages, turning black in my mind, thumping like the heart under the floorboards, until finally she found it, and it was almost a relief when she came crashing into my room, waving the dress in her fist. After, my face bright from being struck, she blew out a mocking laugh and raised her chin proudly. "*You* can't have these. *These*"—she twisted her gratified mouth—"are *mine*."

Every summer, she would set up a tent on our patio and live there until fall. The tent was only slightly smaller than the patio, but still she managed to fit a small beach chair on the concrete near the flap of the tent, and she would sit in it, smoking, in the morning and during sunset. She even made a little campfire in the evenings, lighting junk mail and crumpled paper towels in a pie tin. She called it her "vacation." I didn't realize that this was odd until I was in middle school and a group of girls came over to my house. "Why is there a tent in your backyard?" one of them said. "My mom lives there in the summers," I said. "She *what*?!"

Another thing I learned from her about how to be an artist was this insistence on what made her peculiar, how to turn quirks into terribly important tasks, obsessions into sustenance, this, my kink, produces meaning beyond me, my caprice is my purpose and it has immeasurable value and you should feel quenched by its importance.

She spent most of her time pursuing this purpose in the garage behind our condo, which she converted into her studio and which seemed to me to be the scariest and most interesting place on earth. It was a cave-like room, almost as large as our whole apartment, with wooden walls the color of raw umber. There were no windows, light came from a few fluorescent tubes and some spindly clip lamps. My mother hung her paintings from the ceiling in rows, canvases larger than an arm span in either direction with no stretcher bars, not parallel to the floor but askew and jumbled up like dead skins. They were collaged with feathers, garbage, stuff from the junk drawer, notes in her handwriting that she'd scratched out and layered with sand or dirt or glittering dusts, which she kept in jars along the floor, where they were fuzzed with mold. I was in the garage once when she opened one of the jars and the smell, rotting and brackish, wound around my head and stayed there for years. That stench bled into the pointed, resiny smell of the medium you need to paint with oils, and I can smell it now. I paint with oils, that smell is my madeleine.

She built shelves that went up to the ceiling and I was hypnotized by the stuff on them, straining to see her secret treasures, but she didn't like me looking at her stuff and she'd snarl if I asked to see anything in particular. On one of the shelves was a row of fishbowls, each lit by a small bulb and containing a betta fish a different shade of blue. My mother spoke often of her fish, referring to them by the mystical names she'd given them, Nicodemus, Methuselah, Persephone, I can't remember the others, and they were her confidantes, Nicodemus was telling me that it will rain tomorrow, I was explaining the new painting to Methuselah. They lived in my mind as the tiny sentries to her studio. I was never allowed in the studio for more than a few minutes at a time, but the fish got to live there, got to watch her work, knew her magic, and I was jealous of them. My mother is a Pisces. Was. Is?

In the middle of the room was the table she worked on, large enough to lie on and stretch your arms out like Jesus and still not touch the sides. On the side farthest from the door was a little corner cut out of the table, where she worked on the collaged parts, huddled over the canvas with a frown. When she painted, she crawled on top of the table and, with a paintbrush in each hand, stretched her arms around in arcs and waves. She became covered in paint. It made her out of breath. When I paint, I take great care not to look like her, no windmilling arms, no frantic strokes. My arms are at my sides, I am calm and thoughtful. But sometimes I forget, I get restive, I get stains on my clothes and hands, blood is strange that way.

My mother's birth name was Marianne, but she changed it in her early twenties, before I came around, to Marina. She never called herself *Mom* and didn't acknowledge me if I addressed her that way. Sometimes she'd say, "So should I call you *Daughter*?" with a smile like she'd slashed open her face.

Marina once told me that you can kill someone by holding your thumb against their jugular for ten minutes. But how close—how close!—you'd have to be to hold someone by the neck and flatten their veins with such tender determination. They'd have to let you, want you to. She'd put her thumb into my neck to demonstrate.

Many times, I would sneak into her bedroom and put my face and hands into the clothes in her closet or her dresser drawers. It was so gratifying to see all those blues lined up

45

together. The smell coming out of the closet was heady and dirty, unlike anything I'd smelled at the time, unlike anything I smelled in the years after until I smelled Zinat. In one of the dresser drawers were photographs of my mother naked, grabbing her breasts and crotch. She looks surprised in the photos, as though she can't believe what she's being told to do, can't believe she's consenting to whatever orders she's receiving, she looks as though she's waiting for it to be over. I stared at these photos many times, throbbing with the threat of getting caught. In photos I see of myself now, I have the same expression on my face, a patient squirming, as though I am bearing a cruelty, but because I do appear to be bearing it, the cruelty looks self-inflicted.

SFUMATO

a misty, indistinct effect achieved by gradually blending together areas of different color; from Italian, "smoked."

Elizabeth Valentine was in my third-grade class. She was small for her age, among the smallest of the girls, and wore her blond hair in a sweet bob with a headband. Her favorite color was purple, and she often wore it with pink or red. She never wore blue. She liked the same things I did, books, inventing fantasy games at recess, drawing, and she was good at spelling and reading, like I was. She was one of the smarter kids in class, as I was, but also kind and good-natured, which I was not. We were not friends. She was best friends with a white-faced girl with dark hair and light eyes, like me. They were together always, those two, orbiting around each other, inventing complicated games on the playground, and they didn't include me in their games, they spoke to each other in their own private language, like my mother with her fish.

One day, Elizabeth came up behind me on the playground and declared, "I'm going to be you from now on." I felt that sink in, her body back there, about a foot away, then I took a step forward. I heard her take a step forward, too, and could see her shadow in line with mine, as though she were stitched to my back, as though there were all these tiny hooks of her in my skin, and immediately I hated it. I turned and shouted at her to stop. She turned so that I was facing her back, and then she repeated my gesture and word into the air, at the grass, with great precision. She shouted, "Stop!"

"Elizabeth! Stop!" I cried at the back of her head.

"Elizabeth! Stop!" she said. She somehow knew to lean a little from her waist, and I saw that this was how I was standing, too, and that it looked feeble and ridiculous.

"I mean it! *Don't!*"

"I mean it! *Don't!*"

I started to cry. "Stop! Stop! *Stop!*"

"Stop! Stop! *Stop!*" she said, mocking my sobs.

I reached to grab her, but she knew I was coming and darted away, also flailing her arms.

"I mean it!"

"*I mean it!*"

She danced in circles around me, pitching her voice higher and higher with each repetition and giggling between breaths. How quickly I'd become so powerless. No matter what I did, she spat it back at me, making it stupid. It made me think that I *was* stupid, she was showing me my real self. Then I thought, what if she never stops? What if this goes on forever, my whole life and all its gestures and words swallowed by Elizabeth Valentine? In my belly there was a hot spike of anger. Then her name rocketed out of my mouth with such ferocity, even I was scared. I didn't know my voice could sound that jagged. It gave me power or gave my power back. I lunged for Elizabeth Valentine, catching her arm. I brought it to my mouth and bit. The tension in my jaw thumped in my ears as I held the skin between my teeth, and she twisted and screamed. I bit as hard as I could until I felt better. There was a string of saliva still connecting us when she wobbled back from me in shock. Then she ran away.

A warm calm spread through me, and I spent the next moments as though I'd been happily alone all day. I had been collecting leaves and rocks to make a diorama, and so I started to gather the material that had scattered by our feet, I got onto my hands and knees, picking up my collection, content, even glad, I might have hummed to myself.

Then I heard my name shouted, and I looked up to see our teacher striding toward me. Elizabeth trailed behind with a red, crumpled face, holding her arm as though it were a baby. The teacher said my name again and demanded that I stand. So I did, dwarfed by the teacher's shadow, hanging my head.

"Did you do this?" the teacher said, holding up Elizabeth's arm, which had a bright circle of tooth marks on it.

"Yes," I said.

"Do you know how serious this is?"

"Yes," I said, which was what I was supposed to say. It didn't seem that bad. I looked at the wound. It wasn't even bleeding.

"What do you have to say for yourself?"

I looked at my feet. "I'm sorry," I said.

"Say it to Elizabeth."

I dragged my eyes up to Elizabeth, who stared at me with a bewildered, injured expression. She looked puny, hiding behind the superior mass of our teacher, cradling her elbow and hiccuping with sobs.

49

"I'm sorry," I said, which let the power summoned by my roar slip out of me. I was weightless without it.

"Come with me," the teacher said. She took me by the arm and lugged me across the field. I would've drifted away if she hadn't been holding me down. The other children on the playground looked corrugated through my tears.

I was taken to the principal's office, where I sat at a large table and was made to fill out an "incident form." It asked what had happened, why I had done it, and if I regretted it. At the bottom, along with the largest blank space left on the page for a student's answer, was the instruction to explain why my behavior had been bad. I labored over this, writing with effort, stopping and starting, murmuring to myself. After I filled in the lines, I reread my answer and was horrified: I'd failed to convey how Elizabeth had enraged me. The words I'd written—"then Elizabeth started copying me and I got mad"—were empty of all that heat. I got mad? No, I had been transformed!

I needed to be able to explain that *Elizabeth* had started it, that *she* began the craziness, that it was her plan, masterminded to establish a game beyond normal taunting to launch us into a world of will and rage. I was just reacting to her, I'd had no choice but to be brutal because *she* was being brutal. I tried to add this to my answer, clarifying that biting her was the only way to make her stop because yelling at her hadn't worked. But when I reread this, my stomach sucked into itself. Biting was worse than hitting, I understood, it was grossly worse, I *was* an animal, I *was* bad.

The office was cold and bright. The principal, Ms. Aguerro, looked up from the papers on her desk every now and then to glare at me. "All done?" she said. "No," I said. "Let's go now. Time to finish up," she said. "I'm trying," I said, but as I said it, I realized I was taking too much time to try to convince people of my innocence, which betrayed my guilt. There was no right answer I could use to persuade Ms. Aguerro not to punish me. There was only the right answer in the sense that it was the accurate one. I had decided to bite Elizabeth because it was the only way to beat her and I needed to win, to dominate and hurt her once and for all. At this thought, a vast expanse opened around me, and I felt relieved to have so much room for myself. I erased what I'd written and put a new answer: "I felt like biting her so I did. It felt right and it worked. I wanted to make her cry and feel pain and I did." The truth. I gave Ms. Aguerro my paper. She held it in front of her face for a while, then looked at me over her glasses.

"Do you know there are more germs in a human bite than in a dog bite?" she said.

The next week, I was moved to a different class, and I rarely saw Elizabeth Valentine after that, except on the playground, where I stayed away from her. I pretended she no longer existed, that my magic had worked and I'd vanquished her. I only thought of her when the school counselor, whom I was required to visit weekly for the rest of the year, brought her up, asking me yet again why I had bitten her. My answers never satisfied the counselor. He asked the same questions at every session.

Marina was the only who understood. When I came home the day I'd bit Elizabeth, the school had already called, but Marina was in her studio, and she said nothing when I arrived, so I thought she might have decided it was beneath her notice. At dinner, though, my father was furious. He lifted a big, flat hand and knocked it against the side of my head. "Stupid!" he yelled. "What is it with you and this girl?" Marina sat with her chin on her knees, feet on her chair. Her eyes were swimmy. "She was a threat," Marina said, shrugging. "You had to do something. You couldn't just *let her get you*." She knew. She got it right, without my having explained. And the smile she gave me was charitable and tender. I'd never seen it before, and I never saw it since.

DILUENT

any liquid that will dilute or thin the paint, as opposed to dissolving it; adding diluents allows coatings to flow smoothly through holes or other crevices.

Once when I was nine or ten, just before he left forever, my father and I wandered into a store that sold lava lamps and posters of marijuana leaves, and the man behind the counter leaped up with a hoot, declaring that I looked exactly like his wife. He flashed a photograph from his wallet of a moon-faced white woman with small eyes. My dad said, "Well, look at that," and I said nothing. I resented the man. I did not think I looked like that woman. Although her eyes were hooded like mine, it was clear that she was white, that the skin above her eyelids was only sagging rather than phenotypically folded into my half-Korean monolid, a feature I was very proud of at the time. But I realize now that I did resemble that woman, and I resent that. It wasn't until recently that I accepted the fact that my eyes are small, and since they're the same watery blue of my mother's, I look less like my father and more like a white woman who has been somehow touched with an errant dab of unwhiteness, with eyelids that droop slightly and are already perforated at the corners by wrinkles. Only other

Koreans ever spot them as epicanthic, and rarely, at that, I often have to point it out first. People only tend to pick up on what I don't look like. They'll say, "You look different. Are you mixed?" What I am isn't legible as a distinct otherness but as a weird, furtive force of dilution. There is something that has thinned my eyes at the corners, puffed my eyelids into one creaseless plane, flattened the bridge of my nose into moony cheekbones. My father's Korean-ness lurks invisibly inside of me, none of it enough in itself to create an obvious impression of Korean-ness. Saying that I am Korean American is an act of claiming it, an insistence, it does not seem like it should belong to me because my body was designed according to the instructions instilled into me by my mother's white-mutt genes, some German and Czech, watered down after generations in America. I've always been bitter about being neither one total thing nor the other because, even at the place where my differences converge, it's muddy, I get all smeared. I remember watching a documentary about David Lynch and, at some point, he's shouting into a cell phone, "Get me an Asian—no, a *Eurasian*! Get me a Eurasian!" I wondered if I could get the part. And then, at high school, a group of girls once simpered a new word at me: *Hapa*. When I got home, I asked Marina about it. "Eh, that's just mixed," she said. "Asians mix a lot." She couldn't have cared less about my father's Korean-ness. Or mine. The absence of Korea in our house felt like a subtle, harmless absence rather than an explicit banishment, it was simply the way things were. My mother never talked about my cousins, aunts, uncles, or grandparents in Korea, you'll never meet them anyway, she'd say, and that was that. She forced my father to eat his kimchi outside, squawking about the stench, like a corpse's foot, she'd say. She would occasionally comment on how tall he was, weird for your kind, was how she put it. Later, once he'd taken up with another white woman, one who could realize his first-generation-immigrant aspirations of class and comfort, Marina stopped talking about him altogether, except now and then to mutter that his lifelong dream was to marry someone who owned a car that had a remote-controlled key. This, a couple of bland barbs, was the sum total of her sentiments about half of me, and over the years, without my father around, the paternal side of our family faded, cut down by time and the heavy but insipid silence of racist indifference. What I inherited was my mother's face and hair and dry skin that ages terribly, her poverty, her failures, her narrow opinions, and the onus of it all is whether an inheritance isn't always a curse. From my father, I received only his absence. This means that the spectacle I present to the world is white, and worse, it is white trash, ratty beach towels over the holes on the old couch, sneakers with their soles flapping because we had to wait for a new pair to go on sale, thin, straw-like hair lank with too much cheap shampoo, boxed food heated in a microwave, slurs pitched around for fun, mocking the poverty, the lice, the stinking food of the Mexicans, the Blacks, the Indians, that's what my mother called them, such spite in those unnecessary definite articles, such malevolence in her voice, perhaps because all of them were far cleaner, healthier, and better-educated than we were. I got lice four times as a child, there were stains on the carpet, bad, sallow skin, drugs done without fear of police, used beer cans as interior decorations. Of course, what she hated was herself. What we, hated.

IMPASTO

paint or pigment applied thickly, especially when used to achieve surface texture.

When my father left us, it was like any other day, except he was not in it where he usually was. I was ten. I was sent back to the school counselor, although I can't remember how that happened. I hadn't done anything, as with Elizabeth Valentine, to provoke it, and I've wondered if Marina called the school and asked them to arrange the appointment, though that seems unlikely, as she would've had to admit her defects to deem it necessary.

My mother's blues got bluer. I'd come home from school and have to squint into the shaded blue light that streamed through the air, no matter how many lights I turned on, the air was like a sea fog, and the house was cold and dark and wrapped in a plume. It was like our house was on fire but invisibly so, only the smoke and the damage could be seen as they grew and grew. Marina stayed in her garage. For two years, I don't remember her ever coming out, except some nights, very late, when she'd career into my room, stinking of alcohol and waving her arms with sloppy, chaotic spite, thrashing at my furniture, she'd pull everything out of my closet, sometimes her face would be covered in blood, I don't know how, I don't know, and then, standing in the mess, up to her knees in stuff she'd brought down to the floor, she'd pant with her mouth open, not looking at me, not here, not with me, but somewhere else, and there would be silence for a second. First, a hurt would rush in. But I got good at blocking it. Then she'd tell me to clean up all the shit, and I would.

GROTESQUE

*an extravagant piece of art featuring animals and
plants in fantastic or incongruous forms.*

Before I am born, Marina has a dog named Nyx. Nyx is a rare
kind of German Shepherd, black and silver rather than gold.
She resembles a wolf with a knowing wisdom, the kind of dog
who feels earthquakes coming. There are photos of me as a
baby nestled in Nyx's bed, her majestic face turned to me like
a mother's. Marina talks about Nyx's mother, whose name was
Jade and had won awards at dog shows, and how Nyx cost
eight hundred dollars as a newborn, which was more money
than my mother had ever spent on anything. Marina says Nyx
is her sister and her only friend. One afternoon, after school,
when Nyx is nine years old and I am six, she starts to jerk
violently in her bed in the dining room. At first I think she is
doing something normal for a dog, but she keeps smashing
her head into the floor. I rush to her, watching her claws make
scratch marks in the wall, white foam accumulating on her
black lips. A tightened noise gurgles in her throat. I run to
the garage, shouting, Marina, help, something is wrong with
Nyx, and Marina looks up from her painting, and her hands

grip her jaw, and she blasts past me into the house. She falls on Nyx, scooping the dog into her arms. They rock from side to side, Nyx thrashing, Marina wailing, a mangled song and dance. I help Marina carry Nyx to the car, but we drop her a few times because she swings out of our grip. She is bigger than me. On the drive, Marina says the Hail Mary over and over and over, the only time I've ever heard her do so, keeping her hand on the dog, who flops in the front seat and on the floor, the sound of Nyx's nails scraping at the doors mixes with the prayer. There's the smell of dog piss and shit. I sit in the back seat, watching Marina's searching, frantic eyes, which seem to glow red. I cry and pray in silence, mouthing the words of the prayer as Marina chants them like a hymn. At the vet, I wait alone in the waiting room and hear sharp, throttling squawks coming from behind the door, interspersed with my mother's shouting. I imagine that the doctor has his arms deep inside Nyx's body. I imagine that Marina is lying next to her sister on the steel table, giving up her own organs. After some hours, Dad arrives and we sit together in silence. He is annoyed, already weary at what he knows will happen next. He is called into the room and I hear adult voices talking behind the door, then he comes out and sighs, pinching the bridge of his nose. Marina insists that the dog live. We take Nyx home. She's had a stroke. She is paralyzed. She lies on a piece of Marina's painter's canvas in the corner of the dining room. We have to flip her over every few hours, but still, she grows gaping bedsores that gleam pink in her fur. Marina sits with her, placing the loose head in her lap, and pushes food into the mouth with her fingers. The smell of dog shit settles on the house, new shit that cuts and old shit that's been there for hours, then days. The canvas darkens with puddles of piss. Dad is the one who notices it has stained the linoleum underneath, and he and Marina fight about how the dog should be put down. Marina refuses. The nights after these fights, she sleeps next to Nyx like a guard. At first, these fights are frequent, but eventually they stop. We don't have people over, and if someone knocks on the door, we only open it a crack. I tell my friends they can't come to my house because my mom is redecorating. At some point, I no longer have friends to lie to. Marina starts to smell of dog. Nyx's body flattens. The bedsores grow. I discern shapes in them, continents becoming Pangaea. Marina collects Nyx's fur and tries to weave it into yarn, holding out tufts to show me how soft it is, see, some tribes make all their clothes from dog fur, she says, which is a lie, but she makes a necklace of it that smells like grease and wears it every day. Nyx lives, somehow, for four years in her corner of the dining room. When she finally dies, her stench remains in the house, and I don't think I've ever stopped smelling it. It's why I hate dogs now, that stink, how it settled into my mother's body and became her own.

II

FÊTE CHAMPÊTRE

an early eighteenth-century genre of French painting
showing courtly figures at a garden party.

The Twin appeared in summer, at a party in Silver Lake.
I noticed her hair first, which was tall and messy, like a pile of
wire on top of her head, because I was wearing mine like that.
Summer nights in Los Angeles. The hosts were three men and
one woman, the guys thin and sleek as otters in short shorts,
shirts made into tank tops with ragged holes sagging to their
elbows, and the woman ghostly in something translucent and
puffy. At first, I thought the elaborate black bustier under the
film of her blouse was a scoliosis brace. Basil and mint plants
grew, or tried to, in cracked pots on the long, narrow patio,
and everyone smoked. I was talking about Tarkovsky to a man
whose name was Amadeo. He had long, thick eyelashes, like
swipes of Magic Marker coming off his eyelids. We flirted.
He told me his name meant "loved by God." "So does mine!"
I said, drunk. Another man approached us, handing a beer to
Amadeo. "I'm Anton," he said. We began to speak about heartbreak, Anton was in LA to recuperate from a bad breakup. To
demonstrate his sensitivity, he scratched my name into his

forearm, where it swelled into wormy lines. "You see?" he said. "I'm a romantic." It was then that the Twin wandered into the frame. To my right, beneath an orange tree, with that tall hair. Both Anton and Amadeo turned to look, and it wasn't long before they left me to talk to her.

That summer was the hottest on record for Los Angeles, which happens every summer in Los Angeles. By ten in the morning, the sky was baking, and it baked each day until midnight. Apocalyptic as it felt, there was a window of warm, almost erotic darkness that opened after sunset, when everyone poured out onto their porches or dead lawns or street corners in summer dresses and shorts. During the day, though, it was sweaty bodies in cars, shimmering on the freeway with air conditioners set to high, and if you were prone to migraines, as I am, simply stepping outside without sunglasses triggered the aura. Most days, I stayed inside with the curtains drawn until dark. I slept naked, without sheets. My room, which had terrible ventilation, would climb to 110 degrees Fahrenheit and I'd wake in the night, broiling in my own skin, so I'd rinse myself in a cold shower and go back to bed, still wet, hoping I'd be asleep again by the time the water evaporated. I had a longing to be mildly drunk all the time, so I kept bottles of cheap white wine in the refrigerator and drank them like soda all day. I was preparing for an exhibition in the fall in LA and another one in Berlin the summer after, so I had a lot of time to spend alone. I wore only white and made white paintings. It was my white period. By August, having long hair was insufferable, so I cut mine, late one night in my bathroom, with the cheap scissors I used to cut paper in my studio. I pulled and twirled tufts of it and brought the scissors close to my scalp. Then I didn't look like the Twin anymore. When I was through, I looked like the kind of boy whose parents let him have candy for dinner, the kind whose mother cuts his hair in the backyard. His mother says it's because she can do as good a job as any professional, but really it's because they can't afford it. I looked like the kind of child who tries to grow up from that but doesn't.

After Amadeo and Anton wandered off to talk to the Twin that first night, I drifted away to get a new drink and find a cigarette. I wished for drugs but was too lazy to commit to earning them. I got caught talking to some people who had been in the same MFA program as me. We gossiped. Someone put on a dance record and the night got later. I heard a woman squeal to a man, "Baby, I'm dancing!" He responded, "I can see that." The patio roasted in a dark orange light, crowded with gaunt, nocturnal creatures, eel-like bodies twitching together in groups, collapsed on couches with their wrists flicked up toward the night. I thought of illustrations from centuries ago, showing witches' Sabbaths, peasants and winged demons in a gleeful stupor, feasting and fucking and flying around in dark woods. The bodies in the air or crawling on the ground in Goya's *Black Paintings*, the ones he showed to no one, painted directly onto the walls of his house when he was old and deaf. On a small couch, under a string of Christmas lights, sat the Twin, Amadeo, and Anton, crushed together in a line. Amadeo had a plate of cake resting on his knees. The Twin was reaching across Anton to scoop some of the cake off Amadeo's plate with her fingers. She bent her head back and dropped it into her mouth, exposing her long, naked neck to us all. The Twin closed her eyes as she chewed, and the men did not hide what it made them see, and though I hated it, I couldn't stop watching either.

IMPRIMATURA

*a first coat of color applied to the ground of a painting.
Many artists find it easier to judge color if their painting
surface is not white, so a thin, preliminary veil of a tint such
as red ochre, burnt umber, or cool green is brushed on. It is
particularly effective in the shadow areas of the image.*

In the month before I met the Twin, strange things were
already happening. My gallerist wanted me to meet someone
named Colomba Espinosa, a young, wealthy Argentine who
wanted to buy my paintings but insisted that I first come to
her home to "speak about the work." I liked her name, so my
gallerist didn't have to ask twice. Colomba Espinosa lived in
the Hollywood Hills in a mansion she shared with an old aunt,
who was descended from a lost strain of European royalty. The
house was at the top of a hill, where the winding mountain
road with blind curves turned into a private one-lane driveway.

I rang the bell. Dogs barked on the other side of the door.
A young woman in orange and black with a cracking smile
opened up and let me in. The dogs crawled around my legs.
There were at least four, all large and all black, and I struggled to
keep upright. The woman informed me that she was Colomba's
assistant. "We've been expecting you. Please come in."

The foyer felt like a dark, open mouth. There was the fetid smell of wilting tulips in a vase near the door. I heard a gurgling sound and saw a large room to the right, where there were aquariums along all the walls, glowing green, with little black and orange and yellow fish bodies moving around in the water. As I was led to Colomba's room, the assistant's orange and black clothes hovered ahead of me, the colors blurring as the light grew dimmer, and I thought of Rothko. I had the sensation of being led to the center of the house, deep inside the mountain. But then we climbed stairs.

"Colomba receives her guests in her study, which is also her bedroom," the assistant said and brushed her knuckles against a closed door. When Rothko killed himself, he sliced his wrists *and* took an overdose of pills, just to be sure.

A voice from inside, a bird call, a chattering sounded.

The assistant made herself scarce, and I entered a room that felt like a garage for two or three cars, darker than the rest of the house. I saw that there was a birdcage large enough for four adults to stand upright in, centered in the room. It was filled with tiny fluttering bodies, pale smudges of yellow. Around the cage was a low cloud of fuzz that had come off the birds. Curtains were pulled shut against the windows, which ran the length of the one long wall, floor to ceiling, in a row, so the room shone with a hemic orange light from one side. Diane Arbus, too. She slashed her wrists and took too many pills.

Colomba came from somewhere behind me. She was making a humming noise. When I turned toward the sound, the first thing I noticed was that her jaw was enormous. It stuck out far in front of her face, the bone thick and curved like a Habsburg, but she was somehow beautiful. She was barefoot and wearing a long, loose dress the same honey color as her hair and skin and the shaded light. She got very close, her eyebrows stalking her hairline, and she said, "It is the face in your paintings! The same face! It is you!" She held both her arms out like Frankenstein's monster and tried to grab me. "You have the *exact*, I mean the *very same*, the *precisely same*, *exact* face as my *mother*!"

Colomba gripped my shoulders and I was pulled to the other end of the room, where there materialized a desk whose drawer she tugged open. She dipped her arms into the drawer and pulled out a pile of old photographs, which she let tumble onto the desk and floor as she pawed through them. When she turned around, she was waving a photograph in front of her face. "See! *See*?" Still not smiling. Accusing, as though I'd stolen her mother for myself.

And it was true. I did look exactly like the woman in the photograph.

"She could be *you*!" Colomba said.

"Yes," I said, and though I felt ashamed, I thought, what luck.

PAREIDOLIA

the tendency for perception to enforce meaning on a random or ambiguous image, so that one sees an object, pattern, or meaning where there is none.

Not long after the party where I saw the Twin, I placed an ad looking for models to be photographed wearing all black on a set covered in flour. I wanted to use the photographs as reference for the paintings I'd make for my show in November, and if they were good enough, if they still had me, I'd continue making them for Berlin. I'm not the kind of painter who sees images in my mind and is then pulled toward the canvas to channel them. I need to hold a paintbrush, push paint around on a surface, see the thing struggle to life in front of me. The idea I had for these new paintings, though, was a little hook in my head, a single thumbtack pushed into my brain. I kept seeing white. White as a texture, clotted cream and milky batters, and white as light, brilliant, like a kind of intelligence, something that saw and probed. I wanted my canvases to radiate with it. So there was also black, there had to be. I needed something to give the white weight or, by giving it a ground to stand on, afford it its weightlessness. The force of them together was what was hooking me, what they did to each other and how.

I stitched the ad together with quotes from Genet, Acker, Sontag's "erotics of art," nothing too esoteric but not too legible, either, and I requested that the models only respond if they were okay with being naked but not in a sexy way. I posted on all my social media, so it was public and attached to me, who, what I wanted. The times I'd done this before, I'd been anonymous on a site of classifieds, just a stranger with no name, searching for someone or something. This was the first time I'd used my real name to ask the world for bodies, for muses.

Named or not, I always needed them, I couldn't work without them.

My muses were unaware that they were my muses. I never told them, they inhabited only the world of my gaze, seen from far away, and this was the attraction, the act of looking at them from a distance, so I could reach into the gaps of what I couldn't see and try to guess at what might be in there. It was more fun not to find out. Then they lived in my imagination with and for me, always. I dreamed of them, I talked to them when I was alone, I made social media accounts under different names so I could lurk and screenshot their selfies, I snuck photos of them on my phone, downloaded whatever was posted online, I hid them from my lovers, I lied. Once, a guy I'd been sleeping with for a few months asked about a painting I had made of a male but feminine torso cradling its shaggy genitals with large paw-like hands, filled in with gobs of red. "Is that me?" he asked, the hope in his voice making him instantly irrelevant. "Of course," I told him. My muses were never men. When the work they inspired was finished, I'd invite my muse to the opening of the show and spend the evening watching for their reaction. Once, I approached a muse as she stood in front of one of her canvases and said, "Does it look like anything to you?" She said no with a thin laugh. "It's okay," I said, "just curious." We had an innocuous, polite conversation, which left me safe but bored. Another muse, a young trans girl with metallic-purple fingernail polish and an asymmetrical haircut, didn't pause when I used my courage at a party to ask them to be one of my models. "No way," they said. They shook their head, mouth sucked into a straight line. Refusal only made my appetite more insistent, and insistence was better for the work. Over the next days, I painted a slender trans femme body in stains of green, like a coat of hair, with the limbs lengthening into dog legs, as it bent in half to lick itself, and others where they were being led around on a leash, the skinny neck harnessed in a collar. I would have been too embarrassed of my infatuation to make these if their body had been in my cold painting studio, kneeling with gooseflesh. But alone, I was free to watch and use and take, their body so generous to my looking. My muses came in phases, a few months of obsession that fueled the work when I felt a hunger for nothing else. And then this would dissipate, let me go, sometimes I'd feel as though I was waking from a strange dream that had lasted years, other times it would simply be gone, no longer where it had been, and I would move on.

Making my search for a muse public this time brought a thrill, along with a wider pool of prospects, the potential that someone might arise who was strange and remote yet had heard me call out for them. Also, my gallerist had been suggesting it, saying that it would build intrigue for the next show. I didn't feel strongly about this advice, but I acceded to it because it interested me as opening another kind of gaze. I was looking at my muses, but I was also looking at my audience looking back at me while I looked at my muses. What would they see that I didn't?

Among the replies I got for my ad was a message of a few sentences with eccentric punctuation, slashes for periods and so many parentheses, from someone whose name appeared in my inbox as *Ghost Ship*. There was an image attached to the note, and when I clicked on it, the Twin was staring me in the face. I was returned to the party, her arm stretched out, fingering the cake. The photo was taken during the late afternoon, a wash of golds and blues. I printed out the photo on my expensive printer, using the good archival paper, and I tacked it up on a wall in my studio and stood back to look at it. Her eyes were hooded with half-lowered lids, but her chin was tilted up and she looked awake. Her features were white, she was white. A woman with a proud face is one thing, but a white woman with a proud face is another. The only white woman I'd ever painted before was my mother. She'd looked proud, too, on the surface, but this didn't come from anything proud within her.

Painting is a magic trick, a feint of light, perspective, texture, how to make something shallow gull depth. It is the deceit of the surface that exhibits depth. A painter traffics in this deception, and a good painter makes it seem not like deception at all. A good painter takes you from looking at a painting, from what you see on a flat plane, hanging on a wall, to looking at a being, something that becomes alive in front of you and then keeps living, even when you're not looking at it. It's not that you are looking at a representation of a woman named Mona Lisa, the little square of her image, but that you are looking at Mona Lisa herself. She has an inherent place, and she occupies it. What something looks like becomes what something seems like, becomes what it is.

I don't know if my self-portraits count as portraits of a white person. The thing about whiteness is that it's hard to paint precisely because it's everywhere and in everything, and I mean this in terms of any kind of whiteness. It's the image of the world. And yet no one can see it for itself because there's no such thing as an ipseity of white. Even right out of the tube, there's titanium white, zinc white, foundation white, flake white. There's one drop of yellow, one drop of black, three drops of red, two drops of blue, and then you have ecru, ivory, alabaster, cream, eggshell. There was first lead white, which we used for millennia, but it was poison.

A trick of the trade is that black makes white look more white. All colors do. Put black or red or green next to white, or better, beneath it, and the ontology of each has teeth. This can be done sharply or not, hard or soft, coruscate it or blend. However it is done, now they can define each other because they make each other what the other is not. And I mean this in terms of any kind of whiteness.

I was trying to reach into my own whiteness, where it started and ended, if it was surface or infrastructure, skin or spine. Whitewashed or leaden.

I left the Twin's face on my wall for a few days to see how it made me feel. I'd go over and stand in front of it, letting my eyes fall into hers. I stared and then stared longer. In some dirty part of me, there was a stir of indignity at wanting to stare at a beautiful white face like this for so long. It made me feel guilt and shame, and I didn't like that some part of me liked feeling that way, which was why I kept reaching into it.

CLEAVAGE

occurs where adhesion between layers has deteriorated due to
faulty materials or improper methods of application.

LA in the fall, Berlin next summer. There was a lot of anticipation for these shows, from myself—I am ambitious—and
from my gallerist in LA, Alexandra Nakamura Spector, who'd
recently started to push me more than usual. I hadn't had a
solo show in almost three years, which meant that my next one
needed to bring me to a crest, and to have two within a year
was not an accident. At the end of last year, Alexandra had
called, she rarely called unless in the froth of activity before
an opening, to say that a Berlin gallerist was interested in
giving me my first solo show in Europe, and this was a good
opportunity to start committing to an idea, shouldn't we put
something on the books in LA, too, yes, she knew I'd been
drifting, that was part of the process, I'd been drifting for a
while, hadn't I, but now, now would be good to get back into
it, she was so excited to see what I was working on. Most
LA artists said yes to every invitation that came their way,
shoving their work into whatever theme had been cooked up
by whatever curator. I guess I was lucky to be able to tell my

gallerist I needed more time, to tell her something other than yes, but I knew I had reached the limit of that. Alexandra had been working to build a "journey" for me over the last few years, her hands on my back, moving me up, and it would need to start paying off now. I'd made a little ripple when she'd tossed me into the water three years ago, a splash that surged into more attention than I'd expected, perhaps more, too, than Alexandra had expected, and we'd been surfing the centrifugal momentum ever since, so if we played it right, this next body of work could bring me up to a new wave of career, fame, money, value. My paintings would go from selling for thirty thousand dollars apiece to sixty thousand, maybe even seventy-five thousand. Alexandra never said those numbers outright, but I could see them prancing at the backs of her eyes.

"I want to time it with the fair in February," she'd said.

"Guess I'm moving up in the world," I'd said, letting eagerness get into my voice.

You can tell who's who in LA and how much they're worth at that moment by how close their shows are scheduled to the big art fair in February. I'd always been far. My first solo show had opened in June when everything's dead, but Alexandra gave me the show when I'd been out of grad school for just two years, which was a big deal in its own way, for a young artist like me, it was everything. There was a white guy in my class who'd been picked up right before we graduated, but that was because he made large paintings of foamy silver swirls that would look as good in lobbies as in living rooms, and also he was beautiful and very tall, and also he'd been sleeping with the editor of a glossy art magazine.

It had been a long courtship with Alexandra. She was half Japanese and most of her artists weren't white, so I thought it was conceivable that I might have a place with her, though we would never speak about race. She'd been an architect for twenty years before opening her gallery in her late forties, when she'd bought a space in an industrial part of East LA and single-handedly gentrified the neighborhood. Even though her gallery had since accumulated prestige and a couple of big names, it was still small compared to the established blue-chip behemoths with West LA addresses and annual operating budgets of several tens of millions, and this meant that Alexandra was an outsider, a trait she'd transformed into punkish cultural capital. Her artists tended to be outsiders, too, or were spoken about as though they were, as though they'd been ignored, forgotten, plucked from obscurity, and of course the first one to speak about them this way was Alexandra herself. She'd pick up sculptors when video was the rage, which made her seem prescient when the market swung toward sculpture a few years later. By then, the most interesting sculptors were already in Alexandra's stable.

Alexandra first saw me at my school's open-studio day, then asked for a few studio visits, which motivated her to invite me to be part of a group show. The painting I put in the show sold immediately and several of her friends said I was a good decision (Alexandra told me this later), which led to half a dozen more studio visits, and finally, she consummated our relationship by offering me a solo show two years down the line. This sort of thing is normal. The stakes are high but the flirtation is slippery, oily, it covers you in a thick, fatty film and it's hard to see. But because it feels smooth and slick, you assume you are going some-where fancy.

At the end of every one of our meetings, Alexandra would say something mawkish like, "I'm just *so* glad I got this oppor-tunity to talk to you," as though being in my presence for forty-five minutes was all she'd wanted from me. Her emails would begin, "I'd love the chance to continue our conver-sation," and in the beginning, before I knew how to do it, I always had the urge to respond in all-capital letters: WHAT ARE WE ACTUALLY TALKING ABOUT? WHAT DO YOU WANT FROM ME?! BECAUSE I KNOW WHAT I WANT FROM YOU! But I learned to play along, to be available at all times to meet with her, to know all her references and have something glib and clever to say about them, to be argumentative and forceful when talking about my opinions of another's work, to be determined and charismatic when talking about my own, and to smile and nod when we talked about anything that involved her representing me, in short, to demonstrate my worth to her while performing that we were friends, to pretend that money and business were far from our concerns. The art world, like painting, is a trick of surfaces.

Over the years, I've honed my skills at this courtship, and I've learned that it's less a courtship than a kind of fight, an elegant but still brutal demonstration of power. If you're the one without the power, you have to be especially cunning in stealing it back. For instance, now I know that the best way to meet an important curator or gallerist for the first time is to schedule a lunch meeting with them and order only water. If you miss the international business-class flight that an institution has bought for you, you call and say in your most lackadaisical voice, "I guess you'll just have to buy me another one." It's a fight that isn't meant to draw blood, which makes it even more humiliating for the one who loses, because it's hard to tell why exactly they've lost, there are no corroborating marks on the skin. A trick of surfaces.

Johannes Wiedewelt was named royal sculptor to the Danish Court in 1759, and although he received many commissions and much financial support throughout his life, he supported two sisters, a cousin, and a servant, he was deemed, by all accounts, too generous, and he lived in terrible poverty. What is sometimes called his "final catastrophe" was the sinking of a shipload of marble, which he had bought with borrowed money. Not long after he lost the marble, he drowned himself in a lake.

What I liked most about Alexandra was that, even though we played at being friends, I knew she was predatory, I'd seen her make people cry. I wanted to learn how to do that, be like that, too.

She cut a tough figure: fifty years old, an unnaturally taut forehead, a blunt black bob, and a hyenic mouth painted brilliant, drippy red at all times. I liked that her mouth was the most honestly costumed part of her. She wore angular blazers with exaggerated shoulders and ferociously tacky sneakers with bulbous rubber soles and multicolored stitching, all of which must have cost a fortune and signaled that she paid attention to a certain kind of fashion blog. I'd sometimes let myself enjoy thinking that my paintings had bought this or that item in her wardrobe, and it was an enjoyment wrapped up in a sort of ignominy, like having a fetish for pissing yourself in front of everyone, which felt presumptuous, because that's the secret pleasure in a fight like this. It presumed there would be an everyone in front of whom I'd be humiliated at all.

CRAQUELURE

the fine cracking that occurs in the varnish or pigment of old paintings.

It took me a while to find the right dominatrix. The most beautiful are the most expensive, and that usually means they are white, because often the word "beauty" is a synonym for "whiteness," but I wanted one who wasn't white. And they tend not to be queer. I finally found Mistress Anka. She had a long black whip of a ponytail. Japanese Korean, worked out of her loft apartment downtown. You could also call her Goddess. She stipulated that you pay her "tribute" in hundred-dollar bills offered in an open envelope, which you were to hold above your head while naked, on your knees, at the beginning of each session. You were to kneel in the doorway, your ass and bare feet sticking out into the hallway, before she decided to let you in. You weren't allowed to look her in the eye, but, when booking the session, you could request, by checking boxes in a Google form, what you'd like her to wear. I preferred the nun's habit in latex. I liked the prayer of being on my knees, offering one thousand dollars to a nun with a whip. Although I could not afford it, I made an appointment as soon as I got home from Colomba's. In the

Google form, I checked the box that said I wanted "antihumiliation," a kink where affirmations and kindness are used to shame. You're a great artist. Your next show will earn a million dollars. I broke. Cried for her to hit me harder than she ever had before, and she did.

ISABELLINE

*a grayish, yellowish, dingy white named after Isabella Clara Eugenia, the
sovereign of the Spanish Netherlands in the sixteenth and seventeenth
centuries; the story goes that when her husband went to war, Isabella vowed
not to wash her underwear until he returned (she thought the war would
be a quick one), and Isabelline is named for the color of her linens when
the siege ended three years later. This story was eventually discredited.*

That night, I dreamed about the Twin, although she appeared
in disguise. I was walking through a long hallway filled with
trash and I kept picking up objects at my feet, an old boot, a
dirty bucket, a roll of tape, and at the end of the hallway, there
was an old crone wrapped in a yellow headscarf who told me
that I owed her four thousand dollars. I unwrapped her head
from its scarf for a long, long time to find that her face was
a ball of light.

Colomba was the first to buy a painting of mine all year,
and it reminded me of what was possible. My monthly payment from sales had dried up last year and I'd been scraping
by on fees from old work circulating in group shows. And
I didn't feel like a real artist yet, even though I did nothing but
my own work all day, every day, because I was still poor, too
close to where I came from, a deficiency that was in my DNA.

Looking at the Twin's face now, I knew it would sell, not just as a commodity but as a concept. The face was beautiful in a way that felt wealthy, everyone would agree, the consensus would be universal. I'd never been universal before. Someone like me isn't. I wanted nothing more.

Debt. I had, was made through, as if it were a crucible, debt to the art world: both of my degrees from the two private art schools I'd attended had left me with two hundred and fifty thousand dollars' worth of student-loan debt, more than 40 percent of which came from interest that kept increasing. Every artist my age had this. Unless they had a trust fund, which many did. The art world demanded financial dedition, and this was the price of entry. I didn't know any artist who made a living selling their art who hadn't gone to an MFA program, let alone a cheap one. Although I'd been awarded a few scholarships, they weren't nearly enough, and I'd justified my debt with the understanding that to buy an MFA was to buy my ticket to the circus—but no, that's wrong, I hadn't needed to justify it, I knew this was the cost, and to sign my name on the promissory note hadn't felt like an acknowledgment of my poverty, it never felt like I was the one promising to repay the money, but rather that the document and what it represented were making a promise *to me*, a pledge to pull me out of the penury I was from, a hook in my lip to bring me up from the aphotic zone of who I was and into the light of who I could become.

Alexandra knew about my debt, we'd discussed it one evening, she was the one to bring it up when we were getting ready for that first show together. "I'm assuming you had to do student loans?" I'd told her a little about my childhood, how poor we were, though she'd probably guessed. "You're in for six figures, aren't you, cat?" she'd said. It was the only time she called me by a nickname. I felt her large mouth lift me by the scruff of my neck, then close around me. It felt like a gesture of protection, even though she was also eating me.

The next day, I woke up late, almost one o'clock in the afternoon, sore more from the dream than from Mistress Anka. I made coffee, the Twin's face still glowing inside my eyelids when I blinked. I replied to her email and invited her to my studio. She responded within an hour, saying she would be there. I sat back and looked again at her face on my wall. It flashed me a smile, a little helix of a game.

ANAMORPHOSIS

a distorted projection or drawing which appears normal only when viewed from a particular point, or with the right mirror or lens.

"I think I just twisted my ankle," the Twin said. "In your driveway, getting out of my car." I offered my arm and she clutched it with both hands, putting all of her weight on me. I could smell her sweat, her big bun brushed my face, and we hobbled inside.

I liked that, as our first collaboration, I carried her.

I wondered what she thought of my studio. It was not a very LA studio. Most artists I knew rented large rooms in old industrial warehouses carved up with cheap pieces of drywall that didn't go all the way to the ceiling, and these compounds were owned by older artists who now lived off the rent paid to them by the younger artists, or else by artists my age with trust funds who bought entire buildings and rented them out to friends and said it was about "community." My studio was a small pair of rooms and a bathroom on one side of a little Craftsman bungalow that had crooked stairs going up to a broken porch. Alexandra had found it for me. The house was overloaded with all the paint its different inhabitants had applied to it over the years. None of the doors met their frames.

The Twin did not look at anything in the room or at me. She sank onto the couch, stretching her leg out while I scooted a chair underneath it. She threw her other leg over the arm of the couch, sitting splayed open, legs up, anchored by her crotch, and looked at her injured foot. She bent to rub her fingers against it and I saw that she had unattractive fingers, short and stubby with bitten nails, although her hands, like the rest of her, were long and thin. The thumbs looked especially fat and round. Then I noticed that only one of them was fat and round, the other was slender and half an inch longer than the other. This dissonance felt like a warning, but I didn't know of what. She noticed my noticing and smirked.

"I think this is karma," she said. "This is the gods' punishment. For my sins." She let out a strident cackle, tossing her head back. She had a solid, prominent jaw like Colomba's, with full lips folded like a wide purse around the mouth and teeth.

"Your sins?" I said.

"Can I tell you," she said, "I have a boyfriend, we've been together two years, he loves me, I love him, blah, blah. But I'm a bitch, I'm a terrible person, I'm a whore, I've been cheating on him the entire time. I just came from another guy's house, just now, I was there this afternoon, right after I left my boyfriend's house, where I was this morning, where I slept last night. And of course, here I am, two men in one day, and I get out of my car and step my leg down and my ankle just twists—it's like a hand, ha! No, a fist, *God's* fist, just *pow*, knocks it over and I fall and I'm fucked. It's punishment. It's karma."

She cackled again, a deeper and weirder sound this time. "Of course, I don't believe in karma. There's no such thing as divine punishment. No such thing as punishment at all."

"I've been punished," I said. The purple of my bruises from Mistress Anka had just started to deepen. "I like it when I choose it."

"That's not punishment. That's something else."

"What is it, then?"

"I'm just saying that maybe I want to get caught. It'll get boring if not."

"So you can be punished when you do."

"Punishment means there's a reason. And there isn't. Not with this." She talked as though she'd forgotten I was on the other side of her face.

"Are you going to be okay?" I said.

Now she gave me her full stare. I did my best to hold it. Her face reminded me of a lion's, proud and smart but a little tired. Pride takes a lot of effort. Her big, pale, yellowy-green eyes were turned up at the corners, widely set apart on the face, most of which was taken up by the mouth. Her hair was dirty yellow and her skin was sandy, nearly the same color, it was more ochre than cadmium yellow, I'd have to mix it with a bit of green. She was wearing black, like I'd asked her to. She was my size yet seemed larger.

Otakar Švec was a Czech sculptor best known for a piece in Prague that took nearly six years to complete, the fifty-one-foot-tall *Stalin's Monument* made from granite. A few days before it was officially unveiled, Švec killed himself. The method of his suicide is unknown, but the sculpture was destroyed seven years later by 1,800 pounds of dynamite.

"Oh," she said, her tone modulating from talking to herself to addressing some adorable kitten. "You're a *nice* person. I see. *That's* what you are. It's sweet. It's not what I am, though."

"I hate the word 'whore,'" I said.

"I think it's a *great* word. So many possibilities!"

"I don't think it has possibilities for everyone," I said, but she didn't hear me. She looked like one of those circus girls strapped to the spinning wheel, about to have knives thrown at them but smiling, already victorious and untouched, knowing they will be forever intact.

ICON

a sacred symbol, image, picture, or representation used in religious devotion; anybody or anything venerated or uncritically admired.

She turned out to be the best model I'd ever had. She was confident, staring into the camera without modesty but also without that inane kind of beauty that models sometimes have, bored with their beauty but here it is anyway. My eyes fell along the slimness of her waist that angled out and up into wide shoulders, and with her big jaw and big head crowned with the big bun, the proportions struck me as contorted. Her body tapered sharply as its lines went to the floor in such a way that I could imagine her tipping over if poked with an intent finger. She followed my directions but also extended them, finding more interesting poses, better expressions, than the ones I gave her. She was really good at the degraded positions. Her twisted ankle meant that she had to hobble and lean. It looked great. She told me that her first job had been as a model for an old man who had painted her in her underwear. She'd been sixteen at the time. "The paintings were good," she told me, "but he isn't famous anymore."

I stood behind the tripod, face smashed against the camera, and stared. The camera hid my face so I could gape in a way that I wouldn't have otherwise. I watched her strange head pivot on its little neck and her large breasts move around in her shirt as she leaned over. I didn't ask her to strip, I wanted to wait, I like it best when there's longing. I had her lie on her back with her knees bent at wide angles, legs spread, leaning on her elbows with her head bent stiffly back, I photographed this pose from behind. I had her kneel and reach her arms in front of her, chin on the ground, obviously uncomfortable, trying to follow my instructions, bend your neck more, good, even more, mound of ass behind her head, I photographed this from the floor.

The paintings I would make started to arrive, something I'd never had before, so soon. My thoughts darted through ideas, that line the central thread of the composition, I would add a third shape near the eyes, a rhombus of light that would hint at an organ. The black clothes collected the dusty-white powder of the flour exactly as I had hoped, but I hadn't imagined how striking it would look on skin, so I had her dip her face into it and photographed it, thick and cakey, her eyelashes like little trees in a snowy landscape. It was a surface of whiteness on a surface of whiteness. The only distance between us was the width of the camera and its lens.

When we were done, she went to clean up. I heard her lock the bathroom door, which made me smile, this small act of self-preservation.

I texted Yves, who was the person I called my best friend, sometimes even my soulmate. He lived in Berlin, a Frenchman descended from Martinique-born grandparents, "a colonial Black child," as he liked to call himself. I'd known him since we'd been in the same group show together, almost a decade ago. He was the one I called when I needed a quick yay or nay on whether to buy an item of clothing, or if I wanted to revel in some particularly salacious art-world gossip, or if I needed to borrow money, or be talked out of a depression. He was the one whose smell made me feel protected. He was the one I wanted to see when I was lonely and sad and heartbroken because he had the preternatural capacity to make those states feel honorable and important and like the very stuff of life. He was also the person I talked to about work, even if just to say that I was doing it. Yves would definitely have an opinion on my new work being about a white girl.

"Hey babe, how u?" I texted, then added, "I'm working working, this new show is my life," with the black-haired, pale-skinned, rock-climbing woman emoji.

I watched the ellipses appear and glimmer, and then he replied, "Good to hear from you, mermaid, when's the opening again?"

"November 6, day after my birthday."

Yves texted some gasping emojis and then, "Portentous!" He was into astrology. "And when is Berlin?"

"Opens in summer, July probably."

"When will you get here???"

"After the show. December. Soooooon!"

"Can't wait." Hearts.

I wanted to tell him about the Twin and ask him for advice. Another thing for which I leaned on him was to discuss our lives as people of color, as artists of color, what race meant to us, about us, and how we coped with what the art world said it ought to mean, but I leaned on him for this much more than he leaned on me.

Race was in Yves's work as a lure and a trap. It was something that deceived, it was the most powerful force on Earth, but you could prick it with a pin and watch it fizzle away. In interviews, he liked to say, "Race is a delusion, but it's also the harshest reality, and I want to show you that the nightmare is actually a dream come true. Whose dream? Whose dream indeed." For years, his artist statement ended with: "Black is the color of kittens, weddings, and prom night." One of his dominant themes was his tendency to fall for white boys, how, because he shouldn't, he kept wanting to, and how useless this ultimately was as a political transgression. His most widely known work was a series of videos of himself giving blowjobs to young, beautiful white men, though the frame contained only the torso and shoulders of the white boy and the very top of Yves's head, his hair short and cut in a lineup, bobbing up and down, in and out of the frame. The *Bad B(l)ack* series.

I started typing, "I've got a new" but hesitated about what to call her. Yves knew about my muses, he enjoyed hearing about them, he also read tabloids and followed celebrity gossip, and, in a way, these were all of a piece to him. I tried again. "This time I'm going mainstream. A white girl!" Sent.

The bathroom door unlocked and swung open. The Twin walked across the room without looking at me and gathered her stuff to leave.

How to describe her? I tapped the blond queen emoji, then swiped to the emoji of the hole. SEND.

"Hey, thanks again," I called.

The Twin held up her hand as she went out. It was a wave. She was gone.

My phone blinged. Yves had replied, "Lol I'll pray for you," with the Black hands pressed together in prayer.

Yves and I first met when I was in my midtwenties and he was about the age I am now, thirty-three. It was at the opening for a group show in a gallery in Berlin, my first in an actual gallery, my "international" debut, important enough to me that I needed to fly to Berlin and conduct my inclusion in person, I bought my own ticket. Now I only fly somewhere for work if someone else pays for it.

Yves looked dashing in that room on that first night, wearing a vivid blue suit and hot-pink sneakers, the only Black man in the room, and he'd said so, noticing me, the only yellow person. He guessed this, and when I showed surprise that he would notice something I'd always thought was subtle, he shrugged and flourished his hands around his own face as if to say, it takes one to know one. At this, a small zap spread across my body, like my skin had lifted away from me by a few inches. I looked at Yves's face, his hands encircling it, and wondered if I felt his hands also encircle mine. I peered into him as if he were a mirror, some kind of impossible, generous mirror. Race is not a mirror made of glass but flesh hard as stone.

We snuck out early to drink in a Turkish-owned bar that had a mild brothel upstairs. A few men disappeared through a door. "They only wanted me because I'm Black," Yves said, "and gay, too, ha. Two minority birds with one rock, is that how you say?" Later that night, both of us too drunk and falling on each other, he'd wept hugely, face disfigured with sobs, for many reasons, none of which he explained. He finally bowed his head to apologize. "I don't even know you," he said, "but we're here for the same purpose."

I was not then able to admit anything to myself about my race, who I came from, what I was. Yves's sobs had disturbed something in me that I'd kept—that the world had let me keep—tiny, quiet, and hidden. He was so loud and big with his hurt and all of the trouble about where it came from, it was as if he'd brought race into our conversation as a third entity, a force in and of itself that took up as much space, if not more, than either of us. He had laid his sable eyes on me, wreathed my face with his sepia hands, and it was as though I'd been granted entry to a new, enchanted place of belonging, and it startled me, how good it felt to be invited there. But immediately, because race is not a mirror, I knew I was a trespasser. Being mixed betrays the image of a person, the image of what you think you look like and then what everyone else says you look like, how much of this has to do with what's behind the surface of the image, and how much of it is only surface. Is it who you are or just what you look like? Is this image everything, or is it lying, how will you know? Because someone tells you? It's that slippage from the visible to the affective to the ontological—looks like, seems like, is. The surfaces that trick. Because if you don't know who or what you look like, can you know who or what you are? And if you can't, because I didn't, how can you know where and with whom you belong? It turns belonging into an asymptote: you may get close to something, you may look like it, but you'll never *be* it.

Yves could locate and see and understand how he belonged or didn't, and I've always been jealous of this, even though it's despicable of me. His belonging wasn't an asymptote but two clean lines that would never converge, and so he was disabused of the promise of such a union, which was a form of freedom. He didn't yearn for this impossible thing, why would he? His skin was very dark and his features very African. He'd always say he wanted Isaach De Bankolé to play him in a movie, they looked like they could be twins. Though his parents had been poor, his father had worked as a janitor, his mother as a secretary, and Yves had four sisters and two brothers, the house he'd grown up in was filled with the books of Aimé Césaire and Frantz Fanon, and there were framed images in the dining room of Malcolm X and Assata Shakur. The books by Césaire and Fanon were important not only for representing Martinicans but also for articulating the experience of what Yves called *his people*, and no matter how ambivalent he was about it any other time, no matter how annoyed by politics he could make himself seem, he always said *my people* if not with pride, then with certainty. He knew who they were, his people, and his place with them. This was something I would never have. But I had the hunch that half of me was supposed to have it, though I couldn't say which half, and the question branched, where do I belong became which part of me should, and what if it belongs somewhere, to something, that I know nothing about, or that I don't like or agree with? Do I get to choose, and what should I do if I don't? If the world keeps trying to give you something and you keep saying that you don't want it, does that mean it still belongs to you? Though I would never admit it to him and could barely admit it to myself, I chewed on a feeling that squirmed with guilt, a kind of envy for the clean definitions and clarity of Yves's experiences, how a stranger's fist landing in your stomach can cure you of any delusions about who you think you are, how a child staring and pointing at you and shouting vicious words articulates something indisputable about how people see you, and how this made him know for a fact that this thing the world kept trying to give him was not his. It did and should not belong to him, it said nothing about who he actually was or wanted to be.

This need to keep such violences in the world perturbed me. Which of my colors needed violence so I might understand who I am?

chiaroscuro and tenebrism are both painting styles of high contrast between brightly lit subjects and darkly lit backgrounds, but the difference between them is found in the shadows. Where chiaroscuro uses its light and shadow to create depth behind the subject, tenebrism uses full black.

The evening after my first shoot with the Twin, I came home and loaded the images onto my computer and stayed up late staring at each one, trying to decide which to paint. I liked them all. There was her long, straight, blond hair and pale eyes with lids that creased, her apple-shaped face with tawny skin, she was a classical statue of a goddess from Greek antiquity or a pink-skinned lady with a blinding white bosom from any one of the Masters, how very different she looked from me. She really was beautiful in the empty, vast way that everyone would agree on.

I thought about her status as my first white muse—after Marina, of course. It was naked and sharp, a fact, and it would carry this new series, carry me, the succeeding that whiteness does to beauty.

It wasn't just that she was beautiful or that I wasn't questioning how such beauty was defined. It was that I liked wondering about what was wrong about liking this kind of beauty. It was a kink, whiteness was my kink. I was submitting to it. Like any good submissive, my fetish for giving away my power was actually about controlling it, but in this case, I wanted to relinquish more than I ever had before, I wanted power to scare me again, I wanted it to be wrong in a way that rearranged me, that would leave a more permanent mark. I'd never let myself go to a white dominatrix because it always felt too rote, we'd follow a script that had not been written by us, it would only ever be symbolic. Now, I was curious enough about what damage was possible if it didn't happen within the bounds of a two-hour BDSM session with a safe word. What if I gave it to her—was I making a show about whiteness?—so I could better revel in it for myself—yes, I was making a show about whiteness. Maybe I missed my mother more than I knew.

That night, I dreamed I awoke with my face covered in tattoos. They were ugly, clumsy shapes on both cheeks, a childlike outline of a heart on my forehead, and a weird pattern of blobs on my chin and down my neck. I couldn't look at myself without feeling disgusted. This is my face, this is the face I have to meet the world, no matter what I say or do, it will have to come through the screen of this and look how I fucked it up. I will be judged by everyone because they can see who I really am. I guess I wanted them to.

The next day, as I was eating breakfast, I checked the internet and saw that the prize for the first Los Angeles biennial had been announced. There were thirty artists in this first show, held at the big contemporary art museum downtown. The two curators putting it together had granted me a studio visit in the early stages of their talent search. After a few weeks, I heard that the other nominees were already getting their invites, but mine, I guess, got lost. That's what I was telling myself until I saw the official list of the artists who'd been selected, and my name wasn't among them. I couldn't pretend that I wasn't annoyed.

The prize was already looking to turn into an art-world scandal. Although the nominees were selected by a curatorial committee, the winner was chosen based on votes from museumgoers, the demographics of which were right there on everyone's winking faces. What will the wealthy old ladies of Beverly Hills and Pasadena decide is good art this year? Then there was the hundred thousand dollars in prize money, donated by a private donor. Quite the gold star.

My screens told me that Iris Wells had won.

The image of Iris's bald head and face, shaved so completely as to give her an air of illness, and her luminously dark skin, the color of black calla lilies, sat with distinction beneath the headline. It was the same photo she always used. The first time I saw that photo with all the other profile pictures, everything and everyone else online seemed to pitch toward her eyes, which were enormous, round caves of black. In it, she wore a black turtleneck and stood against a dark background, so the little square representing her was filled with different textures of black, pierced by the two corneal spots of white around the plums of her eyes. I remembered that the first time I'd heard someone talk about Iris, they'd said she wanted to be called the "anti-object" artist. We were still in grad school, she was nobody special then, also in grad school on the East Coast. I'd seen her profile status and her @ handles listed as *ante-object*. The Ante-Object Artist. Every biography and artist statement I'd seen of hers also proclaimed this. It'd made me smirk with admiration, that small cleverness, converging the position of the antagonist with something much more familial, an ancestor that came before.

As the biennial described itself as being for and of Los Angeles artists, her win was doubly dubious, because she had only moved to LA last year. Did she really count as an LA artist, then? Another reason it was perplexing, or so people tweeted, was her expressed militancy against the wealth and precious objects of the art world. In every interview, she proclaimed that she refused to make "expensive collectibles for the master to decorate his house with." So what was the Ante-Object Artist going to do with a cash tip of one hundred thousand dollars?

I got in my truck and drove across town to the museum. It was a reflex action. I had to see. I knew what it looked like, I'd seen her piece in photos and video clips, but at the opening, I'd somehow missed the room where she was performing. As I drove, I thought of her name, so close to Ida B. Wells, and, at a stoplight, I found myself scrolling deep into her timeline, searching her Wikipedia article to see if she alluded to having changed her name anywhere, as an homage or a sign of solidarity, but I found nothing.

The first thing I noticed in the gallery was that the usual museum silence, which tends to impose a kind of sacred solemnity on the space, was, in this instant, less than silent. It was rustling. Iris was sitting on a friable, uncomfortable-looking chair that creaked beneath her weight. She wore the hygienic green smock of a surgeon and latex gloves, bright white. A large canister of air leaned against her front, between her knees, and along all the walls were similar long, silver cylinders. She was holding a white balloon, limp and airless, to the canister. I'd seen online that she'd had the balloons printed with crude illustrations she'd made in scratching pencil of the museum's board of trustees, each head on its own balloon. I watched her pinch the mouth of the balloon around the nozzle of the canister and let the balloon fill. The face of the person on the balloon became legible, a little bobbing head come to life, nodding along to the sound of the hissing, and then it stretched, the expression, a smiling one, becoming grotesque, the hissing a sound of dread. We all knew the loud bang was coming, I leaned forward on my toes. Some people next to me covered their ears. The explosion came, fulfilling and cathartic, and everyone, including me, laughed. Unmoved, Iris reached down and picked up another balloon to go through the mini life-and-death cycle again.

Most people stayed for three or so balloons, but I sat down against the wall to settle in. I started to calculate how many balloons she'd had to print. I timed it, it took about a minute and a half to go through one, and the museum was open eight hours a day and closed on Sundays, the show open for ten weeks, and she was sitting here, on that miserable chair, all day every day for the length of the exhibition. She'd have had to spend her entire honorarium and budget on them, at least. I'd heard that each artist had been paid a paltry thousand dollars to be in the show. If she had a day job, she'd have had to quit it in order to be here every day. Many, especially those without gallery representation, like Iris—part of her politic was that she wouldn't be owned by a gallery, and she definitely

103

never showed at fairs—had gone into debt to buy what they needed to make their work, not unusual in the art world but never talked about in public. So, what was that, one hundred and one thousand dollars' worth of broken balloons? Their carcasses collected around her.

She made no sign that she noticed me, though I was her only consistent spectator, aside from the security guard. The wall text explained that since every day's performance ended with Iris sweeping up and throwing away her trash and the trash was emptied in a dump, there would be no objects or prints of original drawings or anything at all left to be used as documentation. Nothing would be left. Nothing would be sold. When I arrived, there were only a few dozen maimed balloons on the floor, the mess after a birthday party, but as I stayed and they piled up, little shards of white with a deathly texture, it looked like a battlefield heaped with the wounded and their ghosts, a cartoonish slaughter of small things. That they were little, dead, and white made my eyebrows raise. I was impressed she'd convinced the museum to allow her to be so bold, or maybe—white people—they didn't get how it implicated them. White innocence is the other part of white guilt.

In all the time I watched her, she took one break. She seemed less like a surgeon and more like a nurse, attending to her task with devotion, head down, a kind of duty. And the futility of it, hearing those first blasts was satisfying, but after a hundred, two hundred, and Iris still bending to pick up another piece of rubber to be brought to life for a few seconds before it was destroyed, it felt abject, ultimately, she was only exploding balloons, was that enough to explode a symbol of power? The title of the piece was after Obama's memoir: *The Audacity of Hope*.

I went home from the museum exhausted. The drive felt three times as long as usual and there was traffic, not a surprise but not anodynic. The air conditioner in my truck was broken and I didn't have the money to fix it, since I hadn't been making any, so I kept the windows down, getting thrashed in the face by the hot air and bellowing of other cars. As I got out of my truck, the door closed on my shin, and I felt persecuted. I sat at my desk and stared into space. I heard again the rhythmic cycle of Iris's balloons: *Hisssssssssssssss, bang! Hisssssssssssssss, bang!* I nudged the mouse on my desktop and the screen lit up with dozens of images of the Twin, where I'd left them that morning. *Hissssssss, bang!* After what I'd just seen at the museum, my images of the Twin's face, with its white features and what I'd asked her to do with her body, now looked vulgar and slick, like an editorial in a fashion magazine. I tried to imagine my own paintings, based on these photographs, in the gallery where Iris had sat, but I couldn't get the ruined balloon bodies out of the frame. Their deflated white skins merged with the white clumps of flour on the Twin's face, the textures melting into a surface of pale noise, but Iris's piece was good because it had destroyed itself yet withstood its own end. What was I destroying in mine?

SECCO

unaccompanied or with minimal accompaniment; the technique of painting
on dry plaster with pigments mixed in water; from Italian, "dry."

After my first show with Alexandra, I had money for the
first time in my life, but because it was my first time, I did
what was familiar: I spent it until it was gone. I bought
clothes, a pair of thousand-dollar designer boots, a vintage
midcentury coffee table for my one-bedroom apartment,
I dropped a hundred dollars a night on dinner at gaudy
restaurants. This got me into trouble because I had nothing
left when it came time for taxes or to pay my student debt.
With that show, I was suddenly in a new income bracket.
Now, nearly all the money I made went to my student loans
every month because the government thought, based on my
tax return from the previous two years, that I was the kind
of person who could afford to pay them back quicker and
at a higher rate. But I'd only been that person for a brief
moment. And even during that moment, I was not who
they thought I was.

I had no other income but what I made from my paintings,
which had been fine for a while, in the wake of my first show,

there were private commissions that kept me busy for a couple of years, but at some point, they dried up. There were only two paintings left that Alexandra had kept off the market, the usual ploy of manipulating supply to drive up demand, and these were the ones Colomba had bought, so now there was nothing. That first big series had been about my mother, and it had drained me totally. I had to stop, I needed to make new work, make a different, other face, be free of that history, that hole. And I would fantasize about only having to sell three or four paintings to pay off my entire student debt in one go because that was another hole that wouldn't let me go.

For the last few months, I'd taken a loan from Alexandra to pay rent on both my studio and my apartment, and for a while before that, she'd been loaning me the rent for my studio, which was a new development between us. She was fronting me all I needed to make this new show, which was our standard arrangement, and half of this would be paid back from sales, but this was beyond the standard arrangement. Every month, I sank in deeper, first just two grand, now more than fifteen. The debt to Alexandra didn't feel good, but it had a glamour that my student debt didn't, that it was even possible for me to owe money to a successful, powerful person who was pretending to be my friend.

I went to the refrigerator and poured myself what was left of the white wine I'd opened the night before. It was sour and watery but cold, so I drank it all at once and clunked the empty bottle next to the others by the back door. My head swam from the wine, and my stomach clanged against itself. I realized I hadn't eaten all day, I'd watched Iris for nearly five hours. There was no food in the house. It made me even more tired to think of figuring out food to make or buy, so I turned back to the computer as if that were food.

I turned on my camera and tilted the computer screen down so the view was on my crotch. I took off my pants and underwear and selected the filter in the program that magnifies and distorts. My cunt massed into a convex bubble. The black hair swarmed like thickened worms. When I rubbed my fingers into it, the filter enlarged them into gargantuan mounds of white. Cysts in a dark nest. I clicked into a browser to search for images of teratomas, the kind of tumors that grow their own teeth and hair and sometimes an eye. I aligned the grid of images with the window of myself. I got wet. The wetness looked like slime. Near the peak, I thought of Marina and couldn't get her out. The sprouting little monsters and me. There are different kinds of power, most are invisible, all canker. It took me a while, sweat on the chair, but I finally got there, the twitch a heave in the mirror, sick.

FACTURE

*the quality of the execution of a painting; an artist's
characteristic handling of the paint.*

During my second year in art school, I signed up for a studio
visit with that semester's guest professor, Joan Raíz, who was
the chief curator at the biggest contemporary art museum in
California. She was famous and potent and canonical and
rare, a Latina curator with power. She'd started during the
late 1970s, working in a little gallery that represented only
women artists, then ascended through different institutions
whose scale and prestige increased proportionally. Her thing
was to turn each institution she helmed into a place where
artists who usually weren't supported got support, women
and artists of color and especially women artists of color,
but also artists who didn't make objects, whose work couldn't
be categorized by a traditional genre, and queer artists who
were flamboyantly perverted and used a lot of nudity. She'd
give them huge shows and budgets, and nearly everyone she
worked with got famous, either because of Joan and the insti-
tutional cachet she lent them or a causality dilemma: Were
they interesting before they'd had enough money to fill whole

rooms in important museums? By the time she mounted the high throne in the castle, where she'd sat for nearly a decade, she was a legend who could somehow still cash in on her origin in shock. In 1979, she had curated a small show that featured a bucket of menstrual blood at the door. Whether it was real or fake was left to the imagination. Visitors were required to remove their shoes and stand in the bucket before they could enter the gallery. Their bloody footprints dried on the gallery floor and were captured in the single photo of the show that was taken, which became an icon in and of itself. Somehow, everyone knew that all the footprints in this hallowed image belonged to Joan, and the show was considered a failure when it opened. Now that show is taught in every class I've ever been in, classes on installation, documentation, sculpture as performance, the artist's body, feminist art. That bucket of blood has achieved the holy status that only the art world can produce, a type of worshipful reverence people buy into because it's gratifying to be reassured that all it takes for something to be great is for you to imagine its greatness.

When I look back at it, adding my name to the paper taped to Joan Raíz's office door, her list for studio visits, was my first public gesture of ambition. It was a gesture born out of hope that if she came to my studio to sit with me for an hour, power, like a mold, might break off its host and start to grow on me. But it was also a move of survival. Joan was one of the only art-world people I could think of who would genuinely be interested in my work and have the means to take it somewhere.

I hadn't considered my work to be especially political or even feminist, but then several of my professors and classmates told me that by relentlessly painting my own or other women's nonwhite faces and bodies, I was doing something revolutionary, taking up space with something that normally isn't given it. I was insisting that these women be looked at, that they were valuable enough to fill canvases, fill galleries. People were always remarking on what my paintings represented in terms of "the Asian American female experience," although I had no idea what that experience might be, and I hated the word "female." I was just painting what I wanted to paint. It takes hours to paint a portrait, and this was who I wanted to spend hours looking at. My queerness didn't factor into how my work was talked about then as much as it does now because queerness has only emerged in the last few years as being of commercial value to the art world. Before, it had conceptual value, but otherwise, it was masked and abstracted, wall texts in museums using code words like "her lifelong companion," and stationing signs at the entrances of galleries, warning that the contents were not suitable for children. For its practitioners, queerness lived a fuller life in dark little corners of an underground, the kink party, the dungeon, Monday nights at the bar downtown. There, we were happy to look only at each other, the mainstream had not turned its eye on us yet, and we never expected it to.

In those early years in art school, I tried to speak about my work in vague art-historical terms, the Masters, the men. I thought I could legitimate myself there, fit into lineages I had no business being in. I wanted my paintings seen through my facility as a painter, my skill, I didn't want people to talk about what the figures in them meant, their otherness or whatever. I wasn't long into my career, though, before I realized that to fight against this would cause me more problems than cashing in on it. Getting a foot in the door *was* the battle, and I didn't have the luxury to pick and choose which door, only one was, and would ever be, offered to me.

I remember Joan wore a brilliant red suit to our studio visit. She looked like the smear of blood on the white wall in Ana Mendieta's *Body Tracks*. (Later, at a party, I overheard a guy talking about how every time he saw Joan, she was wearing red or some shade of pink. "Like, we get it," he'd sneered. "You're a *woman*.") She had chic black hair cut short and gelled, like Annie Lennox, and golden skin latticed with wrinkles. Her face looked like a fist, tight and capable. She had a tattoo of a spider on the back of her hand. When she sat across from me, I felt I should slouch, sit on my hands, pull in my elbows, as I'd done in Principal Aguerro's office. It was as though we'd agreed soundlessly that she should take up all the space because she deserved it. She was confusingly friendly, grinning and clucking and touching my shoulder as if we were the best of friends, part of the courtship I would come to learn. It was how she bestowed value on me, even if it only lasted as long as she was in my studio.

"So, you're a painter," she said with grave severity.

"Yes," I said.

She let her eyes skate across the walls.

"That you *are* a painter means that your concerns are *different* than other artists," she said. "*And*, that you are a painter who paints *figuratively* means that you are in that peculiar place of being both vaunted *and* esoteric.

"*And!* Of *course*, that you are a *woman*, and not a *white* woman, means that half the time you'll be thought of as irrelevant and extraneous"—she made a swooping arc with her hand—"and half the time you'll be enlightened and prophetic."

"Okay," I said.

"Let's be frank: for the last fifty years—or a hundred, surely, probably two hundred—the entire discourse around painting has consolidated around the question of whether or not it's *dead*. Which means that if you're a painter in the twenty-first century, you're a ghost who speaks the future, but very few will care to hear your prophecies, and even fewer will care if they are right. Now, as a curator, I'm supposed to not be aware of such dirty things as the *market*, but let me tell you, every ten years, the market's pendulum swings between abstract painting and figurative painting, and, lucky for you, in a few years, we'll be in a figurative phase. So, you'd better start finding a way to talk about what you're doing. Now"—here she touched my shoulder protectively—"the primary question for *you* to consider is what will be the contempor*aneity* of your *trajectory*."

She narrowed her eyes and peered into me.

"I'm t-trying," I stammered, "to say something about how bodies are political because of what they are used for and by whom." But I knew and she knew that I didn't have a grasp of the argument, that I was just regurgitating what I'd heard other people say. It made her tighten her grip on my shoulder and crinkle her nose, as if she'd seen something ugly but innocent, something that required compassion.

She left me to circle my studio, putting her hands behind her back and leaning toward the walls. I prattled on, I can't remember now what I said. She didn't look at me, didn't seem to be listening. With each lap around the room, she let her face get closer to my canvases.

When I saw she'd stopped moving, I stopped talking. Her nose was only a few inches from the surface of the painting she'd chosen as her terminus.

"No," she said to the painting. "Your work is about something *very* radical, actually, which is not about a woman suffering because of her desire. But suffering the question of *where* that desire comes from. Why does she want what she can't have? Does she really want it? Or has she just been *told* to want it? Look at how you paint them, like they are standing above you. It's *not* about truth—don't believe what these men tell you. No, it's about lies. And not just your own—but all of ours. Yes."

That final affirmation came in a whisper. She was close enough to sniff my work and did. It was a gentle, thrilling breach. I thought of the sly joy in smelling a finger that's been in an ass.

It was the first time I saw how art allowed you to be not just a freak but a freak with power. Don't hide it in the underground dungeon. Pinch meaning from the dull flesh of the world, here and here and here. Let the light come in, metaphors and symbols in cadmium red and lamp black and ochre, and let them be about something dark in you. They aren't good because you paint like an Old Master, surfaces crusted with history and tradition. They are good because of what lives in you, me, beneath, outside of it, see.

UNDERPAINTING

*paint subsequently overlaid with another layer; the colors of
the underpainting can be optically mingled with the subsequent
overpainting without the danger of the colors physically blending
and becoming muddy. If it seems that one has to fight to obscure
the underpainting, it is a sign that it was not done properly.*

The second time I invited the Twin for a shoot, the week
after I'd gone to see Iris's exhibit, she was two hours late.
She didn't apologize, didn't mention the time at all, just lit
a cigarette, took off her shoes, and strode into the center of
the room.

"I have wine," I said. I wanted to walk like she did.

"Great. I need some." She spread her fingers and laced
them through the hair at her temples, holding her head, she
stretched her mouth open, not to yawn but to mime a scream.
Her eyes looked tired. Now that she was here, I couldn't
remember what I'd wanted to shoot tonight. I brought the
wine like a servant, keeping my eyes on the floor.

She released her head and closed her mouth, accepted the
wine with no thank you, no acknowledgment.

"The photos from last time look great," I said.

She grunted and drank.

"I was planning on using them for just a few paintings in the show, but now I think I'll make more."

"When is it again?" She didn't care.

"November sixth. The day after my birthday." I hated myself for hoping she might rise to the bait. Finally, I surrendered and asked, "Will you come?"

"I don't know. If I'm in town."

"And I have another show in Berlin next year. In the summer."

"Berlin is great in the summer."

"Yeah, totally," I said. "I think these paintings could work for that too . . ."

She moved around my studio, looking at things, walking the perimeter, dragging each leg behind the other. She scanned the titles on my bookshelf like someone watching a bus pull up to the curb, then seeing that it's not the one they've been waiting for. On a lower shelf was a small, square piece of handmade paper with a watercolor-and-ink drawing I'd made in my one of my first art classes as an undergrad. I spent most of that semester learning how to make my own paper, but only some of it had turned out. I'd made delicate ink drawings on the few salvageable squares, and I'd given away all but this one. For ten years now, I'd made a place for it in each of my studios. It caught the Twin's interest, and she deigned to look at it with the whole of her attention, sipping her wine and leaning from hip to hip. I watched her watching, wondering if she liked the drawing, and I felt again how her authority permeated my studio as surely as Joan's had. As an art student, as an artist, it's hammered into you that you must invite people into your studio, your process, your world, people who are important, who can do important things for you, who can give you something and just as easily take it away, even if it's just their gaze, their consideration, and then you watch them decide in real time. Better this exposure than to disappear. In an economy of attention, to be ignored is to be ruined.

The painter Sonja Sekula was one of the few out lesbians in New York in the 1940s and 1950s. She is described as being "extremely" passionate about her work, "extremely" open about her sexuality, and "highly disturbed." She hanged herself when she was forty-five, in her studio.

I was almost too caught up in my thoughts to miss the Twin reaching down, picking up my small drawing between thumb and forefinger, and sliding it into her back pocket.

She took it. She'd taken it. And without doing me the honor of a single glance.

I must've forgotten the exchange we just had, the one where she'd asked me if she could have this beautiful drawing and I'd graciously said of course.

She tipped forward, then, and moved on. She had to feel my eyes on her, wasn't she luxuriating in them? I tried to say something, I liked that drawing, it meant something to me, I didn't want to give it away. What did she think she was doing? Was this a joke? A test?

Then, the thought that she'd wanted it and so, without hesitation or permission, she'd taken it, just like that, stopped me. Her act, in its confidence, was stronger, more persuasive, more correct, than my complaint. I thought of being on my hands and knees and assenting to whatever Mistress Anka thought would best debase me.

Is that what power is? To act as though you own the room and everything in it? Is this what whiteness gives you? Is that why I wanted it? I chewed on my thoughts and drank my wine and kept watching her. There was the fact of my watching her, her knowing it, and whether she wanted this to mean anything, if this was her choice or ours. I wanted it all.

ALLA PRIMA

*a painting technique in which a canvas is completed
in one session, often having a thickly applied impasto
applied in layers; also known as "wet-on-wet."*

"Hey," I said. "I realized I don't know your name."

My drawing was sticking out of her back pocket, hers now, pressed close to her body.

"What should I call you?" I said. "Ghost ship?"

"Eliza Battle," she said. She held out her hand, performing an introduction. I shook it. "The *Eliza Battle* is my favorite ghost ship," she said. She wasn't going to give me anything for free. I pulled back my hand.

She spoke, with long pauses, to the room.

"It's the name of the steamboat that caught fire on the Tombigbee River in 1858. For decades after, people claimed to see it on fire on cold nights, burning people jumping into the water to save themselves."

Then she made long, slow strides back to where I was standing and drank the rest of her wine in a gulp. Our shoulders touched, same height, but she seemed to be looking down at me and communicating that she knew who I really was. She laughed huskily, not the cackle.

"You can call me *sister*. I've always wanted one. And you and I could be sisters, don't you think?" She slipped her hand through my elbow, winding our arms together, and clanged her empty glass against mine.

I wanted her to reach into my pants and grab me or explode a sneeze in my face or ring my nostril with her tongue. Instead, she leaned close and kissed me on the right cheek, the left, then the right again. Her mouth left a dot of saliva on my skin and I felt it.

"There," she said. "Sisters." Her grin was shrewd. She kept her arm in mine and pulled me into her, and a tiny pulse deep in my center, shameful and thrilled at its importance, quivered in reply.

I could smell my own breath coming out of me. Sour, human. I'd never been this close to her before. Her face distorted, like everyone's does, from this view. She seemed not to be looking at me, but I took her relative stillness to mean that she might be ready to listen to me, finally. So I took my shot.

"When my work feels like it's the most terrifying thing I could do," I said, "that's how I know I have to do it. When it gives me nightmares. When it scares me. That's what makes it good. I would do *anything* for my art. I would never say no to it. I would kill for it."

The painter Richard Gerstl took off all his clothes and hanged himself before a full-length mirror, so he could watch, while stabbing his chest with a knife.

"But I guess I've been searching for a long time, my whole life, and maybe now what I'm feeling is that I've found it—I want something I'd be willing to *be killed* for." The expanse of the ceiling brayed down on me. "It feels like freedom. This willingness." Gerstl killed himself because his affair with the wife of his best friend had come to an end. He'd painted portraits of both of them. "I want *it* to kill *me*," I said.

"Isn't that what all artists say?" the Twin said. She was sitting on the couch, halfway through smoking a cigarette, though I hadn't felt her let me go.

"Is that what *you* say?" I said, standing alone.

"Of course," she said, cigarette between her lips. She lifted both of her hands in front of her face and watched herself with admiration as she bent them into different shapes.

"Even if you let beauty make you stupid?"

"Stupidity is underrated," she said. "We could all use a little more of it. The trick is not letting your need for beauty make you tragic."

"Too late for me," I said, which made her laugh, which made me feel something other than the dank, greasy feeling that had taken over.

I went over to her and cracked my glass against hers. The tiny pulse was mad by now, screeching in my ears, and it felt dramatic and benevolent to demonstrate my commiseration somehow, so I wrapped a hand around the back of her neck. The gesture strengthened her. I drank my wine and gave her more. I kneeled in front of her at some point. And I know I said the word, her word, *sisters*, out loud, but I can't remember if I shouted it or whispered it, or maybe I sang it, that would've been the best, then she got on the floor with me.

SCUMBLE

to modify a painting by applying a very thin coat of
opaque paint to give a softer or duller effect.

As it does in Los Angeles, the summer melted into fall. September, if not October, is often the hottest month of the year, and because the last rain has fallen now seven, eight, even nine months ago, the heat is disturbing, as though whoever was in charge of turning it off didn't do their job, pointing to a greater danger, maybe intruders have boarded the ship and started taking out the crew. For as long as I can remember, there's been a drought or drought warning in California by May, sometimes as early as March, so by October, the city feels ravaged, at the desiccated end. The pollution has built up without rain to rinse it, the air is thick, hot, and brown, and the sunsets scorch in reds and pinks the color of skinless flesh. Around dusk, after being in the studio all day, a shot of fear would rip up my concentration, warning me that I might be the last person alive. How would I know? I'd been inside all day, working in a room surrounded by photos of the Twin taped to the walls. What if we two were the only survivors? Or what if she'd perished? These paintings, my paintings, all that was left of her?

I'd shower, standing under the cold water until I was numb with it, then dress without drying off, letting the fabric of my clothes get wet. I'd get in my truck and drive, not somewhere, just anywhere.

You know you're from Los Angeles if you have a favorite freeway. Mine is the 2, the one that starts as a street in Echo Park and widens into a sweeping highway that ascends into the foothills. At some point before it starts to slope up, it dips, like a slide at a water park, between Glendale and Eagle Rock, and you can see the city all around you and the San Gabriel Mountains dead ahead. If you keep following it up the slope and don't turn left onto the 210 freeway, which will take you west through Big Tujunga Canyon, or right, which will take you east to Pasadena then into Altadena, it becomes a curving mountain road and, if you stay on it for an hour, it reaches all the way to the peak of Mount Wilson, almost six thousand feet above sea level, where Mount Wilson Observatory sits at the end of the road. The story goes that the massive, sixty-inch glass mirror lens of the observatory had to survive that mountain road twice: the first time it was brought up on donkeys in 1906, it cracked, so it had to be remade and journeyed again. It's where Hubble sat for months and months, understanding that the universe, already fathomlessly large, was getting even bigger, which eventually brought us to understand that it is somehow doing this with more velocity.

I love this freeway because it's the one that feels least like an LA freeway. It's never congested, and the view of the city is brief, a blip, while a view of the hills dominates. It was also the one Marina used the most, as it connected Altadena, where we lived, to the rest of LA, so we drove it all the time to get anywhere, maybe I'm more sentimental than I'd like to admit. Driving on it always felt like the thing to do and the place to go when I felt restless and cramped by my work at the end of the long day.

One evening, I drove a while, the windows rolled down, thinking of the Twin and my show, and then turned west onto the 134, which I never do. I drove toward Griffith Park and got off at Zoo Drive. The road curved around the cemetery, and I gazed up at the big, bright hill of it. It was a blazing, artificial green amid the brown hills drained by the drought. Some of my relatives on Marina's side are buried there, but I don't know where.

My phone chimed.

An image from Yves. I swiped to see that he'd sent astrology memes for Scorpio, my sign, something about how I'm a psychopathic bitch who will murder you to the tune of your favorite song.

Still driving, I thumbed through Facebook for events that night. I saw that someone I'd gone to school with was organizing a night of performances at a bar in Koreatown. It had started an hour ago but would go all night. I turned left, up over Los Feliz, and down into the city.

The bar was crowded with art people and Koreans who looked blandly bothered at having their bar invaded. The performances, from what I could tell, were spaced out in various corners of the room and one in the bathroom hallway, with someone approaching you and soliciting advice for how to be an art star and then writing whatever you said on their face in

Sharpie: Fuck me, go to school, don't go to school. I ordered a cocktail from the house menu, something frivolous and expensive to break my habit of cheap white wine, and went out back to the patio.

I kept thinking of the painting I was working on, which had the Twin's hands and wrists coiled around smears of crusty white. I looked at my own hands, dim in the shadows. They were not the same. Some people I knew came outside, spotted me, and arranged themselves around the table.

"Your show is soon, right?" a woman named Yu said. We'd once been in a group show of "Asian American women artists" but had nothing else in common.

"Next month," I said.

"Almost at the fair," she said, in place of congratulations.

"I'm just happy to be busy."

"You look busy," someone giggled, pointing at my shoes. They were color-spattered, like the shoes of painters always are.

It was a relief to do and say shallow things. I noticed a white guy sitting at the other end of the table, now talking to Yu. He looked good, red suspenders and purple shoes, tattooed forearms, shaved head, rug of beard. He had pale eyes like mine. I've always found men easier.

We went back to his place, which was small and bare, with a futon mattress on the floor. Thank God he was a service top, which is what all cis men should be.

"You're in charge," he kept saying.

"Yeah, bitch, I *know*."

We stayed up talking until the sky got light. He was an artist, too, I'd heard of him before. Caleb Cooper, went by

Cal. He made videos and performances with his own body in severe situations of tension or duress, hung from the ceiling by his ankles, hands tied around his back, while an opera blared, or long hours where he lay naked on a bed of broken glass while strumming a guitar and crooning, tears pooling in his ears. In much of his work, he was naked, his pale skin glistening with a film of sweat, and he liked to draw attention to his penis, though it was nothing special. In one piece I remember, his cock is hard, a bunch of heart-shaped balloons tied around it, while he carves a name into his abdomen with a razor blade, the blood drooling into his pubic hair. That piece is called *Hanne*.

I traced the scar of the name with my fingers. "You always title your work with names?" I said.

"Mm," he said.

"Who are they?"

"Women I've loved," he mumbled, his Adam's apple dipping. "Should I make a new one with your name?"

"You must say that to all the girls."

He laughed, then sighed and rolled over. The scar on his belly looked like a brand.

"Hanne?" I said. I pronounced it *Hain*.

He corrected me: *Hah-nuh*. "The one that hurt me the most."

"Oh, Christ. Boys are so ridiculous. You always think you're the first and only ones to have felt anything. You know that heartbreak is the most common emotion after boredom and envy, right?"

"Well, she did," he said.

"Well, poor you," I sang, but he was soon snoring. I wondered if my haughtiness gave me away, if he heard that

I related to him, that girls had done nothing but hurt me too.

I closed my eyes and then opened them again. Couldn't sleep. I picked up my phone and googled him. I found a short interview he'd done with an obscure art magazine. It was okay. He name-dropped Eva Hesse, which I liked. The interviewer asked why he so often put himself in submissive or vulnerable situations. He replied, "I can't help it. The name Caleb is Hebrew for 'faithful dog.'"

BLEEDING

the diffusion or seeping of paint or pigment at the edges; often a defect.

Finally, I was painting every day and they were new, long afternoons in the studio, stretching into the nights, and time felt like a warm bath. I'd go till dawn, sleep at my studio on the old couch, and wake at noon with a placid hangover. I'd bought an espresso machine for the studio with some money from a sale a few years ago, so there was no reason I had to leave during the day. I woke up and did nothing else but paint.

It had been weeks since I'd seen her, but that didn't matter. Image upon image, I had her in front of me, for me, in.

Some nights, Cal would text or I'd text him, and we'd meet for a drink, and then I'd go back to his. I associate his futon on the floor with that hot autumn. His white skin and lean arms would amalgamate into the Twin's in my dreams, the lithe white limbs snaking through my paintings.

Alexandra was calling me every day, in the way gallerists do in the lead-up to the opening, where they play at being a friend who is there for you in a time of need, concerned and indulgent, "Do you have everything you need?" but what they actually want is to confirm that you will deliver what they expect you to, which is, in the end, a product they can sell. Gallerists are not your friend, though they perform a sort of friendship, it's closer to that of an invasive, needy, oversharing kind of boss who calls you at three in the morning to say, "I just had a dream of you dying. Tell me you're okay."

Yves once explained it to me, "Gallerists like to blur the boundary between employee and friend because it's what puts you to work for them all the time. You can never clock out. If you're unfriendly to them, you're suddenly doing a bad job. And since gallerists never have a life of their own, some of them actually think their artists *are* their friends. But the power is fucked. It's like a queen who calls her maid her best friend."

"Are we doing frames or no frames?" was Alexandra's reason to start calling at the end of summer. I'd never used frames on my paintings before, but something about this show, its lofty colors, its poise and exaggeration, how it gestured toward a classical tradition of painting, made them fit. I decided I wanted the ornate golden ones, coils upon coils, of the Rococo period. Once I suggested this, Alexandra had to call multiple times a day to go over the details. "So, we'll do the two bronze on the first wall—the bronze is better than the gold for those. I love the one with scrolls for the more abstract pieces, I just think they cushion so well. What are your thoughts on the floral pattern I sent over? So gilded, right?"

On her latest call, she remarked, as if to herself, "Since we're going full baroque, we'll have to look the part. A good, big, fuck-you necklace. And a gown—definitely a gown."

I hung up and texted the Twin. "Hey, I'm going shopping for something to wear to my opening. Wanna come?"

An hour later, she replied, "I'd be down to go to Barney's."

It was our first time meeting outside of my studio, but it was still for a purpose in service to me. I noticed this on the drive over and it made me wince. I decided I'd offer to buy her something if she wanted, but I thought of Zinat and I winced again. And if she'd suggested Barney's, maybe she already had money. I decided I'd invite her to Berlin, not just for the opening but for the months before, so we could work together. I'd already decided I'd keep painting her for the Berlin show. Alexandra had loved the work when I brought it to her, it would be significant, it would be significant, she kept saying, she couldn't wait to take it to the fair, and I'd emailed a few images to my Berlin gallerist, who had also responded eagerly. What I'd hoped for was happening, the Twin's presence in my work, her pride and beauty and white, heart-shaped face, was lifting it and me into a new realm of universality. It was a hunger that didn't have to fight for what it wanted, ambition that wasn't predicated on survival. It could debase itself while staying clean.

I'd never been to the Barney's in Beverly Hills, though I'd driven by it countless times when I used to take Wilshire to UCLA for a couple months of adjunct teaching. The facade of the building was an overworked impersonation of an Italian villa, fake bricks and potted topiary shrubs. The only parking option was twenty-dollar valet in a structure that had fountains near the elevators and curved molding along the ceiling. The valet, a squat, perspiring man, peered into my truck, assessing the empty water bottles and food containers scattered over the floor and seats before climbing in daintily. He tried to drive hovering an inch above the seat to keep his uniform clean.

I lifted my chin a little, put on my sunglasses, and marched toward the glass doors of the entrance. This is how artists are. It's the world that needs *us*.

I found the Twin browsing a rack of coats. She was wearing an oversized men's blazer, heavy brown tweed, threadbare at the wrists, with one pocket safety-pinned on. How she was not wilted by the heat, I didn't understand, but her hair was a matted mess. She looked homeless, yet her big chin was thrust out. Her sense of purpose, of belonging here, filled the room without even trying.

"The fall line," she said to the rack when I arrived beside her.

I trailed my hand across the shoulders of the coats, slipped it between the rich wool to glance at a price tag, $3,500, the same amount Alexandra had just spent on a frame for me, added to the sum of what I owed her, but moved on as soon as possible, as if the price had been as relevant a piece of information as the fact that there was air in the room.

"My gallerist told me to get a big fuck-you necklace."

"The new Givenchy might be good for that," she said without looking at me. She pronounced it *Gee-van-chay*, which I knew was wrong, but I simpered at her little rebellion. It seemed of the same spirit of her taking my drawing.

"I wanted to ask you something," I said. Following her lead, I didn't look at her, I kept scooting hangers across the rack. "For my show in Berlin, I want to continue this series."

She made no indication that I was talking.

"I'd like to bring you," I said, "to keep working together." I could feel the heat of her body next to mine, but now she was looking away. "I can pay for you to come out. And—and I can probably put you up in your own place."

"Yeah, I'd need my own place," she said.

"Okay. I can find something."

"When?" she said and pulled on a garment, fanning out its fabric.

"I'm leaving a couple weeks after my show here. Berlin opens in summer, so a few months before would be good."

"I can't come until February. Maybe April. At the earliest." She moved away to another rack. She passed a mannequin and dragged her hand across its torso, and I felt it as if she were touching my own breast.

"Okay, great. That would be great."

She made a little shrug that I took to be a confirmation, then she floated away around the floor. She came to a slim, shift-like gown cut straight to the floor with long sleeves and a high neck. It was made of something diaphanous that looked like voile, delicate and expensive, the color of bone.

"You'd look great in this," she said to me. She pointed at my head. "With your hair like that, you'd look like one of them." She pointed at the faceless mannequins.

"I love the color," I said. "It's the color of my show." Of you, I wanted to say.

Kay Sage, one of my favorites, died by shooting herself through the heart. It is said she did this because she was devastated at the death of her husband. He was abusive and violent, there are stories of him chasing her through parties

132

with a knife. She'd attempted suicide once before, shortly after he died. She'd worked to make a comprehensive catalog of his work, then took an overdose of pills.

"Try it on," the Twin said. She looked around for help, then whistled with her finger and thumb, the fat one, in her mouth, like men do to call dogs or each other. A saleswoman came over, her eyebrows raised. "She wants to try this," the Twin shoved her chin at me.

"Of course." The saleswoman grimaced.

Alone in the dressing room, I loved the dress. It was dignified and collinear, covering my feet, but it was semitransparent, my underwear and nipples clearly revealed, like the thin washes of white I'd used on a few paintings, as if raising a fog from their depths. It cost $1,500. I had one credit card left for emergencies that I could use, I'd have to max it out, I calculated in my head how much I owed the bank, Alexandra, my new promises to the Twin, but the numbers didn't take shape, they washed out in the fog too. I used to be uncomfortable in spaces where the art world's money took up all the air in the room, when I walked in, I felt the number of my debts blaze above my head in scarlet, but once I started buying very expensive clothes, telling myself that they were materials like my paints and stretcher bars and canvases, it made me feel as if I was enough of who I was supposed to be, of who I wanted to be, in that world.

I stepped out into the dressing-room hallway, where the Twin was sitting in a chair with curved wooden arms. She was sipping from an espresso cup. The saleswoman fidgeted behind her.

"It's perfect," the Twin said. "I think it's obviously a yes."

The saleswoman took this as her cue, rushing me and clucking her tongue. "Now, you can pull this off," the saleswoman said. "Not everyone can."

"Have you ever *not* said that?" the Twin snapped at her. Of course she was a top.

Once the saleswoman's speechlessness had persisted a few beats, the Twin spoke to me. "It's rad it's so see-through. Will you shave your pussy?"

"We have plenty of nude lingerie that would go nicely," the saleswoman said.

"None would also go nicely," the Twin said.

"What about a slip? A long slip, to the floor?" I said.

"Of course. Let me check what we have," the saleswoman said and disappeared. "Nudity is not my look. I'm not a model like you," I said.

The Twin looked as if a sound had buzzed in the distance. She watched me in the mirror. I felt her eyes slide around my body. I put my hands on my hips and posed. An exchange passed between us. We'd been inverted.

"That dress could easily be wrong," she said. "Like, if you tried to make that yourself, it would look *awful*."

"Why would I try to make this myself?" I said with too much ferocity. I thought of my mother's lumpy homemade dresses.

"All women artists go through a making-their-own-clothes phase," the Twin said.

"I didn't," I said, remembering how Marina's stolen, hand-dyed dresses had felt swelling around me.

"You're smart, then."

I twisted my body around and looked at myself from different angles. I emitted the kind of sigh I'd heard wealthy people make, as if I were tired from a long day of manual labor, though I'd just been standing in front of a mirror.

"Yes, it's perfect. Okay," I said.

I started to move toward the dressing room, but the Twin reached out and grabbed the dress. She pulled me close to her and whispered in my ear, "I know how to remove the tag so it won't buzz when we leave."

Mirrors surrounded us, and I looked at our position reflected in multiplying fragments, heads together, hers tilted up toward mine, me bent over to be closer. I could feel the heat of her face on mine like when she'd kissed me three times, it was not just our bodies being near to each other, but combinative, referential, and I felt as if I understood it somehow, where the heat came from, what it made her want to do.

"I can't do it today, though, didn't dress the part." She made a face of regret. "It'll have to be you."

I looked at her. Her beauty could not be disguised by an old men's jacket and uncombed hair.

"I can't do it either, though," I whispered. "Not, um, not dressed for the part either." I swept my hand around my face, trying to communicate that my whole body was wrong for the part.

"What do you mean?" she said.

Did I have to say it? I don't look like *you*. I may be able to pass as white, but that didn't entitle me to its perquisites, and I could never pass as beautiful, and not, though I tried, as rich either. I'd worn an old T-shirt and jeans, a dirty tote bag slung over my shoulder, the haircut I'd given myself, the round, fleshy face that looked like a swollen moon, washed every

135

night with drugstore cleanser. And if I got caught, I wouldn't be able to cry my way out of it.

But in that moment, while she looked up at me in a beseeching sort of way, I wanted the world she lived in to be mine too. How I looked revealed nothing about me, other than that I ought to be protected by everyone. Who needs who?

Resolved, I looked around to see if anyone was watching us. I must have done it wrong, though, because the Twin sighed and shook her head.

"No, no, you blew it," she said. "So obvious." She made a moue of distaste.

"I can afford it, though," I said. I made myself smile, as if I'd accomplished something.

The Twin released the gown. "Oh, okay, then," she almost shouted. "If you've got it, flaunt it."

Recognition, I realized on the drive home. I'd wanted to see recognition in her face, she looking at me, me looking at her, both seeing something familiar. A magic mirror of, not facsimiles, but what was possible. Why did I feel like I'd failed, and not both of us?

That night in my studio, I worked on the largest painting of her, part of a diptych, the last pieces to finish for the show. My desire troubled me. That we recognize each other, an impossible thing to want. In the painting, I made the light come from below, casting shadows near the top of the frame, which made it seem as though she stood on a plinth, above the viewer. She did. Stand above us all. This was how it felt best to me, the most inherent. The painting was taking me weeks, using everything I knew about underpainting to get the most radiant light and shadows, to make her flesh tactile, using green underneath to make her alive with rufescence. But I itched to mar the beauty I was coaxing out of my paint, something to collide with it, it couldn't be too easy. I mixed charcoal dust with water and sprayed it around her eyes. I did it over and over. It made it look dirty. I stepped back and looked at it, looked at her. The impossibility of seeing, the stygian fog between us. I wasn't seeing the way I ought to, I wasn't seeing what was clearly there. I didn't want to see it. It was a dazzling misunderstanding, voltaic in its wrongness, what it brought to life. Maybe she *had* seen me. A me I wasn't yet. A me which, through her, for her, could be like her. She would take me there, but it wasn't enough only to want her to.

FORESHORTENING

*to portray or show an object or view as closer than it is, or as having
less depth or distance, as an effect of perspective or the angle of vision.*

I made eleven paintings of the Twin for the show that
November, with three of them to save for the fair. I'd never
worked that fast in my life, they came as if they'd been waiting
in me to simply hatch. They were oil on linen, five feet high
by six or seven feet long, except the classical portraits, which
were eight feet high by five and a half feet wide. All the paintings, but especially the portraits, were the largest paintings
I'd ever made because, for the first time in my career, I could
afford to be that large, and, more than that, I wanted to be.
I used the most expensive linen and pigments and I heaped
the paint in places, using dozens of tubes for a single painting.
It cost thousands of dollars in materials to make the big ones,
my loan from Alexandra climbing ever skyward, but I knew,
and so did she, that I was making the kind of paintings that
art collectors wanted to buy, so we let it rise, and I felt almost
giddy at how high it went.

Half of the paintings were more abstract than I'd ever
gone, the photos of the Twin's flour-covered figure drifted

into hazy fields of whites, creams, and grays, with snaky lines and thin shards of black as shadow, the paint heavy and chunky and built-up on the fabric, like the flour had looked on her skin and clothes. There were a few expressive ones, closer to the style of my past work, where I let her whole body appear, though I fractured it, many-limbed, headless, a creature from an underworld, a chimera without heads, a basilisk with seven arms. The classical portraits were the centerpieces of the show, a diptych for the biggest wall. They were my most overt nod to the tradition of painting beautiful white women, the kind who always had more money, beauty, and power than the painter. They were outliers, with their neoclassical realism, in this show and in all of my work, but they were so forceful, like a magnet, the whole room would pitch toward them and bow. All three for the fair were variations of these portraits. First I'd painted two because I'd loved the feeling of painting her this way. I finished one, then started the other almost immediately, just to keep the feeling in my hands, and then I painted three more. When I showed them to Alexandra, she had snapped her fingers three times to indicate done deals. I'd thought of ghost ships while I worked, wrecked, the Tombigbee River fire, her skin wrapped in ropes like rigging, her arms hoisting the flesh of her breasts, the sails, her spine a mast. I titled the show *The Eliza Battle*.

The dress the Twin had chosen for me made me look glamorous and commanding, like the captain of the ship, I loved it. I cut my hair to the scalp again, though this time, I went to a salon that charged me one hundred dollars for a haircut that cost forty dollars for men. I stood in front of the mirror and inflated my chest. I felt accomplished, good, the sweet sting of the whip. Yes, I was a good artist. I was great.

I texted a selfie to Yves and he replied with the heart-eyed smile, which gave me enough pluck to post it online, one of only a handful of selfies I'd allowed myself over the years.

Then he texted, "Do you have help for tonight?" which meant, did I have any drugs to calm me down. I sent him the OK emoji. I didn't need drugs for my openings, though Yves needed them for his. It made me feel cared for, though, that he'd make the mistake of us being the same.

CAPRICCIO

a painting representing a fantasy or a mixture of real and imaginary features;
a kind of free composition, not keeping to the rules of any particular form.

The last big opening I'd been to was last year in Berlin, for Yves. It had been the biggest show of his career, a solo exhibition at the contemporary art museum, albeit in their smallest room, reserved for what they called "emerging" artists, which had needled Yves, who was in his forties and had been working as an artist for more than twenty years. All of his friends and I had made appearances that night in our finery, surrounding him at the entrance like a movie star's entourage. He'd worn a cobalt suit with matching lipstick. He'd darted through the crowd like a fish, with an air of desperation, as though pausing for too long would make him vulnerable to attack. I knew that to keep his face and hands from trembling, he'd started drinking early in the day, and on the way to the gallery, in the cab, instead of the U-Bahn he would've taken any other time, he'd swallowed a Klonopin and squeezed my hand until it felt gone. Yves wanted the nights of his openings to be about triumph, but instead, they always ended up being a trial he had to endure, performing that he was equal to a crowd to which he could never hope to be equal. He'd endure this theater with grace, wearing a persona of contempt and flippancy, laughing too loudly, as though it were all a joke.

One of the most important things I'd learned from Yves was how to project a version of oneself that could perform the kinds of behaviors that didn't come instinctually, that you hadn't been born with but needed. It was the right blend of traits and quirks and mannerisms that, as a whole, provided an armor that appeared decorative, even frivolous, but whose function was to protect the places that felt too tender to reveal, a way, even if only for an evening, even if just by wearing the right shade of lipstick, to parry the fist of the world's scrutiny as it came right at your face.

Like most working-class dreamers, Yves had concocted his persona from stuff he saw on TV, which meant that some mismatched bits ended up in the mix. I always enjoyed a thrill of pride when I noticed one, like a connoisseur who spots a jewel in a bargain bin. The fact that they were all old and mostly forgotten references only added to my feeling that we were special together, that we could see and know each other where others could not. We were old-fashioned queers, which made us glamorous and fragile, the keepers of the past, and our references were from real people as much as fictional characters because the whole thing was a fantasy. This made us lonely, but that, too, felt defining. There was an arrogant frown of Norma Desmond's and the cigarette held aloft, which came from Bette Davis, as did the way he'd snap his head from side to side to reject an idea before it was even presented in full. There was the leaning against doorframes, chin down, gaze serene and predatory, the move Lauren Bacall did in her early movies. At the end of delivering particularly excoriating sentences, he'd channel James Baldwin, his favorite writer, by vaulting his eyebrows toward the crown of his head and lifting his chin, as if it wasn't sufficient for his words alone to ascend above his enemies but that even his face shouldn't be on the same level as theirs.

They weren't all of queenly scorn. The way he twirled his hands through the air reminded me of the stories he'd told me of how, as a child, he'd ached to be a dancer. He was always in the mood for dancing, spreading his arms out and smiling hugely, like Diana Ross. When he was at home, he sang aloud in a booming Broadway vibrato. His laugh was full and generous and cute. And when he allowed himself to fall in love and get drunk enough to talk sweetly about it, he'd put his hand across his sternum in the gentle, injured gesture that politicians do when they speak at memorial services for massacres.

Years ago, Yves and I were in the elevator of an apartment we sublet together in New York, we were there for a group show that had a lot of funding, a few stressful, decadent weeks. We were going out, dressed up, already a bottle of wine into the evening, and a stocky white guy in a backward baseball cap, about my age, got in the elevator with us. Yves and I talked and laughed for twelve floors while the man kept quiet, until, upon reaching the lobby and taking our exit, the man said to us with a jumpy grin, "Jesus, you guys are assholes." I don't remember what we'd been talking about, but I remember we shouted a "Ha!" and I'd felt very gratified, as though I'd achieved something I'd been striving for.

SOTTO IN SU

Italian for "from below to above"; extreme foreshortening of figures painted on a ceiling so as to give the illusion that the figures are suspended in air above the viewer.

I arrived at the gallery as I'd been instructed by Alexandra: at six-thirty, half an hour late, alone. Cal said he'd arrive later, toward the closing, and we'd go for drinks afterward at Foxglove Bar down the street. Alexandra gripped my elbow as soon as I walked in the door, pushing a cup of wine into my hand and leading me to a well-dressed couple whom she had groomed to buy the work. I chatted with them as I let the wine handle me. They asked about Turner and storms, ideas planted by Alexandra, she'd told me, in so many words, that we shouldn't speak too openly about the comments I was making on whiteness in the work. So I said I was interested in ghost stories, mermaids, sea monsters, women who've drowned, where beauty comes from. Their faces showed the confused performance of fascination. "How interesting," they said. "Yes. It is interesting," I said. Alexandra steered the conversation toward the question of which of the pieces would look good in their foyer, she pointed to a painting with a skull-like wash of white over a torso that had fine sutures of black around the nipples. The woman shuddered, her earrings swinging, and said it would startle her every time she walked inside her own house. "Then that's the one," I said. No one laughed. Alexandra moved them toward one of the more abstract pieces, with a bulky, boatlike veil of white over a stark gray background and a pair of thighs and bent knees delicately visible beneath. They bought it. I wandered away to refill my drink.

A procession of friends and acquaintances filled my time, approaching me with wide smiles and light hugs, saying congratulations over and over. The gallery filled, people clutching their cups, kissing cheeks, looking over their shoulders, glancing at the walls and around the room, trying not to look intent. Some rivals came, artists whose careers had paralleled mine. We were often lumped together in the same group shows, they were women who were also not white and who painted figuratively, or made sculptures with legible faces and bodies in them, or were photographers who primarily made portraits, and I resented them not because I thought their work was bad but because it was always tied together with mine, and I'm sure they felt the same about me.

I saw Iris Wells for a second, alone. She zipped around the room, spending a few seconds in front of each piece. I felt a tug to extricate myself from whatever conversation I was in, but then she slipped out the door.

Alexandra came every few minutes to pull me toward potential buyers or other people she deemed me worthy of knowing, the editor of this magazine, the curator of that museum. When a work sold, she would come up behind me, put her hands on both my shoulders, and whisper in my ear, her mouth stained with lipstick and red wine, a feasting hyena. I went to hover around the few people I'd known the longest from grad or undergrad, cool and free from the circus, wearing sneakers or clogs. We went outside to smoke and sigh.

Throughout the evening, I waited for the Twin to appear, knowing my glances toward the door were too eager. As I watched for her, I saw myself as though from far away, standing in the room of my paintings, her face and body everywhere, eight huge canvases, as if the walls of my inner theater had been cut open and bled out. I was flayed for the whole city to see, me and my work, here it is, my desire for you, come see, look at it, it's for you, you, you.

Half an hour before the end, Cal arrived. He put an arm around my waist, kissed my neck. It was nice to have him there. He looked good and interesting, but not, I thought, as interesting as me. He presented a sprig of eucalyptus wrapped in a black ribbon and said, "Hey, baby."

Then he shrank away from the two portraits in front of us.

He swallowed a nervous laugh and said, "So you found my girl."

"Your girl?"

"That's *my girl*, my"—he pointed at his belly—"Hanne."

"Hanne? *Hanne* Hanne?" I said, also pointing at his belly. He shook his head. "Weird. I didn't know you knew her."

"I didn't know her name. I didn't know *you* knew her."

"Well, I guess everyone knows her."

"What does that mean?"

"Of course, she wasn't ever mine. I mean—Haaaaaa-nuhhhh."

"What is that? What is that bullshit?"

"Well, let's just say you're not the first to do something like this. Make a *whole show* about her." With its new scoff, his voice deviated from the one I knew. "Yeah, Hanne," he sighed. "She's quite the femme fatale."

"Hanne," I said. That was her name. So like mine. Almost mine. And she was carved into my lover's stomach. With balloons attached to his hard, bloody cock. And he had nothing but clichés to account for her. Femme fatale? God. She appeared before me through his eyes, my desire for her infiltrated by his. I wondered how he had looked at her, and my stomach lurched when I thought that he had been inside her, *inside*, his cock, his fingers, his tongue, he had penetrated her, he'd been wet with her, smelled of her, and the smell had dried on him, covered him like a skin. He'd worn her like perfume, and me—I'd only looked. My lonely thoughts, imagined, craving, flaccid.

I felt silly, crushed in my long gown. My paintings were stupid, late to the race, just gossip that would help drive up the price of each painting, artist in abject love, queer mourning and unrequited desire, I guess everyone knows her. I tried to tell Cal I was going to have a cigarette, but my throat pinched around my vocal cords and no sound came out, and, of course, as if on cue, as if I'd conjured her, there she was, just coming through the doorway fifteen minutes before the end, indifferent and gorgeous. Her dress was high-necked and long-sleeved like mine. It was just like mine, but it was dark red, as though she'd emerged from a pool of blood. She must have gone back to Barney's and asked for it in a different color. Or did she buy the same one as me and dye it herself? It showed something sweet in her, that she'd do that for me, sweet and cruel. It threw me even more. She wore high heels, her hair, tied up in its bun, was grand and elevated like a queen's. She seemed colossal, striding over to Cal and me, swinging her arms, pelvis thrust forward.

"Well, hello," she sang, amused.

Cal rose to the occasion with, "Hey, Hanne. Fuck, it's been a while."

"Yes, it has. How's the stomach?" She cackled her cackle and reached out and patted his belly just below his belt, where I had been putting my hand for the past month. The two of them talked. Mouths opening and closing. I watched. Two white bodies, the same color, shoving themselves against each other, pushing and pulling and grinding, sucking up each other's saliva, plunging his cock into her, pumping his cock in her fist, I thought of how he liked to push my face into the pillow, to pull my mouth apart with two fingers, had he done that with her? She had probably instructed him to do that, it had been her idea, and now he was using it on me. What belongs to you first belonged to someone else.

"Well, I'll let you girls talk," Cal said, placing a proprietary hand on the back of my neck, then walking away. I wanted to tear his throat out.

Hanne put her face very close to the portrait, her nose almost touching the Payne's grey I'd used in a shadow. "Wow, I love these," she said. It stared back at her, a mirror. "They look like the insides of a body. So visceral."

I said nothing. What the inside of her body felt like.

She started talking about how she'd been on a road trip through the South, how the car had broken down, how the Grand Canyon was actually really cool. I barely listened, but

I watched her mouth. Someone walked past us then stopped abruptly, arms out, as though to embrace us. It was a tall, thin man in his forties, I think he was a dance professor. He looked from her, to me, to the paintings, and his plucked eyebrows arched up. He grinned conspiratorially at us. "Ah!" he cried. "The artist and her muse!"

"Oh, ha," Hanne said.

SELF-PORTRAIT

a portrait the artist makes of themselves; there is an
adage that all portraits are self-portraits.

Everyone came to the Foxglove. Hanne walked in front of
me, talking to someone whose name I'd forgotten. I watched
her ass swaying in the rich fabric, her big, imperial head. At
the bar, I ordered a martini. A skinny man with a mustache
remarked that it was a sophisticated drink. "But your paintings aren't. They are so raw, so, so"—he waved his hand—"so
filthy."

"Does that surprise you?" I said. There was bite in my voice.
It was late.

"Not necessarily. It's surprising how unsurprising it is,
actually. You make very *female* art, I would say."

"I would say you can suck my dick." My head throbbed with
irritation as I walked away. I saw Cal smoking on the back
patio, wedged into a group of people I knew but did not want
to talk to. I decided, in a swarm of drunken resolution, that
I wouldn't call him anymore.

The bar was dark and loud. Red light outlined lumps of
heads. Everyone looked tired, rolled into their own dreaming

strangeness, faces wrinkling and hanging slack, making words but not sentences. I couldn't find Hanne. What would I have said to her? Her name?

I went out front, stumbling onto the sidewalk. I leaned against a streetlamp and smoked and tried to inhale as deep a breath as I could, but it felt cut off at the top, and the air cramped in my chest.

A timid voice came from behind me. "Can I smoke with you?"

I looked up and, like a pair of wings in a small cage, the breath inside me thrashed. It was a small, light-eyed girl with dark hair and milky skin. She looked like me. She *was* me. She was young, in her early twenties, me at that age. She had different eyes, I recognized it, something about them was different than the rest of her face.

"Hi. I'm Lea. I loved your show."

It wasn't me. The wrong name, and this girl had a sweet face, thin like a sparrow. Mine was more round, but faces change, maybe one day, she'd have mine.

"I really liked it," she said. "I'm a big fan of your work. I've saved all the images I can find online. They're my screen saver, actually. I did a presentation on you in class this semester." She paused, then giggled. "Sorry, I don't mean to freak you out. I just wanted to say I really love your work. I love what you do with women's bodies. There's so much beauty, but it becomes ugly. It's like you carve them or something."

"Cool. Hey, do you want to get out of here?" It made me cringe, saying it. Only straight guys used lines like that.

"Okay."

"Where?"

"I don't know? Where, uh—where do you want to go?" She bowed her head and rubbed the screen of her phone with both thumbs. "There's a party in Boyle Heights, some people will be there. I don't know them, but we could go if you want."

"Good, I live in Boyle Heights. Let's go." I lurched away, and I heard her trotting after me. I walked as the Twin—Hanne— walked. I felt Lea's eyes on me, wishful, pining. It felt good, I was getting close to something far away from here.

"Are you okay to drive?" Lea asked.

"Of course!" I crowed. "I always drive better when I'm drunk! I was born and *raised* in LA, that's why." We got in my truck, and I stretched my arm out and felt the dry air press against it as we sailed onto the freeway.

I thought of what the Twin—Hanne—would do, how she would command more and do it with more ease, how she would know her place and not question if it was right that she had it.

Constance Mayer was a painter who fell in love with her teacher and acted as his assistant and maid for twenty years. When his wife died and he still wouldn't marry her, Constance cut her own throat with his razor. He organized a posthumous retrospective of her work.

Lea seemed to understand that we were driving to my house and not the party. Lea said, "I read an interview with you once where you talked about your mother being like a ghost demon from fairy tales. I related to that. My mother was a monster too."

I pinched my brow. A migraine was gathering itself impressively. Mothers and fathers and monsters and daughters.

I pulled onto my street, which was shadowed, the one street-lamp broken.

"In Japanese folklore," I said, "there's a female ghost who appears as an old crone carrying a baby. Ubume—she's called Ubume. She keeps trying to get people to hold the baby for her. But when they do, she disappears, and they're just holding a rock." I got out. "The baby would get heavier and heavier and then, when Ubume disappeared and they were left with the rock, it was so heavy, they'd drop it and it would roll away."

After a series of four successful solo exhibitions, the Russian painter Véra Rockline killed herself at the peak of her fame. No one knows why.

I went through the gate and around the house to the apartment I sublet in the back. The night was downy, like a thick skin. I saw Ubume without her baby, her ghost body clear and alone. I heard Lea follow me, coming into our house, then I reminded myself, this is my house, mine.

When we get inside, I tell her to lie on my bed. Just like that. "Go lie on my bed," I say. My voice is ambitious, I need it that big all of a sudden. Every movement I make is large and important, a choreography that must be executed without mistake, but I don't know why. Monsters and fathers and daughters and mothers and, which is worse, the ways they are marked or the marks they make. I wonder what Marina would think of Hanne, I see that my mother tongue is one of brazen, bankrupt need. I see my mother, my mother's shit on the floor, her wriggling, reddened eyes. She would sometimes smell so sharp and sweet, which drugs smell like that, I'd sometimes get up the courage to ask Google this, and other things, how to stop your mother from hurting you, how to exorcize a demon, what to do, what should I do. Sometimes I'd google her. All that came up was her arrest records, court dates. If she googled me, as Lea had done, what would she find? Paintings of her own face. What could Lea know about it, what does she know about my mother and me. It is dangerous that I should be so legible. I need to control the pace of her recognition. She doesn't go to my bed but hovers near the bookcase like Hanne did. I feel the little hole of where my drawing used to be, the one that belongs to Hanne now, then I feel Lea looking at my books as though she's reading my thoughts, maybe she can read the special language they are written in. To be deciphered. That's all I've ever wanted. No, I've wanted most of all for my deciphering to be needed, for someone to need to do it, and for its discovery to reveal the other to themselves, that we need this to be who we are. Suddenly, I feel flushed with my boiling need. It hurts. "Was your father depressed?" I ask. Her shoulders flinch. I feel quick, sharp sorrow. "Actually, yeah." "Mine was too. That's a male Asian immigrant thing." She nods her little bird head. "Social defeat, masculine honor. I agree." "Mine left us, finally." "You must hate him." The thing about having a father, and then not having one, but having one long enough to understand that he sucked, means I'm not fucked up about men. I think I say this out loud. I think I tell her I'm fucked up about women instead. I want her to understand. Our fathers were both depressed, and she says her mother is a monster, but did she have a mother like mine? What is Hanne's mother like? I realize I don't know. But I understand that Marina would envy Hanne, too, yes, she'd want to ruin her too. "Isn't it weird that our moms are white?" Lea says. "Normally, the moms are Asian and the dads are white. Yellow fever or something." Then Lea moves away from me. I spin around and try to find her in my house. We are playing hide-and-seek. I need to decipher her. What would Hanne do. Her name is Hanne. This is her house. Small bird girl at her feet, she would probably command Lea to open her mouth so Hanne could spit in it, something Mistress Anka makes me do, I love it, press the high heel of her shoe into the soft indent of the temple, tighten her knees around the ears, and shove her cunt into the thankful face. I could get her to pull me by a chain on a collar, or by my hair, but then I remember I don't have any. Mistress Anka charges extra for that. I defile Hanne's beautiful, wealthy hair, I sneak up behind her with my cheap scissors and grab it all like a rope in one hand, I put my knees into her armpits and push my weight into them, and she doesn't want me to, then she does.

I sail into my bedroom with this image. Lea is lying on my bed, her feet still on the floor. I kneel and start to take off her sandals and socks. There is a sect where the women wash the feet of the men with their hair. But my hair is gone now, I can't do it. She does not look like me at all. I feel explosively alive with this, too alive, a voice in my head demands to know: how can you be sad when you do things that are so alive?

Lea sits up. "Lie down," I bark. She does, but then she sits up again.

"Um," she says. "But I don't know if I want to."

I snort my disapproval. Hanne wouldn't let that stop her. No, she wouldn't. I put my hand flat between her breasts, they are so small, and push. "Yes, you are," I say. Her face changes, a decision passing over it, as though she has resolved to obey me. It changes me too. Faces change.

I make her feet bare and look at them. They are bony and fragile-looking. I feel pierced by a wild pity. Is it for me?

"You should run," I say, watching the feet. "I want to but I can't," she says, or maybe I'm imagining that. I pull down her shorts and underwear. She has a thin, shaved cunt. It looks like a child's. I resent her for it. I slap the cunt. Lea flinches. "Wait," she says in a small voice. It's that, by trying to ruin her, I shall ruin myself. I am teaching her, teaching both of us. "You're such a *nice* person," I sneer. "You're so *great*." I want to make her cry because I want to help her, I want to give her what she wants. I pull her shirt off. She raises her arms in meek compliance. Her chest is flat, her nipples sharp, stuck out like thumbtacks.

"Let me look at you," I say. She has the body of a young boy. "You look like a boy," I say.

"Really?"

"Tell me what I look like," I say. I am in my fifteen-hundred-dollar dress, the Twin's washed-out sister. "Tell me I look beautiful." Hanne had looked so beautiful, installed in her bloody dress, entering the room crowded with paintings of herself.

Lea is not beautiful. Neither am I. "Do I look powerful?" I say.

She nods. I see that she is confused. Good. We're in this together.

"Tell me again," I say.

"You"—her voice hits a minor quake—"look powerful."

"Am I like a dog?" I say. The room slides. "We should run away."

Lea crumples her face, embarrassed, embarrassed for me. Hanne sees me like this too.

"Am I the one who has hurt you the most?" I shout. "I'm the one who hurt you the most!"

"I want to stop," she says, and she starts to reach for her clothes and scrunch her feet toward her sandals.

"No—you're going to paint my portrait. I want you to paint me."

She is pulling her clothes back on slyly, if she goes slow enough, I won't notice. "I—I, um—I don't know how." She makes her voice calm.

I realize I have no paints anyway, I only have myself.

"I want to stop," she says again. She is standing over me now, walking backward. I'm still kneeling.

"Yes, let's stop. I'm sorry," I say. "I'm so sorry. I'm sorry I am—" Then I cough on a sob and reach up, maybe for God, but I fall around the corner of the bed, spilling onto the floor. She slips away and stands in the doorway.

"You can still stop," she says, her generosity constricting around my heart. "If you keep going, you'll regret it."

"I'm sorry," I say. "I'm so, so sorry!"

In the doorway, she doesn't move, but I see one of her hands wrap itself around her phone.

"Come here. Please. Look at me. You can take my photo if you want."

I pull my dress up around my waist and it rips. The sound tears a hole in the most frightened part of me. I stick my hand down my underwear. My hand moves.

Lea shifts her weight, and her eyes fly around the room, my house, my crotch to my bookcase to my front door to my windows. She doesn't want a picture of me.

"Look at *me*," I cry out, my voice high.

She gives a little nod, but she is metabolizing her fear, she is waiting for it to be done, I'm the only one of us still in my body, and I hate being here. I see myself from her perspective, down, across the room, and I know what she feels, that inherence, I gave it to her, someone gave it to me. Maybe Ubume had a twin who rescued the child: which one of us had been left in the road: my name, people know my name, but I don't: kneeling at the feet of a twenty-year-old, straining to insert three fingers but the fingernails catch: ruining something: a ridiculous gown with a rip in it: debt: cracked lips: debt and pain are the same, weights that need you, keep you: this sweet young thing in my house, she'd gone to the opening because she loved the work, what I do to women's bodies: what I owe: the marks I want to make are not the ones I am making: I was dry and drunk and I couldn't, and this was how I would stay in the world, and all of this was me.

III

STILL LIFE

the class of pictures representing inanimate objects. Many theories have suggested that still-life paintings, despite the word life, are paintings of death.

I hear the ocean. There are howls from coyotes in the foothills nearby. The air is close, the salt collecting at the edge of the Pacific. Marina has found a beach house for sale in Venice. It's empty, being renovated, most of the walls stripped to their studs. One of the back doors, covered with a plastic tarp, is left unlocked, so she drives out here late at night, an hour from our house, and sits inside, dreaming that the place is hers. She's an old painter living alone, and her life has been lucky. She does not want for money or fame because she has enough, she is only honored when they happen to be delivered to her, and when they are, she accepts them because she knows what is hers. She uses all the rooms of this house as studios for her work. She has a beautiful, regal dog, all white with blue eyes, named Athena for the goddess of wisdom, who was born to no mother and never wanted for one. Athena will live forever, so when Marina dies, it is Athena who will ferry her along. Marina's children call her often, not too much and not too little. Love makes their voices full and calm, and Marina understands how, although sometimes the words love and art are synonymous, it's not all the time, and she can tell the difference. Her children ask her for advice and she always gives the right kind. She is selfless, and yet the self she does have is articulated and inviolate and gentle.

My mother taught me never to judge myself against the successes of others. My mother taught me to love and cherish my craft and to be in service to it. My mother taught me to be grateful for all experiences, the painful ones, too, because even pain is a gift, an invitation to know myself and deeper, and this wisdom that comes from wounds, I can use to help others. It's not necessary to make art, but it can be useful to put pain into something other than one's own body.

There were some years, as a young woman, where Marina felt disappointment, but she learned how to dispel it and was granted the grace of not regretting this time, for it was causal to who she became. Heartbreak happened only to show her how resilient her heart was. She does not, will never, inflict pain upon others, but she understands that pain is no different than any other emotion or experience, and if it moves between people without aim, it can show us ourselves, and she is grateful to have the knowledge it's brought her and secure enough in her purpose to know that it is not the element by which her life will be most marked. The road she is walking on is hers; she belongs to every place along it, no matter where it takes her, and over and over and over, her name is a truth that the world speaks clearly, not too loud, not too quiet. It is changeless, permanent, and only sometimes, at the right time, does she feel the need to say it back.

VELATURA

*is a milky, translucent glaze used in intermediate layers or as a top
coat to adjust colors. For example, a velatura tinted to the color
of flesh can be spread over the face in a portrait, to create a more
opaque mass. Velatura is applied with the artist's fingers.*

I began to draw when I was very young, four or five, and soon
Marina bought me proper sketchbooks, and I was given charcoal and colored pencils and watercolors that I cherished and
kept in slim metal cases in my backpack at all times. When
she said I'd been good, she'd bestow a used, twisted tube of
her oil paint on me, which I'd squeeze and squeeze to get out
the last drips.

Beginning in fifth grade, I enrolled in art class as my elec-
tive every semester, and in the contests held in class at the end
of each term, I won for best painting every time. It continued
through high school, only art classes as my electives, winning
each semester's contest, and in my room, my paintings and
sketches began to pile up on the floor, and I covered every
inch of wall with my work. I didn't have as many images of
the ocean as Marina did, but my room started to look like a
smaller version of her studio. One of my art teachers asked
to buy the painting that won the contest of the fall semester

when I was in ninth grade. It was a portrait of a woman with green hair and yellow eyes with lumpy tears of sandy paste creeping down her face, against a muddy black background created by gluing dirt from the rosebush to the canvas. I sold it to my teacher for fifty bucks and Marina took a photo of the check for me, which she framed and hung in our dining room.

The secret was that Marina had painted all of the paintings that won the contests. I didn't paint them, but we said I did.

It was our secret.

In the days before the first contest, when I was ten, I made many sketches of a woman carrying a bundle of irises. I wanted it to be a portrait of Marina but slightly disfigured so that her face was concealed by the clusters of blue. I tried to make her hands and arms so intertwined with the stems that they blended in, but I couldn't get the flowers right. I wanted their petals to look like tongues, but they kept coming out like popsicle sticks. And the hands of the woman looked like popsicles half-melted, fat and lumpy, too short. The night before the painting was due, I crept toward Marina's studio door, carrying my stack of sketches and a canvas with several attempts I'd had to paint over. I think I was crying. I don't remember what I said as she looked at them or if she said anything in response, but I remember that she kissed the top of my head and the kiss had pain in it, a sting of need, hers and mine.

The next morning, I came downstairs and saw a painting leaning against one of the dining-room chairs. It was my iris woman, but she was shining and warped with light. I didn't understand what she was made of. When I leaned close, I found that Marina had covered the canvas with something metallic—gold leaf? where had that been hiding on her shelves?—and had painted the blue tongues of the flowers and thin arms of the woman in gobs of oil paint that rose off the surface like frosting. The painting on the canvas I'd brought her was nowhere to be seen, I think I'd hoped only that she'd fix mine, but upon it now was this new, stunning creation. I remember thinking it was too good, too good of a lie.

She was out in the studio already, and I went there, skittish. "But everyone will know it's not me," and to this, she slammed the table with one flat hand and spat, "Not even a thank you, and I worked *all night*! Such a fucking ingrate you are! Get the *fuck* out of my sight!" But when I returned home that evening with the blue ribbon of first place and showed it to her, she wrapped me in her arms, a long, pink smile on her face, and said, "I *knew* you could do it. And you did it."

No one noticed that the paintings I made myself and the ones I turned in to the contests were different from each other. That's because they weren't, not yet, we still needed each other too much.

GRISAILLE

a method of painting in gray monochrome, typically to imitate
sculpture; when done in yellow, it is called ***cirage****.*

My first memory of Marina is of an event that I've come to
realize also ended my childhood, troubled it, perhaps there
had been a period where I was Marina's daughter before this,
but when I think of that time, I don't know when it could be,
I think I had always been enemy, equal, something else. She is
standing over me, staring down into the crib, but she doesn't
look at me. I can't be sure if this is because she doesn't notice
me or because we are sharing an unspoken moment together.
The scene is silent and still and dark. Marina doesn't speak.
She may be smoking or drinking from the mug of whiskey
she carried with her throughout the day. I try to will her face
to change, to throw back the emotions she is sending to me
through the air between us. I want to tell her there's been a
mistake, Dad was a mistake, I was a mistake, it was all a mistake, and I was trying to fix it, I'm trying, I tried, but I tried.
I remember she turned her face to me, finally, and it seemed
as if her head was on backward. She was walking away from
me, but I could see her face, she didn't look at me, but I could

tell she knew I was watching her, and she kept her emotions for herself. The face showed me nothing but the intent to be closed. Then she opened her mouth and said, "It's a lie—I've been lying this whole time—I've done nothing but lie to you. Telling you I love you. It's a lie—I am—yes, yes, I am." And then she was gone.

BLOOM

a phenomenon that occurs with varnish on paintings. The condition appears like the bloom on a black grape. If it is on the surface of the varnish, it can normally be removed by gentle wiping with a soft, natural fabric. If underneath the varnish, which is rare, the only cure is to remove the varnish and to revarnish.

The Eliza Battle was a success. It sold out. Money arrived in my bank account, tens of thousands of dollars. I'd never imagined my work would sell for this much, and now came the fair. My text thread with Alexandra was full of diamond emojis. She wanted to organize a dinner for me at the fair, important collectors will be in town, it's the perfect time for it. She sent me the menu of the restaurant she would buy out for the night in my honor. Ostrich egg with truffle, eighty dollars. Fifty plates of it. We would need to calculate what I owed her in loans and production budget, but I didn't need to worry about it now. This first payment was plenty for the next months, and as long as I continued to make the work I'd made for *Eliza Battle*, following the trajectory it had set me on, I would never—thinking of it made a part of myself narrow and sharpen—have to worry about money the way I'd always worried about money.

Over the next weeks, my inbox swelled with a dozen invitations. They were from people I didn't know, for shows, interviews, talks, whatever, I'd do as many of them as I could, more for the momentum than the money, but the money was good too. I still had to reply to all the ones I turned down, saying I hoped we could find another way to work together in the future. That's how you know you're a success in the art world: how many emails you have from people you don't know.

I had a little less than two months before I left for Berlin, and I didn't need to do anything to get ready for February, although Alexandra was happy to remind me that if I felt like making more paintings for the fair, the more she could sell. Thinking of my two hundred and fifty thousand dollars and all the rest, I churned out two more like I was taking aim, it was easy, a couple of trigger pulls. Otherwise, I spent the time in a fog of getting stoned and lying in bed in foul pajamas and having food delivered through an app.

Of course I googled Hanne, now that I knew her name, though I didn't see or speak to her. I found her Instagram, she had twice as many followers as me and half as many posts. There were only images of her, selfies interspersed with images other people had taken or made of her, photographs, paintings of different styles, from many different hands. Some of them were more artistic than others. In one, she was a model for someone's handmade fashion line, wearing a pair of bumpy, red-canvas overalls, the hems wobbling in contrasting thread. The two portraits I'd painted of her were the most recent posts she'd made, with no credit or mention of me, my name nowhere. I scrolled far down and found the photo documentation of Cal's *Hanne* piece. She'd posted it without a caption.

When I closed my eyes now, Hanne's face smeared into Alexandra's, the mouth flaming, the color of blood, and there was Lea's frightened stare. My head started to nurse an ache, a stiffness in my neck, pain in a glittery vein kept pulsing above my left eye and over the crown.

I was tempted to search for Lea, but. I couldn't. My dreams found her, those big eyes, and I was overexposed, my gut dropped away from me with guilt. It wasn't that I needed to hide from her, but from myself.

I—it was not me, who had done that. Who it had—had it?—been.

On the plane to Berlin, I drank a lot and updated my CV, another necessary artist's chore. Almost every artist I knew complained about having to do it, but many, myself included, took a shrewd pleasure in it. One of my professors in grad school had a CV that was a hundred pages long and could be downloaded from her website as a PDF, .doc, or .txt file.

I'd been to Berlin a lot, more than any other city after LA, first visiting the summer after my senior year of college, when it seemed that everyone I knew from school or met at an opening or a party, and everyone they knew who was an artist somewhere, was going to Berlin. Over the years, Berlin became my place for retreat when LA got too hot or started to feel claustrophobic, and because I was being invited to show in Europe more, my career was starting to take root, and this next exhibition would secure me there, but it had been a year since I'd last been here for Yves's show. I was coming back to Berlin different, mutated.

I could always stay with Yves, and there were plenty of sublets from people out of town, for this was a city of transience, expatriates, gig-economy nomads, but this time, flush with new money, I rented an entire flat for myself, in a different part of town than most of the people I knew. When the plane landed, I was still sort of high from an Ambien I'd taken, that hadn't made me sleep but hover in a twilight of hypnagogia that I'd jerk out of when I felt myself to be falling, the bottom of the plane suddenly dissolved. My head throbbed and I felt sick, so I went into a bathroom at the airport, thinking I might throw up. The bathrooms at Tegel were incomprehensibly small, your body barely fit, you had to leave your luggage outside the stall. My knees wedged against the toilet and my back pushed into the door, and though I didn't vomit, I hung my head at the toilet for a while and it felt good, the tiny space of my sick and pain was lustral, something from within would soon get out. Flashes of Lea, the chill of guilt. In the cab from the airport, the Ambien and hangover swayed me, I couldn't hold my head up. It was nearing four in the afternoon, Berlin time. The sky was steely, already night. I was able to make out the drab buildings with their box balconies, the typography of the street signs, the black coats being dragged around by little moons of grim faces, Germans get so grim in the winter. I watched the Muslim women in their headscarves and long dresses that dusted the ground as they walked. I felt a long way from home, which was consoling.

I arrived at my flat in Mitte, the posh part of town, and found that the heater hadn't been turned on. The rooms felt

171

like a morgue. I switched on all the lamps, but the weary light only made the place seem more like a tomb, filled with a cold that had been living there, undisturbed, for a long time, and wasn't about to vacate for me. I called the landlord, no answer. Left a message as I flicked off the lamps and gave in to being claimed by the rules of the place. I fell into the bed with all my clothes on, my coat, gloves, scarf, and hat, and slept hard. I half woke a few times in the night, stiff and frozen, my eyes parched where the lids met.

At some point, the migraine, finally assembled in full, wrenched me out of sleep. Red wine always did it, I'd pushed my luck. I opened my eyes to see the Mitte flat pulsing with stars. The aura had spread to both eyes, and the tingling vein had shaped itself into a hammer. I thrashed through my bag, trying to find my medication. It wasn't anywhere. How would I last? I took another Ambien and got back into bed, curled like a pill bug, taking shallow breaths as the pain and then the dark leaked through everything.

SFUMATO

*the diffusion or seeping of paint or pigment at
the edges; often a kind of paint defect.*

When my eyes creak back open, I feel like a tunnel has been carved through my head by some machine with metal teeth. The time on my phone is confusing, it takes me some moments to count that I've actually been asleep for fifteen hours. It's sometime deep into the next day, but I don't know which day. On my phone there are a dozen notifications, emails, texts, alerts. They are urgent, many from Alexandra. The one from Yves says, "Timing has always been a bitch," and then, "I'm here if you need."

I open the most recent email, which is from someone I don't know. It asks if I care to comment on the Iris Wells situation.

The Iris Wells situation?

My thoughts try to pull me toward Iris, searching for her face, but instead, a huge image of Lea's face rises in my mind, shouting my violation from behind my eyes, what did I do?

My head beats out a rhythm that fits between Lea's blinking eyes, blink, stare, blink, stare, throb, stare, throb.

I search for Iris Wells, but I only have to type Iris W before Google fills in the rest of her name.

Several different headlines announce the same thing, all published in the time I've been asleep. Iris Wells has posted a callout.

"'The Boycott of an Emergency We': A Message from Ante-Object Artist Iris Wells"

"Artist Iris Wells Calls for Boycott of Commercial Art Market"

"Why Iris Wells's Boycott Doesn't Matter—and Why Everyone Should Care"

Photos of her face accompany each headline, so Lea's vanishes, and in its place, Iris and her large black eyes are installed in my skull. The throb adapts, Iris, Wells, throb, throb, Iris, Wells, throb, throb.

"Wait," I say out loud—like Lea had said—to no one. "Please, wait."

But I open my eyes, click on a link, and read.

The artist Iris Wells, who refers to herself as the "Ante-Object Artist," has issued a statement calling for the boycott of art fairs, major art museums, and all commercial art galleries with an annual operating budget of more than one million dollars. She has asked that her boycott be joined by artists who "share [my] . . . racial and ethnic background" and other marginalized identities. Wells is a female African American artist born in New York City. Within twenty-four hours of its posting on Wells's social media accounts, close to one thousand artists have publicly declared that they will join the boycott and cease exhibiting in the institutions named in Wells's statement. The

I drag myself up to sit. I realize I don't remember what's
happened since the night of my opening, since Lea was
in my house. It's been a few days, no, weeks. It's January.
Right, I was making more paintings of Hanne's gleaming
white skin.

The making of meaning, which is to say, the unmaking of
meaning, becomes ever more perfunctory. The aristocratic
land- and life-owning white corporations-as-men consume
our work, our art, our bodies, our intellectual property, our
means of production, our land, our planet, our hope, and our
death, and we do not rebel against this gross exploitation but
rather serve him up our labor on a white tablecloth. We are
happy to be his court fools. We post and like the dates and
times for the rally against gentrification, then we congratulate ourselves when curators and gallerists gather us to their
bosoms and offer us shows in neighborhoods where the blood
runs in the street. We make work about the blood that runs
in the street. We say it is meant to "provoke discussion." We
say it is meant to "challenge viewers to think." We say we are
critiquing the norms of domination, but we gather cultural
capital to *our* bosoms and keep it close. We call it our identity,
our birthright. We claim it is our wealth, wealth we are owed
and which we deserve. By doing this, we perpetuate the only
law those in power understand: the law of ownership, the law
of who owns who, which is to say, what owns what.

175

The museum is a slaughterhouse and the galleries feed it with the meal that is us. We go willingly as sacrifices, martyrs, cud to be chewed, and our only hope is that our names are sprayed with glitter before they're covered in shit. Our identity is a meme, a currency, a performance, a scapegoat, a hero—our skins and names mechanisms of neoliberal self-actualization—and none of any of this is, in fact, ours. We are invited by the institution to critique the institution. Our critique is a cannibalization of critique. We make the institution look better while we make ourselves look worse, and we should be doing the opposite. Our labor shores up the institutions who dominate us, who exploit us under the mandate of diversity, who cash us in like tokens at the fair, who have appropriated our value under the costume of a moral action, but which, of course, is all a lie, a farce—and we let them; indeed, we say we approve, even that we want it.

But *do* we want it? Are we so compliant, so desperate? If we are, it's because we are not yet a *we*. I am aware of the epistemological failure of this text because I am presuming my reader is a *we* when in reality it is a *you*. I'm talking *to you*, not *for us*—and I wish I wasn't. I want there to be a *we* between me and you.

YOU, who share with me the skin color and the so-called ugly bones and facial features, the racial and ethnic backgrounds of the wretched, the genderfuckery, the social defeat, the dirty poverty, the monstrous sexualities, the temporality of ontological death, who suffer from the instruments of oppression but who have chosen to step in line with such weaponized instruments—all of YOU, who come from lineages and ancestries, backgrounds and bodies, histories and traumas of political oppression, domination, violence:

I hereby call on YOU to join me in creating a WE. We are not yet a WE, but in this moment, *we should be.* I am talking to YOU about creating a WE for US.

Let us be a WE:

WE who refuse to produce art objects to satisfy the wealthy, the kings and dictators, the Master. WE who reject the aestheticized collision of our bodies with our value with our skins with our misery. WE who will not bend at the knees to make objects whose value is determined according to power's law of tyrannical beauty, for the hope of being granted a stay in our own executions.

The struggle to become *us* is the struggle not to become *them.* It is an emergency because if WE fail now, it will be the final failure.

WE is born when we boycott the slaughterhouses.

WE is born when we withhold our genius.

WE is born when we keep our lives alive on our own terms.

WE are more than meat for the table of tonight's dinner party.

WE ARE NOT ingredients on the shopping lists of—

—and there follows a list of museums and galleries.

All the major museums and commercial galleries are on it, all the international art fairs, the ones that have loomed like triumphs we could reach for, what I've been reaching for.

Alexandra is on it.

So is my Berlin gallerist.

The only places in the art world where I have hoped to belong.

The ones with the blood on their hands.

The list of art fairs has LA at the top.

Then there is the list of names of artists who've joined Iris. It is the same as the lists that accompany the group exhibitions I am in, the panels I speak on, the artists I am associated with, the ones who came to my opening, my rivals—my peers.

Where I belong.

What if you've been telling the world you want something, and it keeps refusing to give it?

I cannot locate myself.

I close my eyes, and the river of migraine courses through my head. The words of Iris's statement constellate on the black of my eyelids, and I tell myself I should focus, I should think, I need to be alert, the world keeps trying to give me something, but I can't remember what I asked for, there is only the rush of my head's sturdy pain.

Where *do* I belong?

I open my eyes and look around the room of this strange, bare flat. It is icy cold, the squares of the windows black with night, and I will live here for six months, making paintings that will sell for more money than my entire family has ever known.

I say out loud: "I am here." My voice falls through the empty room. I wonder what time it is in California.

I look through my inbox, emails sent to me directly, many from mailing lists I subscribe to, blaring Iris's name and her demand, if they don't ask me outright to join, they imply that I should.

I should, I think, shouldn't I?

Is there a way to know when one has stopped wanting to be something because they have become the thing? What I mean is—if the only people here are outsiders, who decides what's inside the gate?

I see an email from Alexandra that I'd somehow missed, sent the day after the opening. It is buried in my inbox, short, sent from her phone. It says only: "I'm so proud of you."

Her mouth. A lion mother holding her baby in her big, safe mouth. My head hurts. I see Marina, the queer, curled smile she'd given me about Elizabeth Valentine. What would Marina do? Did she teach me anything I could use now?

I think of Marina feeding me, telling me I would be great, her hurt my hurt. Marina loved me so much, too much, she coiled around me and her loneliness as if we were treasure, a fathomlessly breakable egg. She taught me everything, I am her egg.

I go back to the article. I read again the list of artists who I'm supposed to align with, I try to envision myself there, too, because I feel my own clinamen, it pulls and leans and yearns toward belonging, I do so badly want to belong.

I think of all the money Alexandra has given me, paying for my studio even when I had no work for her to sell, paying my rent so I could live, the plates of eighty-dollar ostrich egg with truffle. I think of her typing my name into emails, saying it over the phone, as if her mouth were a calefactory, warming us both against the cold.

I reply to Alexandra's email. I write, "I love you too. Thank you for giving me a home."

I go to my contacts and scroll to Marina, she is listed as M. My mother. Should I text her? Call?

What could I say to her, after so many years of not saying anything? I try to assemble her face, but I can only see the round, startled eyes that Lea gave me and feel the pit of how I've failed them both.

I start typing a message. "Hi. It's been so long." No. How can I know what to do with, for, her, I haven't ever known what to do.

I try again. "Hi Mom, I miss you. Hope you're okay." I type, "Where are you?" but my phone autocorrects it to, "Who are you?" I press SEND before noticing the error.

My phone squirms alive in my hand. Revolted, I drop it. It thuds on the floor and I am up, pacing. I look down to see the screen, black and covered in a lacework of fractures, the names of my family, the names of the galleries, the names of the other artists, the names that are not my name, all swallowed into the dead metal, inert and micrified, leaving me alone.

ULTRAMARINE BLUE

a representation of the Holy Mother with the dead Christ across her knees.

"Is it *you*?" Yves's voice, cool and low, gave away his smile.

"God," I said into my new phone, "it already sounds like you're not on the other side of the world." I clutched the machine, wanting to pull Yves close and have him in my hand, let him slip into my head.

"So," he breathed, "my wife, you have arrived. Amid such drama!"

"I know. Fuck."

"Well, how is it in your chichi headquarters?"

"The heater's broken, says the landlord. And I've had a migraine since I fucking landed. But I just keep reading all the Iris shit online."

"Same," Yves said and sighed.

"I'm kind of fucked up," I said. "About it—about Iris."

"Yes, it's a mess."

"Can I come to yours tonight?"

"Should we have a party?"

Hilarious, Yves.

"Come whenever," he said. "I'm working, of course."

"I'm just going to swim first."

"Have fun, mermaid."

Later, when he opened the door to his apartment, his large hands enveloped my head. Immediately, the throb in it vanished. "Your hair!" he said, kissing my face. "You look like a boy!" His body was graceful, thin, and ropy, and his hair had grown, it was starting to curl around his ears. There was a lot of gray in it now.

I held onto him and said his name.

"It's so good to see you," he said, stepping back and curving his frame to the door like a ballerina on her barre, "even if mermaids can't have hair like this."

The lambent light in his apartment bronzed his mahogany skin, his loose, Prussian-blue clothes, and I smelled his cedar cologne merging with the odor of food. His apartment was warm and lit by candles and small lamps, the heater murmuring reliably like a big, hibernating animal, and I could hear Nina Simone's regal sadness being voiced in a room somewhere. I wanted to cry from the swelling of gladness in my throat. Returning. He started to talk, taking my coat, moving into the kitchen, bringing out the wine. I'd always loved his voice. It was deep like a cello, and he spoke British English through his French accent, which made him sound elegant and always a little disdainful. He'd lived in New York for years before I'd met him, so he could pepper his speech with American slang, which somehow added to his elegance. He folded himself into a chair, stopped talking, and lit a cigarette, letting his onyx-colored eyes rest on me for a while. We could go for long periods of easy silence and tender looking, and

I nestled into my chair, smoking, too, and returned his gaze. I shouldn't have had wine, but I did anyway, here we were, together, I could be happy.

Between our faces was Iris and her callout and all that it meant for me, for us, and what had happened to me, what I had done, I had to tell him, but I didn't want to yet.

"I had an extraordinary experience at the pool today," I said. "In the showers, there was a woman, very large, doughy. Lumpy and pale, one of these German ladies—"

"—salty pillars of the earth," he said.

"Yes. Like the color of chicken broth. She had that gray-blond hair, that *un*-color, you know? And she kept her back to us the whole time. She never showed her front. Even as she went out, she pulled her towel around her and waddled out of the stall like a big baby. On the left side of her back, near her shoulder blade, was a scar—but, like, an intense scar, Yves. I've never seen anything like it, I couldn't stop staring at it. It was like a whole chunk of her had been scooped out. It was the size"—I looked around for a piece of fruit, then held up my fist—"like, this big!"

"The size of the fist is how big the heart is, you know," Yves said, making his own fist. His fingernails were painted indigo.

"Yes." I nodded. "It was like her heart had been scooped out of her but from the *back*. Like they had gone in from behind, when she wasn't looking—or she'd asked them to do it that way because she couldn't handle it from the front. There was another woman in the showers who was staring at it too. I caught her eye, and she looked away. I had a thought"—I paused, feeling a crease in my memory—"I don't know. But I—I wanted to lick it."

"Lick her scar?"

"I know, I know. It was so smooth and shiny, but it was also just so—I don't know—empty."

Yves smiled at me and then let it fade from his face. I knew he was about to remind us that we needed each other, he wanted a friendship of commiseration, an exchange of secrets. He reached across the table and took both of my hands.

"So, what will you do?" he said.

"What are we all going to do?"

"No, I asked you first," he said.

He went to the stove and stirred something in a pot. He set out bowls for us the size of dinner plates, dirty colors of earthy blues, and I recognized the rough, handmade grit of them.

"Did Alain make these?" I asked.

"Yes. The only good thing I got from him, probably." We brought spoons to our lips, and he let his eyes lower from mine, giving me a stay. The broth had oily clusters of gold on the surface.

"This is delicious," I said and wanted to cry again.

"You're really evasive tonight."

"I'm—Yves, I think I'm lost. The fair is in a month, and I could make real money there—I'll have five pieces, and Alexandra has raised my prices, like, a lot. She's doing a dinner for me. And there's the show in summer, which could—I can't even say it out loud, what it could do. It's not just that I'm broke. It's not just that I have debt. I spent nine hundred dollars just in overdraft fees last year. And that's how it's always been for me. Everything hinges on this—my career but also my life. Who I am. But Iris did something for me. She—she explained something," I said. "But Eliza Battle's face fucking sold like *that*." I snapped my fingers.

"Of course it did, babe, just look at her."

"I wanted to paint a beautiful white woman as if we stood on equal ground, as if we had equal access to the meaning in the image, and we—"

"Don't tell me you're craving subjectivity. You know that's impossible for us."

I didn't like hearing that.

"Yves, you're becoming a packrat," I said.

"Stop changing the subject. We're talking about whiteness right now, it's very important!" Which was worth a mutual chuckle.

"But I don't want to make work for white people anymore," I said.

"Who bloody does? But they're the only audience that matters, even when you pretend otherwise."

"That's what *The Eliza Battle* was about. The *failure* of my desire for whiteness. It was about how all that I've hoped white women could do *for* me is why I've let them do so much *to* me. It was the most political thing I've ever done, actually. Why can't Iris see that? That I *am* on her side?"

"Are you? I mean—do you want to be on her side?"

"Do you?"

"You know how I feel about these things," he said. "I've told you before."

Yves had a militant position, which was incongruous, there was nothing obviously militant about him. But he had a rule of turning down invitations to shows and events if they were organized around politics. He was always being asked to contribute work about postcolonialism or Blackness or queerness, whichever term had visibility at the moment, and even if he was making work that dealt with those topics, and even if the offers came with prestige or money, he'd politely decline.

"It's not that I want to make race my explicit subject—it's that I don't need to," he said. "It will be put upon me, no matter what. I could make a painting of birds in a tree, and the white art press would say it's about how I'm reclaiming empowerment about my people being animals. Or whatever. But bitch, I'm no self-hating Black man either. Of course I want to talk about Blackness. But I don't want you to know it's coming! I want my Black work to slide into you and start eating away at your insides. I want you to see me in a show about, oh, some white-artist concept—the picture plane, the history of two-point perspective—and then I want you to go home and find that your sugar has turned black. The world is bizarre and destabilized—that's what I make work about. None of us stand on solid ground, not least on the ground of identity, of all the artificial things."

I nodded along, I liked this speech, but I often wondered if he shouldn't relent a little; either he could make a statement about it and foreground his politics and integrate it into how his work was read, or he could ease his principles, at least so he could afford rent without having to do freelance graphic design gigs, which he hated.

Yves drank the rest of his wine. "I know I'm not respected in the way I want to be. But I don't want to be respected because I can explain someone's racism to them with eloquence. Gilded *guilt*? What a cheap form of respect. And even though it matters to me—because it so very painfully does matter—they'll never let me have it on my own terns. There is never going to be actual liberation."

I said, "There's only going to be bullshit like 'inclusion' and 'diversity,'" but as I said the words, I realized that I'd been relying on them.

"Yes," he said. "But Iris is asking that something be at stake. She's making a point that a boycott is not something one can participate in easily. The point is that it's a struggle. It matters *because* you can't afford to do it. And, you know, she's a firebrand. She would give us all guns if she could," he said. His eyes got dreamy. "She reminds me of my parents' generation. They would sometimes have gatherings at home where everyone called each other 'brother' and 'sister,' and they spent the whole night talking about the 'movement.' Can you imagine what my parents and their friends thought when they found out I wanted to be a *ballerina*? Of all things? That I wanted to be wrapped in furs and driven around in a limo?"

I tried to imagine Marina calling someone Brother or Sister, belonging to something called a Movement. She had no one to call anything, except me. Sometimes I'd go to the grocery store with her, she'd make one trip a week, very late at night, right before they closed. She'd wear her sunglasses the whole time, cheap ones from the gas station, and she'd be wrapped in many layers of tattered blue clothes, her bathrobe belted like a coat and ripped at the elbows, her cheap sandals held together with duct tape. She'd pile our cart with frozen dinners and cans of SpaghettiOs, boxes of macaroni and cheese, and bottle after bottle of whiskey. The only day this menu deviated was her birthday, which was the saddest day of the

187

year. She'd bake herself a cake, blow up one balloon and tether it to a chair in the dining room. Instead of eating the cake, I'd watch her cry and speak the litany of the many ways she was alone in the world. Sometimes, she'd seem to remember I was there, and then she'd ask if I loved her. "But *you* love me, right?" And I'd say yes. And then she'd forget and ask again. She kept asking.

"Iris came to my show," I said.

"She did? What'd she say?"

"We didn't talk. I saw her looking at the work, though. If she was on the fence about her position, I think my show being so white was the last push she needed. She was probably like, Goddamn it, that's it."

"It's eclipse season." Yves shrugged. "Sudden chaos."

"Ugh. It's just—again, it's me read as wanting something I can't have. 'The Asian American woman striving to paint like the Old Masters.' But they never question the Old Masters, they only question me."

"What did you expect," he said.

"I expected people to see that I'm *trying* to deal with whiteness."

"Yes, but the thing about whiteness," Yves said, and we sat back in our chairs, and his voice became slow, the room still, "is that it needs Blackness. It's never just white supremacy— it's always also anti-Blackness. But the thing is—what's really fucked up—is that Blackness needs whiteness too. This is the trick. All of us—we all measure ourselves by these two poles. How Black, how white. How *not* Black, how *not* white."

"Doesn't that feel like what Iris is doing?" I said. "Us versus them? It's still the colonizer's system of organization."

"It's crude, yes. But"—he made a face of giving up—"she's also speaking truth. She's dealing with the world as it is, rather than how we'd like it to be." He paused and cocked his head. "You have to respect that. It takes courage. I've never had that much courage, mon dieu."

"Do you have anything that was on the boycott list?" I asked.

Yves shook his head. "Only next year. I'm in a dry spell."

I winced and apologized.

"I had to take some shit gigs last month to make rent." He pouted. "The logo for a queer film festival."

I knew he'd been having to do that more and more because the art world was tilting toward being explicit about politics, which meant that Yves's position of being implicit was falling out of favor.

"My year was pretty dry too," I offered.

"Seems plenty wet now, mermaid." He smiled, but his eyes were glassy and faraway.

I glanced over at a small framed drawing on his wall. It was a black piece of paper framed in thin black metal. You had to get very close to read what had been typed on it with an old typewriter, black ink indiscernible, only the indents of the paper with just one word: *white.* He'd never shown it. Too political, he'd said.

"But *of course* we have to join Iris," he said. "There's no question, mermaid. We must not be on the wrong side of this, despite our narcissisms of small difference."

He put out his cigarette and didn't wait for me to respond. He assumed I agreed. I assumed I agreed, too, yet as my mind reached for the solid thought of my allegiance, nothing was there.

The music from the other room reached its end. I made gestures of trying to do the dishes, but Yves waved me away, pushing me into the living room, where we sat on the sofa he'd reupholstered with the gray wool Swiss Army blankets of one of his heroes, Joseph Beuys.

"What we really need to talk about, though," he said, "is that I can tell you've had a heartbreak."

"God," I groaned. "Let's not talk about it."

"But you made work about it, I presume. I *hope*."

"It didn't help. The opposite, actually."

"That's the risk, always."

"No, not like that. It's just—" I saw then, like a phantom had risen in it, that I would have to live with Hanne's face on the inside of my head for six more months. It felt like grueling discipline, a lesson I needed to learn. "It's the woman in these Eliza paintings. The white girl. But—but I was late to the race."

"Ah." Yves started to chuckle. "So you fell for a *slutty* white girl?"

"You know I hate that word."

"Yes, but it's different for me."

"Why, because you're a man?"

"Of course, my love—that's always the reason things are different for me, isn't it?"

I hoped he didn't notice how my laugh at this was so much limper than his.

"I've fallen for another slutty white boy myself," he said with a smile that was equal parts sorrow and mischief. He laid his head back and went into a mushy story about the new fling, a young Adonis, white, twinky, named something like Timmy or Timo, a dancer, perfect shoulders, hung, and I floated away on the days of wine and Ambien, my headache feeding from its familiar trough. My mind flipped through images, Lea beneath me, Hanne standing over me, Hanne and Cal's tongues in each other's holes, and then the woman at the pool, her heart being dug out with a long spoon, the kind Berlin cafés give you with your latte, then I thought that maybe she had been shot and they'd had to tunnel into her to get at the bullet, I gulped the last of my wine and saw the woman on her soft, big stomach in bed at night, nightgown undone, the hole in her back stinging, the bandage sticking to it, and then, when it had healed into the shiny, concave pit, how a nose, a tongue, a gentle fist, would've fit there perfectly, when Yves touched my knee and said, "You're tired. You should sleep."

I let him lead me into his bedroom.

"Aren't you coming?" I said as he turned to shut the door behind him.

"It's Berlin, remember? We're nocturnal, you barbaric American. I'll try not to bump you when I crash in here at dawn."

"Bump me all you want," I said. "Love you."

He shut the door, and we were—I was—alone. I spread out on the bed. The room turned slowly and I felt like I might vomit, so I turned on my side and hung my head halfway off the bed. The next thing I knew, I heard the click of the bedside lamp being turned off and saw Yves's sinewy chest and wiry arms folding back the covers in the dawn light. He burrowed into the bed, and I heard him sigh. The trace of stale cigarette smoke was all that was left of his cologne. In the colorless light, I saw that the skin on his face had sunk into the cheeks. He looked much older, gray in his stubble too.

Soon he was snoring lightly, a lowing rumble in his chest and throat. I pulled the curtains closed and the room was shadowed a sooty violet, like a bruise. I felt a sharp tingle in my cunt. Went to pee and felt a burning. Held his shaving mirror between my legs and saw that I was swollen and bright red. Must have been the pool, or the plane ride. Or the drinking. I don't know. My shoulders drooped. I hobbled to the kitchen, underwear around my knees, found yogurt in the refrigerator, and scooped with my fingers, pushing it into myself as far as I could go.

GRISAILLE

a grayish, yellowish, dingy white named after Isabella Clara Eugenia, the sovereign of the Spanish Netherlands in the sixteenth and seventeenth centuries. When her husband went to war, Isabella vowed not to wash her underwear until he returned. She thought the war would be a quick one. This story is now understood to be apocryphal.

Silke Stuck, my Berlin gallerist, wore leather pants to our first meeting, which I took as a good omen.

As soon as we sat down, she commenced: "Perhaps it is not the most easy, but we would like to begin by offering a space to let us discuss what to do about Iris Wells."

"Great."

"Even if that means we decide not to do anything."

"Right."

"We are, of course, hoping you will continue the work of *The Eliza Battle*, which we found to be so, *so* brilliant." Her German accent susurrated. You vill continue ze vurk of Ze Elisa Battle. Zo, *zo* brilliant. "We found the questions in *The Eliza Battle* to be, to the current discourse, quite relevant."

"The questions," I said.

"So relevant," Silke said.

"To the current discourse," I said.

"Yes, the current discourse," she said.

I let too much silence happen because Silke pulled out her phone and said, "Let me read now out loud a quote from an essay that we think is articulating an important but so far unspoken position. I will email you the link. 'A boycott is nothing more than a withdrawal and is decidedly not a form of activism. The demands of a boycott are always both too specific and not specific enough, depending on the scope of the reading. Questions such as 'Whom are you punishing?' and 'What price are you prepared to pay?' are seldom raised. Imposing one's moral judgment unto others and asking them to act upon it is a slippery slope that can easily, if not inevitably, lead to hypocrisy and double standards.'"

I shifted in my seat and my cunt scalded, a wave of burn up through my belly.

"But what is the difference," I said, "between being punished and being held accountable? Like, what is the difference between symbolic violence and actual violence? I mean, isn't the performative also something that really happens and leaves marks and is in the world?"

"We are so excited to be supporting your process through these questions," Silke said.

On my way home, I saw a batch of sparrows stipple the branch of a bald tree and took this as another omen, but if it was good or bad, I wasn't sure. I couldn't walk more than a couple steps without my cunt catching fire. I thought of RuPaul saying, "Your pussy's on fire!" and then the word "rue."

I went inside the nearest pharmacy. The pharmacist was a young man, probably my age, and I watched him shrink under

194

my stare as I told him my symptoms. "There's a lot of chalky white shit coming out," I said.

"For this, we have a cream and some—some—" he struggled to find the word, held up a finger, then brought out a small box and opened it, showing me pearlescent, ovoid tablets to insert.

"Yes, fine," I said.

"Three times a day, you put these inside"—he paused and made a gesture with that finger—"inside yourself."

"Obviously," I said. He started to peck at the cash register.

"Oh, and, um, Miss," he said. "It's—it's—um—it's advisable not to have intercourse penetration for several days."

"Jesus, man, I *know*."

He lifted his hands in mock defense.

"Oh, but, also," I said, trying to make my voice inoffensive. "I forgot my migraine medication. In America. I take—I can't remember the name—I take something for migraines. I get the aura really bad. I can't—I'm not able. Do you have something? For migraines?"

He lifted his gaze at me, and there was something hot and new in it. "There have been studies done," he said, "about 'migraines.'" He made air quotes with both hands. "We have found that the best thing is rest and acetaminophen—Tylenol, as you call it."

"Tylenol," I said.

"Yes." Now he was standing straight.

"Tylenol doesn't work. At all. I need something a *lot* stronger. I'm taking six ibuprofen and nothing happens."

"You can take two pills Tylenol as many as three times in one day," he said, a generous offer, and punched a button that made the cash register fling itself open with a clang. "In Germany," he went on, pleased with how this had turned out, "we do not take so many pills to solve our problems. It is eleven euro forty."

I stared at him. He stared back. It wasn't working, I would not win.

"Please," I said. A man—he might be swayed if I begged. "I'm in horrible pain."

"I'm sure it will go away," he said. "Maybe you should have less stress."

My eyes started to burn, but I would not let him see me cry. I fumbled with my wallet and let some coins fall on the counter, then I grabbed my yeast infection medicine, clutching it as if it were a small fortune in a paper bag.

DILUENT

*paint or pigment applied thickly, especially when
used to achieve surface texture.*

Now Alexandra was texting me and emailing about the fair.

"When you have a moment, let's do a call. I want to make sure the dinner is perfect."

"Happy to loan you anything you need to buy an outfit. The fair is the perfect place to splurge."

"Saw this and thought you'd kill it" with a photo of a beige latex dress that looked like skin.

"Or I can pick something for you? Remind me your size?"

"I'd like to confirm the titles of the new pieces at your earliest convenience."

"Would like to book your travel back to LA ASAP, can we speak tomorrow re dates? First-class is not a problem."

I stared at her name in my phone, the words she was typing for me.

What should someone who doesn't know what to do with herself do?

I read them, and she knew I'd read them. The two blue checkmarks burned in our thread for days.

But I could only type, "I don't know. I don't know. I'll try to decide soon."

Alexandra, her cardinal mouth, replied with the sparkling heart, and more, if it was possible, of me unraveled.

CRAQUELURE

occurs where adhesion between layers has deteriorated due to
faulty materials or improper methods of application.

My yeast infection was interminable, as yeast infections are, and all I could do for my migraine was take Ambien every night, which asphyxiated my consciousness enough that I was not awake for when the pain was the worst, but I only had a few left. Despite this, I let Yves and his fling, whose name was Theo, drag me out nearly every night to a bar, a club, a party. I'd watch them frolic with each other with their giddy, newborn desire, wrap their arms around the shoulders of their friends, and, as the night wore on, become attached to each other with more and more suction. After a few hours of this, I'd depart, smiling against their drunkenly glittery eyes and operatic pleas that I stay. I'd sink into the luxury of the cab that sped me away, even if it only took me a few blocks.

In my flat, the medicine's hot slime oozing out of me, I'd spread out on the bed, or sometimes the floor, and rest my phone on my chest, so if I fell asleep when Hanne texted, I'd feel it in my bones and wake up.

I'd emailed her to say I needed her to get here soon. For the work, I said. Even though I meant for me. She'd replied vaguely. "Oh sure, cool. Will let you know when soon." But she never let me know anything.

The days stretched into weeks, then, about a month later, a text came: "I got some photos of myself, wanna see?"

After waiting a few painful minutes, I mimicked her tone: "Oh sure, cool."

No response for twenty-four hours, then came six in succession with no words, only the photos themselves, and there she was, no more staring at my own reflection, I was staring at her, in the phone, in the palm of my hand, there she was. She was nude, prostrate on a bed, in dim light. The bed was a mess and the room looked destitute. She was wearing a harness, on all fours, and her hair covered her face. Then she was spread-eagle. The dark line between her legs was perfect. Then she was shot from behind, a flawless little circle of an asshole. She had tattoos in crevices, little nests of black near her crotch, on her ribs tucked close to her armpits. Who was I to her? Who was she trying to be for me?

The photos arrived while I was at a quiet bar with Yves, Theo, and some of their friends, and the dings and buzzes from my phone came during a pause in the conversation, so everyone turned to me and watched whatever fluttered in my face, indicating I'd received something of value. Yves reached over and snatched the phone out of my stupid hand. I didn't, couldn't, protest but fell back in my chair as the group pawed at the phone, rectangular blue glowing on their faces as their aw-ing morphed into twittering, and Hanne's face shrank the world around me. I was alone with her in a room with glowing walls, ceiling, and floor, and her face curved around us both. I had wanted a world of her, for us. Instead, I'd let her become *the* world.

I looked up at the ceiling.

The pain in my head moved, as if to breach. I pitched forward, then backward. A mistake. To look up. A huge cavity opened above me, behind me, cracking through the ceiling and into the low-hanging sky. It had always been there, and now I could feel how close it had been to me the entire time.

It was my head, she was springing out of my own head. Fully formed like Athena, motherless.

Yves and Theo took me to the hospital. I had to have stitches, a diagonal line across my forehead, which would, Yves said, give me a "fine and charismatic scar," but they gave me painkillers, thank God, so I finally had a buttress against my migraine. I also had a concussion, they told me, from cracking my head open on the floor, and so would probably feel strange for some days. "Ha," I said, which provoked quizzical looks, "then I'll feel like myself!" Yves started in with German, trying to assure the doctors that this didn't mean anything pathological. He always took care of me. They asked me if I had allergies, if I was taking medications, if I had any ailments. I told them about my yeast infection, that I had a migraine that was blinding me, that I'd had it for weeks, that it had started last summer. "I've had a migraine my entire life," I found myself saying, "My head is giving birth! I inherited a family curse!" This got no reaction, so I raised my voice, saying, "My mother—my mother was fucked up—she was cursed!" I had trouble breathing, and a nurse stroked my shoulder.

I wrote a text to Alexandra. I'm sorry, I've been ill. I don't think I should travel. I won't be coming to the fair. SEND.

She called, the sound banging against the linoleum and fluorescent lights of the hospital, and I watched my hand, as if in slow motion, tap the DECLINE button.

Then I put my hand on my heart, felt the gloating of it. There was all that I owed, I could feel it breathing behind me and on top of me and beneath me and also in me, for it was in me, money, vows, debt, void, this thing called my career, my work, but was it mine? Really, now, who was I, and what, if anything, belonged to me?

Yves took me home without Theo. I've always appreciated his perceptiveness. When I'd climbed into bed and he'd patted the blanket up around my neck, he pulled my phone out of somewhere.

"At least now I know why you're such a mess," he said, holding it up. "She *is* quite beautiful. But straight, no? Tsk, tsk."

"Oh, fuck, I didn't respond yet!" I lurched up and grabbed for the phone. He waved it out of reach.

"I'll write it, I'll write it. You just rest, sweetheart."

I waved my arms. The contempt in the word "sweetheart" caught my fear. "But what are you going to say?" I cried. "It has to be the exact right thing!"

"Mm, I'll just say that seeing this side of her put you in the hospital."

"Fuck! Stop it! *Yves!*" My voice was violent and pathetic, and I stretched forward with enough force that Yves stood and backed into the wall.

He said my name in a low voice, not as an address or a question but as though to describe the thing he was looking at. "I've never seen you like this." We stared at each other, a minor battle. When he decided he'd won, he said, "Take your pain pill. I'll come by in the morning."

He left the room with my phone and was gone by the time I'd flung myself out of the bed and flailed into the living room. The blood that rushed to my forehead crashed into the wall behind my eyes, and I pitched forward, hands dropping into the cushions of the sofa. I vomited a bitter, clear liquid, the expulsion after weeks of retching deterged me. I dreamed of Hanne again that night, but the medication strangled my memory of it, and I awoke the next morning as though I'd fallen out of time, but I hadn't, I was here, here I am, and there was the stain on the couch I had to get out.

CLEAVAGE

*an early eighteenth-century genre of French painting
showing courtly figures at a garden party.*

Yves decided to throw a party to combat the winter, but really, it was an excuse to get everyone together to dish about Iris. We had it at mine, the heater had been fixed. I barely agreed to it, my forehead thick with a bandage and stitches, though my painkiller high was strong enough to deaden the dread I felt about everything. The fair was two weeks away, and I still hadn't answered any of Alexandra's calls, there were seven of them on my phone, so I'd started turning it off for days at a time.

Yves invited Theo and our mutual friends, all artists, living in Berlin, but of course from somewhere else, and traveling all over the world most of the year. We had careers that were in similar places, so we could enjoy each other as both competition and commiseration, we played the same game. Most of them would soon be flown by their galleries to LA for the fair, they were the kinds of artists who had solo booths, reasons for the excess. Perhaps some of them had even been invited by Alexandra to the dinner in my honor.

In this room now, though, my attachment was not where it had always been. I looked at everyone through the clarity of my new face, my clean damage, and saw their self-satisfied faces as vile, their ostentatious eyeglass frames and designer shoes frivolous. All of those who belonged there had added their names to Iris's list. Except me. I weighed myself against them, and I looked at those who didn't belong with Iris's WE. There was Tamás, who had not added his name to the list and was perhaps the most successful of us because he was a very beautiful white man and also very tall. He brought a woman named Celeste, from New York but "based in Berlin and London," who had brassy golden skin and called herself a "mutt"—"you know, *post*racial"—and everyone laughed at how that didn't mean anything, she had the smallest hands I'd ever seen. Her name was with Iris, she said she made videos about colors and capitalism, a phone went around showing an image splintered into many shades of beige. There was Agata, from Poland, who made work in the empty, ruined buildings of former war zones, where she broadcast radio shows or made and screened 16-mm films. She came alone, wrapped in a camel-hair coat and black leather gloves, and she looked like an oryx. Her name, too, was with Iris. There was a couple I'd met the last time I was here, Jack and Clemens, American and Dutch white boys, respectively, who made abstract De Kooning-esque paintings and abstract Johns-esque paintings, respectively, and whose names were not part of the WE. I had little respect for them as artists, mediocre white boys getting away with it, but I enjoyed them as people, we'd bonded at a drunken dance party one late night, the last time I'd been here. They brought with them a

guy who looked white but mixed with something, black hair
and eyes and olive skin, and a dignified air, a little too preppy
but I assume intended for me, whom I'd heard of, an artist
who'd recently exploded in New York, everyone was talking
about him, he was also a figurative painter. He painted lan-
guid people with refined hands, reaching for each other while
reclining, there was a melancholy loneliness with a satirical
humor, the art press loved him for his wit, and he enjoyed
the role of the intellectual painter who knew his theory, he
liked to quote Bergson. He kept his black scarf on the entire
evening, I could tell it was cashmere and that this was why
he kept it on, his new money.

I didn't know if he had joined the WE because I thought his
name was Jonah, and I called him that a few times, but then
Yves pulled me aside and whispered, "His name is *Dominic*,
what's the matter with you?" We both laughed into our palms.
I was uninterested, anyway, my vagina holding the dregs of my
infection, my head thudding with images of Hanne.

The conversation got going when Clemens, the Jasper Johns
mooch, asked Yves what he thought about Iris.

"And why do you ask me first, darling?" Yves said.

Clemens tried to reply, but Yves laid one of his hands on
Clemens's shoulder, and Clemens stayed silent.

"What do *you* think about Iris?" Yves said.

Jack cut in, "I don't think it's our—our place to say anything."

"No?" Yves said. "Why not?"

"We shouldn't—shouldn't take up space in this dialogue,"
Jack said.

Yves giggled. "Don't you people love to take up space,
though?"

"Ultimately"—Celeste smirked—"Iris's boycott actually gives all the space to white people. If we withhold our work from these places, who's going to be in there, if not us?"

Tamás nodded gravely. I'd seen white men be like this before, on their best behavior for their new nonwhite girl-friends. I'm sure Celeste had already had to deliver long racism-101 lectures to him, explaining how reverse racism wasn't real, that kind of shit.

"But there has certainly been a change," Clemens said. "Now, so many artists like you"—he waved his hand at Yves and Celeste, and I sucked in my breath at the insult—"are being given shows. Big shows!"

"Listen, darling," Yves said, "when I started, the only thing curators ever wanted to know—but could never bring themselves to ask—was how my art was about being Black and gay. That was my entire worth, which is to say, my entire poverty. But not one institution in all of Europe could bring themselves to say those words. The number of times they said the word *identity* at me—you'd have thought my mother named me that. How often did I hear about quote-unquote universal themes, about how these fools could or could not relate to my work. If they could not, this was because my work had failed to transcend the wretchedness of my oh-so-specific identity. It had been too fucking Black, too fucking gay. But if they *could* relate, well, this was clear evidence that their enlightened institutions had taught me right!

"It used to be, 'Oh, he's a fag? We can't show fags! We're already showing one!' Now, ten years later, 'Oh my God, you're a fag? We need to show more fags! We only have one!'"

He knit his brow into the tight little Norma Desmond frown. "And, darling"—he inched his hand up Clemens' neck, curled his fingers in the blond hair—"nothing has changed. That's still the only thing they want to talk about, only now they can bring themselves to say the words. It's, in fact, all they want to talk about these days. They have their trendy terms for it now, but they still have no idea what any of it means."

"But aren't you happy about this?" Clemens said. "Isn't it better to have them at least know they're being racist? Isn't that the way to fight racism?"

"Bitch, please," Yves said, and Theo whooped. "Knowing that racism exists is not fighting racism, that's just plain education. Including me in their museum is not fighting racism or even about race, any more than when I *wasn't* included. Somehow, they missed the fact that, back when they paid for galleries and museums full of white men, there was still *just as much race* in the room as there is when I'm included. A room full of white artists is an exhibition about *whiteness*, even if none of the whites can see it."

"Because whiteness gets to be blank and invisible and fucking universal," I said.

Yves snapped his head in my direction and twirled his face in endorsement. "Which is why white people can't ever see their own race," he said. "They're taught that it's empty—universal!—just waiting to be filled in with the fine strokes of their individuality." He paused to shake his head mournfully. "For centuries, white people have gone around insisting, 'It's not about race, it's not about race,' while they slice babies in half for no other reason. They say it's science, or anthropology, or what God wants. They build institutions of quote-unquote civilization on quote-unquote universal principles that somehow always puts whiteness on top, while slaughtering everyone else."

"But you still show your work in these institutions," Clemens said. "How do you reconcile that?"

"The real question is," I said, "how do *you* reconcile it? You show *your* work in the same institutions." I thought, I really can't talk anymore about this because I'll start screaming, which startled me, my outrage, it had never stormed like this before.

"It will always be us"—Yves motioned at himself, Celeste, and me—"who have to do the labor of fixing the world. That your people broke, by the way. And bitch, I'm tired. I'm a fucking Pisces!"

Yves was smiling at me, but it was weird, voided, and tension was thronging in me, bitterness spreading through my mouth.

Clemens looked down in his lap and drank his wine haughtily, as if he deserved it. I watched him, thought of him brushing his teeth at the end of the day, climbing into bed, listening to his inner voice work through its troubles. I envied him with hostility, that not only the world but someone, a parent, a god, a quote-unquote civilization, had let him define himself on his own terms.

"I can't help but point out," Jack said, standing up, "that this is the same artist who was just awarded one hundred thousand dollars by the museum she's now boycotting."

"So, she can't critique the institution—she should only be grateful?" Celeste said, raising her voice after Jack, who was now going into the kitchen to get more wine. They started bickering, voices getting loud, someone saying something about "hyperrepresentation," but I couldn't listen.

Arshile Gorky, his studio burned down, his wife gone with their children, and his painting arm paralyzed by a car accident, hanged himself at the age of forty-four. Why be an artist at all, who is it for?

Yves and Theo got up and disappeared into the bedroom. Agata pulled out her tarot cards and everyone turned their attention toward her, relieved to go back to their personal agons. I watched her hold up her ornamented hands and start to speak about fate, but my head was pounding with itself, with this new anger.

I wrapped myself in a blanket and went out on the balcony to smoke.

It was late, two or three in the morning, maybe later.

There was a light on in the apartment across the courtyard. I could see straight inside, no curtains against the naked glass. I saw a woman, white, older, skeletal, with gray hair fuzzed out around her head like a ball of dust, on her knees in her living room. She was turned away from me, digging with a small spade into a huge earthenware pot of dirt the size of a washing machine. Her back was hunched over her work, she looked like she was kneading dough. She put the spadefuls of dirt into a pile next to her, but I couldn't see if they were being deposited into another container or onto the floor. I watched her for a while, feeling my body's throb start to concentrate, the prickling in my scalp awakening the rip in my forehead and the bacteria in my cunt. She stopped to rest, sitting back on her heels and wiping her forehead with her sleeve. I couldn't see her face. I tried to will her to turn around.

But—

"There you are," someone said, so I was the one to turn around. It was Jonah. What was his real name again?

"Mm," I said. I looked back to my woman, but the light had gone out, she was gone.

He slid next to me, lit a cigarette, asked what I was looking at.

"There was a woman there in her apartment, digging in the dirt."

"Dirt?"

"Yes, on the floor of her living room. She had a huge pot of it." I searched the facade of the building, forgetting now which window had been hers. They all looked the same, still and black.

"It's kind of late, don't you think, to be gardening in your living room?" I could hear the bemused disbelief in his voice, his method of flirting.

"Whatever. I saw her."

He held his hands up, okay, okay, and I saw he had a silver watch on his wrist. Its large face glinted at me, impudent, wanting too much already. "Hey, I heard great things about your show," came next. "Very visceral, was what my friend said. He was there. Sexy, he said, but in a fucked-up way. It takes a lot of courage to paint what you did."

"And what did I paint."

"Beauty is the most radical thing of all."

"Says who? I mean, who *decides* what's beautiful?" I stayed turned away from him.

"Didn't you? Decide?"

"I don't think a decision is what I made."

"But how could you not have made one?"

"It was impossible, what I wanted, it wasn't ever going to work." I wished my woman would come back to her window.

"To chase something so impossible, to insist on it—is that not a decision?"

"But it was the wrong decision."

"The great horror of being an artist," he said, "is that you spend hours, months, years, pouring your intention into something, and then you bring it into the world and declare, 'This is what it means,' and someone can come along and say, 'No, it doesn't, it means this other thing,' and that is also true."

His black eyes were odd to me when I couldn't help but meet them.

"What am I going to do?" I heard myself say.

"What are you going to do?" he asked, but his mouth hadn't moved.

"I don't know what to do," I said.

"You're a painter," he said. Suddenly I felt loved in a way I didn't earn.

"No, I want to be someone else."

My blanket had fallen off my shoulders. "I can't trust it anymore," I said, trying to make my voice convinced, which startled me, that frailty, its truth.

He took a step closer. "Don't be afraid," he said.

"I'm not afraid," I said. I did not want this. "I'm not afraid," I said again. I pulled my blanket up and closed it around my neck.

"Congratulations," he said.

"Why, thank you."

"No, really. I'm not eating your ass," he said, and he took another step closer.

Don't say it, I thought, don't you fucking say it.

"At least, not yet."

I let out a retching sound and crashed inside, *fuck* this, storming past the fortune-telling to the bathroom, whose door I slammed and locked. I sat on the toilet, pulling my underwear off, and felt my cunt throbbing with distaste. My underwear was stained with new lumps of white. I wondered desperately how this yeast infection could last this long. Maybe it was becoming my cunt's natural state. I turned on the shower and stayed in there, under the hot spray, for as long as I thought it would take until they were all gone. There was a bar of soap from the landlord, the only thing in the apartment except for the furniture. It was brown and angular, shaved off a block, and smelled loamy and ripe, like wet wood. I used its weak lather to wash my hair, since I'd cut it all off, I didn't need much. I brought the rough rectangle close to my face to inspect its striations, how much it looked like wet dirt, why had she been digging?

I must have stayed in there for an hour, but of course, Berlin, there were still people in my living room when I got out. I kept my face down even as a voice said my name and went straight to the bedroom. Theo and Yves lay in my bed, braided together, resting. The room smelled of sperm.

"Hi, darling," Yves said, lifting an arm toward me. "We've taken your bed."

I went to the window and turned the well-engineered German latch, cracking it open. The frozen air streamed in, clean and fast.

"I'm coming in. I need *out* of there," I said and tunneled into the blankets, still in my bathrobe with a towel embellishing my head. Yves rubbed my shoulder.

"Mmm, you smell good," Theo mewed.

"I hate artists," I said.

They both laughed. Yves turned to Theo. "I told you, she's in a heartbreak."

Theo clicked his tongue. "Poor you," he said. From the way he said "poor," with the long *o* like a *u* sound, I suddenly recognized that he was German.

"Oh, you're from here?" I said.

He confirmed this by lowering his eyelids and face in mock prayer. "The only one who's original."

IMPRIMATURA

*if the overpainting is not thick enough, ghostly
figures will appear in the image.*

February froze, time froze. It was impossible to remember
a time when it had not been cold, and I was confused that
people could live here at all. The darkness relented only a few
hours each day, but even then, the sky wasn't exactly light
but a dim gray, which made it feel like the night wasn't on the
other side of the world but close, just resting so as to return
soon with full force. The trees stood crookedly, denuded of
their leaves as though they'd been violated, and there was
nothing to look at that wasn't black or gray or the color of dirt.

I found a studio to sublet. It was at the south end of
Neukölln, the neighborhood of Turkish immigrants that had
been invaded by young expats freelancing as something that
used "creative" as a noun. No matter where they were from,
they all spoke English. A decade earlier, when I'd first come
to Berlin, these gig-economy kids had lived in Kreuzberg, the
neighborhood north of Neukölln, also alongside immigrants,
but had inevitably started to creep south like a cluster of
herpes sores.

I saw Hanne's face in my dreams, hovering in the air before me when I woke up, and in people I passed on the street, their jaws big and curved and their skin and hair washed with pale gold. When I got close to them, they revealed themselves to be dark-haired or weak-chinned, and questions would start to sprout in my mind about who they were, where they had come from, and where she had gone, but I'd squash them and keep walking. There was my headache, my wound and its small bandage, the big hole of debt that followed me, but these did not belong to me, I felt invaded.

The fair—it came and went. I turned off my phone and shut down my laptop, so it expired over me as a stretch of meaningless days. I checked my face in the mirror a couple times, as if to make sure I still existed, and I did. It was oddly still there, I, for such an obliteration. My dinner had been canceled, though Alexandra had still taken my paintings. She couldn't *not* take them with how much she expected to make from them, but I imagined them installed on those fluorescent-lit walls of the great bazaar, secreting something that stank.

The last email from her had been the angriest I'd ever heard her be: after a terse hello, it was the itemized bill of what she'd loaned me. The total was more than my monthly payment, so she'd written that, this month, nothing would be deposited into my account. *I'd very much like to speak with you after the fair is over.*

My new studio was through the courtyard, on the top floor of the hinterhaus. I rented it through July, paying all the money up-front. The fourth of July had been decided upon for my opening at Silke's. As I handed over the envelope of cash to the artist I was subletting from, I said with extravagance, "I have a show on America's birthday," but his mouth only twitched, and we said nothing else to each other. Maybe he hated Americans, or maybe he himself was one. Probably both.

It was not the best studio I'd ever had, and though it was technically more spacious than my studio in LA, it had a distinctly Berlin air of desolation. Its walls were old and crumbling and felt too far from each other. The only thing in it was a flimsy IKEA folding table that slanted to one side. The floorboards had been ground down over the decades, broken in places and filled in with cheap, uneven concrete, and if you were barefoot, you would've cut your feet on splinters and jagged corners, but I was never barefoot because the heater failed to bring the room above fifty degrees. The building had been bombed in the war, and you could see the exact place where it'd been rebuilt, there was a raised vein of wall in the corridor where the color shifted between beige and light brown. Where they met each other, this seam of right and wrong, I couldn't bear to look at it.

On my way to work there for the first time, I stopped at the art supply store and bought an armful of oranges, yellows, reds, chartreuses, and pinks. It reminded me of what I loved most about painting, to be absorbed into how pigments changed if you put them next to one another. This yellow becomes entirely different next to this blue, or this red, or another yellow. But I couldn't even untwist their caps. *The Eliza Battle* was far away, selling at a fair I wasn't supposed to be in on the other side of the world, a strange blip in my past that didn't fit anywhere. Who had made those grand, masterful paintings that had sold for so much? Expensive decorations for the Master's house.

When I arrived in the cold room and spread out my new colors, they looked frantic and exhausted, like drugged ravers who'd been dancing all night and now spilled out of the club into the harsh sunrise. I stood in the room as if in the center of wreckage.

Suddenly, Marina's paintings reared up and I saw them everywhere on the sad walls, plastered on the lenses of my eyes.

I had to get out of there. I rushed outside and stood in the courtyard. I let time pass, trying to breathe.

My phone started ringing. The sound tore through me.

Unthinkingly, I brought the phone to my ear, an escape portal. It was Alexandra.

"*There* you are!" she said, her voice thundering through the phone. "My *God*, I have been so worried! *What* is going on?"

I looked up, following the dark building to where it met the dark sky.

"I am somewhere," I said. "Somewhere I've never been before."

"I thought you were in Berlin?"

"Alexandra, I don't know."

"Kitty cat, you have had me so fucking concerned, I've been going out of my mind!" I could tell that she was shouting loud enough for her assistants to hear.

"I don't want it anymore, Alexandra, I don't want it," I said, but she didn't hear me.

Her voice mowed over me. "The paintings all sold at the fair, I'm pleased to report, though I'm not surprised. But really,

I wish the dinner had happened. It is *really* a shame we missed this opportunity, but I am hopeful we can keep the momentum. We definitely need to. Let's plan for a dinner in Berlin for the July show. We won't have as many people in town—this is why fairs are so good, everyone's in the same place—but we can make it work. I'm confident we will still have interest."

I pulled the phone away from my head and held it out in front of me, Alexandra isolated to this small rectangle. Was it as simple as tapping the red hang-up button? Would I be free?

"Alexandra," I said, keeping my arm straight, the phone distant, "you have been so good to me. But I need to be different now."

I hung up. The fizzle of her voice cut off, and the silence of the courtyard came into the new space. I touched my bandage. I'd made a new space. I tapped the options near Alexandra's name and selected BLOCK. Then I went to my contacts and found Marina. I stared at her name, a strand between us that was limp and cold from unuse.

I started writing a text to her. Everything I needed to account for, all the deeds and their terrible counterparts, the absences, the things I hadn't done.

"First of all, I am sorry. I am so very sorry."

I felt the phone's weight in my hand, the mass of time.

"I abandoned you and I've never forgiven myself for it," I wrote. SEND.

"I'm sorry, I don't think I can thank you enough for what you gave me." SEND.

I thought of Lea, how she'd snuck away from me and pulled her clothes back on. She'd given herself what she knew belonged to her.

"Sometimes I feel like you infested me and I can't clean you off. But sometimes I think it's the other way around. I let my dirt get on you too." SEND.

Into the empty field on the screen, I wrote, I miss you, then hesitated at its possibility. SEND.

"I wish I was close to you now. I want you to know who I am now, I am an artist. Do you want that too?" SEND.

I looked around for something to sit on, but the courtyard only held bicycles chained to a metal pole.

"Mother daughter enemy stranger lover muse. Pick one." SEND.

The phone felt like it would fall through my hand, through the street beneath me, cut through the earth.

Then I saw a little door I hadn't noticed before, under the staircase. It was barely high enough to let a hunched old woman pass through. It framed a rectangle of black that was blacker than any black I'd seen, it seemed to make a noise, like it had a throat with a voice in it. I went closer. The air at the threshold was warm and smelled sweet, of aged decay, the kind that's done most of its disintegration already and now takes its time. The noise came again, like it was calling my name. Was it Marina? "I need help," I said to it, and it was instinctual to go inside because that's where I would find what I needed. I walked down the stairs, which were oddly sound-less, no creaking. There was no light switch. The blackness was total, quivering and thick and soft as fur. The heart of the building's furnace was down here, I could sense it nearby in the darkness, it made a lowing hiss and rested in its scent of old metal. It was warmer here than any place in the building, any place in Berlin. I unburdened myself of my coat, sweater, and gloves and went forward into the black with my bare arms and neck. I held out my palms. The space was magnificent. It felt boundless. But it also felt very close against me, as though my skin were soaking in it. It was the space behind my head, the one that had attended my whole life, but here it was, with me now, with me in a new, essential way. I lay down. Don't be afraid. The ground was comfortable somehow. It fit me. I'm not afraid. I held up my hand, stupidly, to see if I could make out its edges, feel the distance between it and my face, but the dark was so complete, my hand and arm and then the rest of me went extinct in it. I lay there for a long time, breathing quietly and not knowing if my eyes were closed or open. It was relentless and ample, like a big whip held in an expensive glove. It was home, and it had been right under me all along.

VELATURA

Painters dislike working directly on white, so they
brush on a thin veil of a tint of color.

It was very late when I came up from the basement. It had rained and the streets were soundless, black, and glossy, like the world had been smothered beneath an oil spill. I swerved along the sidewalk, the wound in my head like a weight, and the greasy black was also inside me. Only the night trains were running. I descended the stairs into the subway station, hitting a wall of stifling, heated air that smelled of urine and smoke.

The train arrived with its thuddering *whoosh* of air. A few people hurried out of the car in front of me so that it was empty. I was the only one who stepped on. I sat down and, within a moment, understood why. Stretched out flat on the floor of the car was a passed-out white woman in a short summer dress. She looked as if she'd been flung there, neck bent as if broken, arm fallen over her face. Her dress was thin and stained and flung back, showing smears of dried shit on her bare thighs. Her feet were bare, dirty, and red, on the verge of frostbite. She was probably a junkie. She was not the first junkie I'd seen in Berlin, passed out on the street. All the junkies here were white. She smelled sharply unwashed. I couldn't see her face. Her thin legs and arms were covered in what looked like dozens of bunches of spindly tattoos in pale black ink. No, she had written on herself. Or maybe someone else had. With a ballpoint pen, it looked like. Having had to press hard to make a mark. There were invented letters and shapes, like a child's doodling, maybe they were sentences in a secret language. Maybe she was a painter.

Was this Marina lying unconscious in front of me? Maybe she had tried to find me after all this time, called around Los Angeles, have you seen my daughter? You may know her work, she paints my face, she can't stop painting it, yes, she's a painter like me. Maybe she'd sold enough drugs and sex for the money to fly to Berlin, but when she arrived, she'd gotten lost, gotten high, never made it past the train station. The skin of her neck looked defenseless. She breathed lightly and rearranged her limbs, as though she were trying to get comfortable on a couch. Her hair was stringy and thin, but it was blond, so this wasn't my mother.

I pulled out my phone. It bit at me, I remembered the text messages I'd sent.

I just saw someone who looks like you. You should come to Berlin to be with me. I need you. SEND. For a second, I listened for a bell from the phone of the junkie, but there was none.

Hello? I typed. Are you there?

SEND.

Then—a brief streak of light and movement.

223

The little bubble of ellipses popped up. It changed everything, that she might be there, that she might come back to me. She was pushing toward my heart.

I watched the ellipses ripple on my phone. Getting close. They bubbled. But then they faded. Nothing came.

ALLA PRIMA

the condition appears like the bloom on a black grape.

The next stop is mine. I search in my wallet for some money to give the junkie, but I don't have any coins. I hold a twenty-euro note in my hand, hesitating as the train pulls into the stop. The woman sighs in her sleep, her breath scratching in lungs that sound damaged. She doesn't have pockets or anywhere I can slip the bill into, it will probably be stolen if I leave it with her, so I put my money away and step over her carefully as I leave.

I try to forget her as I walk home, but there comes a noise, a hiss. *Ssss.* I feel it slide into my ears. I look toward the street. It is empty, still, shining with blackness. When I come to my building, dismal and looming in the night, I feel a cold thought scrape out my mind.

I should have given her my coat. I left her there, in that paltry sundress, to freeze to death with shit on her legs.

The noise comes again. *Sssssssssss.*

I run back to the train station.

Sssssss sssssss ssssss.

An animal of regret squirms in my belly. I wait twenty minutes for the next night train. *Sssssss SSSSSS sssssss.*

I get on and off a dozen times, different stops, different trains. I am a fist punching through the stations, swinging at the bodies of the trains, but I never land on anything.

She has disappeared. I tell myself she has woken up and gone home. She's tucked herself into her bed, the bed that is just her size.

I go up to the street. The buildings look like the outlines of trees, hundreds of feet above me. The noise gets louder, insistent, as though it is trying to get my attention. An appetitive tingle is spreading through my limbs into each finger, the tips of my ears, the dark seems to move with it. I start walking, I try to follow it, but now that I am in the middle of the dark, it comes from everywhere. It is behind me and above me, in front, in the street, up toward the black sky.

Sssssssssssssss.

"Mom?" I call out.

The hiss gets louder, as if in response. *Sssssssssssssssssssss!*

I cross the street and walk faster, almost running. There are more tall buildings here, but they have no lights on, and they have accumulated as if I am in a forest.

"Mom?" I whisper. I want to see if she can hear me even if I whisper. The hiss comes again, also quiet.

sssss

I go up a hill, which slopes sharply upward, getting closer to the sky, but then it turns downward on a steep decline. I stumble and slide down it. When I land, a hundred years have passed and I am a thousand miles away from anywhere I know. I clutch my belly, it is flabby and soft, then my head, an empty mouth, wanting to find things to fill it. There is the smell of garbage and sewer, the dead things of the city streets, the forest floor, the rot and fungus of everything beneath each other. I can hear myself panting, I'm sweating. My head—my head.

"Mom? Where are you?"

I listen for the hiss, but it is silent. I scramble to get up and cut my hands open on the concrete.

"Mom!" I shout. "Mom!"

I realize she isn't answering me because I'm not calling her actual name. That bitch, I think.

I inhale to start shouting her name, but I stop. My mouth is hollow. I can't remember it, I can't remember my mother's name. I know it starts with an L. No, that's not right, that was Lea. It starts with a V. Does it? I inhale a big breath and blow it out with a cry and I hear myself not knowing what I should know. What is it? What is my mother's name? I start to run. I make sounds that an animal makes, I feel nothing other than the brazen, reckless fact that I exist. I am lugging dead weight behind me, then I lurch, no, it's inside of me, it *is* me. My face is wet and twisted, and my head is the heaviest, weakest thing in the world. I inhale and inhale and can't breathe. I fall and hit my chin on the street. I rest my head and whimper for a long time, facedown on the empty sidewalk. When I stop crying, I lift my face and feel in front of me with my hands. There are cobblestones holding me, but there is one large, smooth rock beneath my face. It has been carefully placed there, smooth and round and flat as a dinner plate. It is a mirror, a mirror that reflects stone back to you. How merciful, I think. That I wouldn't have to see my face right now, the face that looks exactly like my mother's.

And then her name comes back to me, so true it feels like my own spine, and I say it into, out of, the dark, and I wrap my arms around my body against the stone.

ICON

the tendency for perception to impose a meaningful interpretation on a random or ambiguous image, so that one sees an object, pattern, or meaning where there is none.

Hanne arrived.

I picked her up from the airport in a car I'd rented for the occasion, an overblown excess, as Berlin's public transport system is clean and swift and never breaks down. But—I'd wanted to impress her, I was appurtenant to her. I'd gone to the airport the day before and waited two hours, but I'd had the day wrong. The impassive German at the information desk had shaken his head at me. "Nein. No flights from Los Angeles now."

Hanne stepped through the gate with one small bag the size of a microwave and a black wool coat that went to the floor, the collar pointed up to her ears. Her face didn't change when it saw me, she only came closer, dragging her little suitcase, coat flapping around her like bat wings, and said, "Fuck, I gotta smoke. Now."

We didn't speak much on the drive back to my flat. The city was gray and tired, and the thought poked at me that I'd dragged her away from LA and its yearlong warmth. She set her knees wide apart, looking out the window with her big chin skirting the glass. I thought of lionesses napping behind a glass wall at the zoo.

Her large head turned toward me and stayed turned toward me. She was looking out my window. She had blobs of mascara under her eyes that made her look drugged. I looked back to the road, then she said, "It's great how fucked-up your face looks now. It looks like a monster leaped out of your forehead. Like *Alien*," she said.

"I thought more Athena. It's my wisdom and my wound," I said.

She spoke as though I'd said nothing. "There was this guy I used to know who was so pretty, like one of those boys who's prettier than a girl? Like, what the fuck? Then, one day, he shows up with this tattoo of a line across his face. Like, the line of a black pen, ear to ear, right in the middle." She traced her finger horizontally on her face. "So fucking rad." She turned back to the window, closing her eyes without me.

"What did it mean?"

"Oh." She waved her hand drowsily, the lioness flicking its tail at a fly. "Who cares?"

The image of the face sliced in half took me to the photos she'd sent me of herself in that grimy room.

"What do your tattoos mean?"

She popped a piece of gum in her mouth and rotated her head in a slow circle, the way yoga instructors make you do, then bent her head sharply to the side. A moist *pop* came from her neck. She sighed and said to the glass, in one exhale, "I don't know you well enough to tell you that yet."

.   .   .

The next morning, I invited her to breakfast at a little gentrified place near the canal with menus printed in English and tealight candles on all the windowsills. The walls were painted the German-gray of places like this, my flat was the same color, jail-cell chic. Berlin made her face look different, still regal but with some sludge on it. I hadn't really seen her, faced her, since we'd stood together in the room of my *Eliza Battle*, when I'd careened out of the Foxglove. The last part of her I'd seen had been her blood-colored ass.

"So, I'm going to visit some friends in Rome in a few days, and I'll be back in a couple weeks," she said.

"Oh, you didn't tell me—"

"—just decided. Hope that's okay with the sublet. If not, I can find something else."

"No, I think that's fine. I'll check, but it should be fine. Who's in Rome?"

She blinked, a response, then said, "Tell me about this summer show," stirring her latte with the long spoon. "What are you trying to do this time that you didn't do last time?"

What I didn't do last time. I thought of Iris calling artists like me ingredients on a shopping list.

"I'm starting to hate the last one," I said. "Well, I don't hate it. I hate what it means. What it did."

"Which was?" She sounded bored. "I thought it was a hit."

"It was. Sorry, I'm—I'm a little disoriented." The wound in my forehead itched, and I wanted to claw at it. "It's been a weird few weeks."

Hanne waited, her face empty of complexity, even more beautiful.

"Whatever, sorry." I exhaled. "Sorry. I'm not explaining this well."

"Don't apologize so much. It's unattractive."

"Well. It's that I'm having an existential crisis about beauty."

"Still?"

"Beauty and power. How they are the same thing. What they are synonyms for."

"Beauty doesn't mean anything. I already *told* you that."

"Right." I nodded. It could've been my thought, but it happened too fast, and someone other than me had said it. Maybe this was just more evidence that we were connected now.

"There's drama happening too," I said. "I've been called out."

"Yeah, I know," she said.

"You do?"

Hanne's face contorted with excitement. "Yeah, how invigorating! Now you have so much to work with."

I was nodding without knowing why I was nodding.

"The first thing I want to know about anyone," she said, throwing her arms open and then folding her hands behind her head, the same wanton confidence she'd displayed in my studio that first time, when I should have thrown knives at her, "is who do you *resent*. That's everything. You can make an entire life's work from that."

"But—I agree with the callout," I said. "I understand Iris's position and I—"

"Well, of course you do. That's what makes it so fun. It's important to always have an archnemesis. To define yourself by what they are not. It's how the universe stays in balance."

I sat back and tried to fit myself into what she said, to interpret this as a gesture of her being careful with me.

"Can I ask you something?" I said. "I've been thinking of what you said about punishment. When we first met. You said you didn't believe in it—divine punishment, or any kind. What did you mean?"

"I don't think things are beyond our control. What happens to you is what you make happen. You make your own bed. Isn't that what Hegel said? No such thing as punishment because even a slave needs its master to have an identity."

She pronounced the name *Hi-gel*. She wormed her nubby thumb and her long index finger in and out of the coffee cup's handle.

"You make your own bed," I sounded out, staring at her, as if I were trying out a sentence in another language.

She nodded at me her authorization.

"Yes," I said, and I knew, because it wasn't a no, that it came from the place that I'd been understanding as love. In that moment, I felt so close to her, it was as if I was inside her, that all I had to do to take up the space she enjoyed was to superimpose myself on it. Maybe belonging, maybe love, was a trick of surfaces too.

I pointed at the candleholder on the table. "This is nice," I said. It was metal, dirty gold, and held a tapered candle with a saucer and loop for your finger. Its candle was burning low in the hole.

"It is," she said. I watched her eyes move over it too. Her face was good and open now.

"I've always wanted one like that," I said.

"Oh yeah?"

"They remind me of *Jane Eyre*—like, you carry it in your white nightgown to inspect the strange moaning in the east wing of your mansion."

I looked over both my shoulders, first one and then the other, performatively, then at her. I made sure her eyes were on me, then I reached across the table toward her and grabbed the candleholder. I pulled it close to me, blew out the flame, then buried it in my bag. It made a small lump in my sack, its presence a kind of whine that only we could hear.

Her face changed. I decided it was the recognition I'd been wanting from her.

Two tables over, a man was watching us. He'd seen me steal the candleholder. My cheeks got hot, and I looked away from him. He had a long, ugly face and a dark coat drawn around him like a blanket. There was an air of dejection about him, or maybe it was only the fact that he was balding.

Now Hanne looked at him. Everything about her body started to say *me* but not out loud, directing the attention away from my little theft. A large piece of chocolate cake, half-eaten, sat in front of the man. It was preposterously large, like birthday cake in cartoons, this was his sad birthday, alone. I looked to see if he'd tied a lone balloon to his chair. In one graceful sweep, Hanne moved to sit at the table next to the man and extended her long arm to his cake. The bend in her arm was exquisite, it made him even more ugly. She plunged her fingers into the cake, fondling clumps of it, and I watched him watch her put large pieces in her mouth, filling her mouth so that her cheeks puffed out, then she tilted her head back, as though in ecstasy. Too much, I winced. But still I watched.

Where had I seen that before?

I thought of Hanne stealing my drawing, back in my studio in LA, the $1,500 gown I'd bought to look like her, how she'd gripped it between her finger and that repulsive little thumb. And now this candleholder, whining in my bag.

I had the fast, brutal thought that all the people I knew were beautiful. I didn't know anyone ugly, not one. And sometimes I used the word beauty when I should have been using a different word, but not always. When not? Iris would use this as evidence of my—my what, exactly? Maybe she really was my twin.

SECCO

Italian for "from below to above."

Hanne returned from Rome later than she'd said she would. At first, she said it would be a couple weeks, but that came and went, so I texted her, asking where she was and if she was okay, and didn't receive a reply until the week following, saying she'd been visiting an old convent in Portugal and was going to keep traveling around into Croatia, some Greek islands. She wrote that she'd met someone and he was showing her the country. I had a vision of a farmer with tattered pants and bushy, black eyebrows fucking her in the hay. She didn't wind up back in Berlin until the winter was over, mid-April.

I spent the weeks without her in my basement, letting myself be eaten by that consoling dark. I didn't answer when Silke called. I deleted the social media apps from my phone, swiftly, the boycott disappeared, its chatter silenced.

My friends came back from LA to their flat, and because Hanne had not really lived there at all, I ended up paying the rent she was supposed to pay. Upon returning, she informed me coolly that she'd spent more money than she'd planned on her travels, so she had to move in with me. My account was getting low now, and I didn't know when my next payment would come from Alexandra.

Now that Hanne was here, really here, the question of who she was had not moved toward an answer but away, troubled, conflated with the question of what she wanted from me. I'd walk into the living room and find her there, taking up the entire couch, an odalisque, and my thoughts would bounce with confusion, why wasn't she looking at me? It was all I wanted, for her to look at me, for her to see not just who I was but who I was for her, because I was so many new and terrible things. I'd fractured my allegiance to the world I was supposed to belong to for *her*, but then I'd wonder if it really was *for* her or *because* of her or worse—*about*? There was her beauty, her whiteness, her disregard for everything difficult and ugly that crawled around my life, and I wanted this, yes, but how and why and was that all? I was hoping she'd be a map or a key to a place I could never belong to, and instead, this hope had razed that place. It felt lewd. It revealed my hope to be callow, made my desire conspicuous and artless, like a man who exposes his penis to you on the street, a gesture he performs to feel powerful or get a thrill, but which instead reveals his genitals to be like all other genitals, so ordinary, banal. The mundanity of them is what is most harmful. What a weird mistake that the world can be terrorized by such a wrinkled little worm.

After spending the first week sleeping day and night on my couch, she woke up.

"Do you want me at the studio today?" she said, not looking at me but at her phone.

237

I had no intention of painting her again, of being captive to that face of hers. But I supposed I'd need to perform it to keep our charade going.

"You could come see this cool thing," I said. "In the basement of my building. Where the studio is. There's a cool place I found." The black started to sing around my head, reminding me of the world I preferred to be in. "I've been going there a lot, every day. It feels so—it's not in this world. Or of it. It could be the afterlife. I've always believed that God was just death. Just nothingness, you know? *No-thing-ness*. Am I making sense?"

Hanne's face flattened into its feline aspect, a regard so calm it bordered on somnolence. She said nothing, which I took as a yes.

"Is this it?" she said when we were sitting on the floor in the black of the basement. "This is your cool place?"

I shut my eyes, which felt no different than when they were open. "Doesn't it feel good?"

There was silence. I envisioned our bodies together, close and slender and horizontal, like two sightless fish packed in a can of oil. The painter Christiane Pflug killed herself when she was thirty-five years old by taking an overdose of Seconal at the beach that was her favorite place to sketch.

"I don't think I can do this," Hanne said, and her voice sounded strange, different than I'd ever heard it.

"Does it freak you out?" I said, but then I heard scraping against the cement floor, her footsteps up the stairs. She was scrambling to leave.

Outside in the courtyard, she wouldn't look at me. I could see that her hands were folded into her chest as if her heart hurt.

"Are you okay?" I said.

I got close to her, but she jerked her face away and walked out to the street. There was a little spark of light near her eyes, and I understood that it was a tear. Its presence was shocking, an error. I'd made her cry? She could cry?

"Hey, I'm sorry," I said, finding her already down the block, at the corner. "I thought you might like it. I've been sitting down there every day. I find it really meditative. The dark—I—"

"I've had enough of places like that in my life," she said in a severe voice, her back turned to me.

"Places like what?" Was she afraid of the dark? That seemed too dull for Hanne. "Places like what?" I said again, but she moved quickly away, crossing the street without me.

It felt wrong to follow her, so I stood there, but I was too thin to be standing without her. It was colder today than it had been, the winter was making a last stand, and the air got into me, I hadn't brought my coat, the one I should have given to the Marina on the train.

I felt a *plop* on my chest and looked down, certain I would find a healthy drip of blood leaking from my head. But my shirt was clean. I snapped my head back up to look at her. But she wasn't there, she wasn't where I'd left her. The spot on the sidewalk across the street was empty. I wondered if she thought she was treating me with love, if this was a kind of respect. My mother would often tell me she loved me while she punched me in the face, but I've touched my canvases gently and carefully and with precision while resenting their very existence. There is an aim with love, a telos, what is love but a kind of intention driven by the force of its aim, but meaning is slippery, it has no end, it looses itself into the world but keeps slicing into you. I thought of whether I could forgive myself for what I'd done to Lea, if there had been anything venial in me then, any intention that wasn't about power and pain, but even if there was, did it matter? The marks that were made were made. Desire is a tragedy of telos. Aim is a need. Is this how Marina thought about me? Was I the product of her need, some art she'd made?

An itch burst into the space where there should have been blood. As though it had been carved by a surgeon, I felt a precise, straight line spread itself like a slice into the top of my head and down the length of my body.

"I got it!" I said aloud to no one. "It'll be about how desire *itself* is punishment!"

"Who are you talking to?" And there she was, behind me, very close.

"I just had an idea!" My voice was loud and high.

"Oh, really, me too."

"Painting is all I have because painting was the only thing *Marina* had! Like mother, like daughter—like you said! But I also took what was hers and contaminated it with my own, my own—"

"What are you talking about?" She was pulling away from me.

"How I'll respond to Iris—it's not that I can't say no to who I love. It's that what I mean with my art is meaningless because art is so many different things that are and are not what they say they are," I grabbed for her, but she stepped out of my reach.

"Okay then," she said.

I didn't know how to explain without going on for a very long time, and it wasn't going to be possible because Hanne was never not walking away. Keeping just out of reach.

"Whatever you want," she called back at me, her voice drenched in sarcasm. "You're the artist."

FORESHORTENING

the colors of the underpainting can be optically mingled
with the subsequent overpainting without the danger of the
colors physically blending and becoming muddy.

I started walking alone, without Hanne, anywhere else, I didn't know. I was in a neighborhood I'd never been to before. The streets were crowded. I wondered where my coat was, but with relief, I remembered that I had given it to Marina when I'd found her the other night.

I turned quickly down into the nearest U-Bahn station. I read the sign as I ran down the steps, but its letters looked like hieroglyphics and made no sense to me. People, anonymous, indiscrete shapes, waited for the train. An electronic display said the train would come in five minutes. I stood on the platform and shivered.

Out of nowhere, a shrill, infuriated voice flared at me, so close it seemed to sound from within my own body. It screeched, "You!"

I started, looked up to see a pale, wrinkled face wreathed in a purple headscarf with wisps of black hair vibrating around the face. The mouth was flapping open. It belonged to an ancient, ragged-looking white woman. Several of her teeth

242

were missing, the teeth that remained had dark spots of brown, black, and gold, the mouth looked like a drawer of broken junk. She reached for me with her hands. I felt a rinse of fear at being touched by her and leaped backward. Her nails were ringed with black and the knuckles were swollen. She was wearing frayed fingerless gloves, and when her hands landed on my shoulders, she pinched them and shook me hard. Then she hit me cleanly across the face, not with malice but with a tortured longing.

Was *this* Marina?

I tried to pull myself away, tripping on my feet and hers. We were entangled for a few seconds, but it felt much longer.

She cried at me, "I see you! I am psychic! I read for you! I know! You from California—only twenty euro!" The voice was still shrill, but now it rose with a tone of confidence, a certainty, not a question, I know you, you owe me, but, how—who—did she know?

"Fifteen euro! I am psychic! I see you!"

I stumbled away. I imagined what we must look like, two women locked together, one shrieking, beseeching, one flailing, refusing, mother and daughter, enemies, strangers, artist and muse. I started to run up the stairs, not looking back. My face burned from the mark she'd made on it.

The voice yelled after me, "I can see your love is not good! Your *love* is not *good*!"

My running delivered me onto the street. I breathed deeply and started walking with purpose.

Her phrase began to repeat in my mind, a lot, too much, was crawling through me.

Your love is not good.

Did she mean I was doing my love wrong, or that what was not good was who I had chosen to love?

I came home and found Hanne reading a book on the balcony.

"Hey," I said. She made no move. "What a weird afternoon."

"This book is really good," she said at it.

"What is that, Stephen King?"

"I love it," she said. "Horror is my favorite."

"I hate horror. White people love it. They can afford to be scared for fun."

"Or do you just not like that it shows you who you really are?" she said, snapping the book shut and standing. "Hey, I have something I want to ask you," she said, coming close to me. She was moving faster than I'd ever seen her do before, and she was staring at me, this concluding stare that brought me in.

"What?" I said.

"I have an idea. For your show. Something I could put in as my own work."

"Your own work?"

"Since my face will be everywhere and you'll be doing whatever you want to it, I was thinking there should be art I've actually made myself. Then we'll be even."

"Okay," I said mechanically.

"I do shibari, rope bondage—it's what I'm into," she went on. "And I've wanted to do a series of self-portraits where I'm tied up. I need a photographer to take the pictures because obviously, I can't do it myself when I'm in the ropes."

"Okay." There was a throb in my cunt immediately, the first one that was distinct from infection, but it felt just as sick.

"You can say no, of course."

"No," I said. "No—I mean, yes."

"Cool."

"What do you want them to look like? The photos, I mean."

"Like Araki. Film, of course. Black-and-white, grainy, low light. We could do it in the bedroom here. And I'll be wearing a mask."

A mask. "Okay."

"And there might be other shit. Kinky shit."

"That's okay." The idea was for my okays to brace me.

"Tonight."

"Okay."

PENTIMENTO

to modify a painting by applying a very thin coat
of opaque paint to give a duller effect.

Hanne appears in the doorway of my bedroom. She is nude, holding a bundle of rope.

"I'm going to need you to help with the ropes," she says.

I wonder where she got those ropes, if she brought them with her from California. Maybe she planned this, she'd thought of our future together.

There's an odor to her nakedness. My head swims with it. She wraps the rope around her body, through her legs, down her back, around her stomach, between and around her breasts, over her shoulders, making knots and doubling back, asking me to hold this or that piece, pull on this or that end, holding a piece with her teeth while she stretches another, until she is encased in a web of it, all knots and windows, tight against her skin. As I pull on them, the ropes lance her skin with red welts, and her body looks like how I'd made it look in *Eliza Battle*. But had I done it myself, or had she been telling me what to do from the beginning? Here she is in front of me, Hanne This, Hanne Now. She raises her arms to collect her hair and holds it in a mass atop her head, then she slides a black leather mask over her face. It has small circles of mesh for eyeholes and is split by a large gold zipper with shiny teeth that are grotesque in their size, a toothy grin vertically slicing her head in two. Around the head and ears of the mask are more zippers crisscrossing the head into patches, like pieces of the bones of the skull. I stare into the mask, smell its strong scent of skin, then let my eyes fall over her body, woven into its net. I think of fish dragged up from the sea, big animals yoked by ropes and diminished by whips. I don't know what to do next.

Her voice comes out of the mask. The mask doesn't move. "Where's the camera," she says.

Right—the camera. I stumble to get it. I am clumsy, I am not the one with authority. I look through the eyepiece of the camera and see her in its frame. It looks good, vivid. It's more than just sex and leather, I think, but meaningfully about power, and pain, and thirst, the debt of want. I know her then, all at once, her right to exist, the bright, white light shining from her, she is someone who we look at, black and white, and in this looking, we are taught how some of us, but not all, can dare to be. As much as a self can be bought, it can also be stolen. Meaning is slippery, whatever you want it to be, it's whatever.

She positions herself around the room and I take photo after photo. She directs me with short commands, over here, now here, make this one a portrait. I say nothing. I kneel, stand over her, lie on my belly, on my back beneath her. She turns away, back to me, bends over, leans on the wall. She lies on the floor, on the bed, on her hands and knees. Our choreography is finally in sync.

She tells me to sit on the bed. I sit on the bed. She comes close to me, looking down into the camera, the black mask a hole. She lifts her legs and straddles me, one leg on either side, like Zinat did.

"Do you like me like this, Daddy?" she says, but her voice is different. It squeaks, and now she's making a whimpering sound. "Is this what you want, Daddy?" she says.

I snap the shutter quickly, in a fluster. Is this the kink she was talking about? Really?

"Daddy, I want you to like me," she squeaks again. Her voice is cloying. It sounds like every straight porn star I've ever seen. She arches her back, and now she's wiggling her ass. "Daddy, Daddy." She starts to rock on top of me.

I am snapped out of the scene. I see us from across the room. Her little shimmies atop my flat body. Daddy, Daddy. Oh. So she is just a straight white girl.

"You don't like me, Daddy?" she simpers. "Have I been a bad girl? Daddy, did I do bad?"

I understand now. I am repelled by how ordinary it feels, how ordinary it reveals her to be. And—she has dared me to want this.

"Yes," I manage to say. "You're very bad."

This seems to thrill her, and she wriggles faster on top of me. There's the sharp smell of her BO, which makes me scrunch my face.

"Daddy, you need to punish me, don't you? I did bad."

"Yes," I say. "You did bad." You're the one who hurt me most.

She stops wriggling and sits up straight. She starts to tug at the zippers on the mask around the head and pull pieces of hair out of the newly opened holes. Her head is now the head of a doll, the kind that belongs to a violent child who has cut chunks of hair away. She reaches over me, to her nightstand.

"Here, use this," she says. Her normal voice is back, flat and hard. She is pushing something into my hand, and I see that it's a lighter.

"What?" I say.

"Use it to burn my hair," she snaps, all the simpering drained out. "And get the shot when the flames are tall." She pulls more hair out of the holes in the mask.

"You want me to burn your hair?" Maybe I was wrong.

"Then I'll look like you," she says and starts making a grunting noise through the mask. I understand that she's laughing, I hear in it a pure and cutting sound of contempt, she is tricky and strange and changing and I am mislaid, did she simper for me, is that what she thinks I want?

I put the camera down and feel an appalling confusion. Maybe I don't know her or myself or anyone. I fumble with the lighter, drop it.

"Come on, you're ruining it." Her voice is harder. She reaches over with irked swiftness, pushes the lighter into my hand. I feel that my palms are wet with sweat, the lighter is a silver Zippo, cold and heavy. She wraps her sticky, hot fingers around mine and clicks the lighter on. Still holding my hand, she guides the flame to the ends of her hair.

"Get the camera ready. Don't miss the shot," she says. "Come on, look at me."

She taps her hand on my face, I can't remember if it was my forehead or my nose or my cheek, but I remember she taps it hard enough to be a slap, yes, it was actually a slap, there was a viciousness to it that I've tried to forget, like my mother, like the woman on the street, like who I was with Lea, and then she says, "This is *my* fantasy, *not* yours," but as I am telling the story now, I want to change the word "fantasy" to "art," because it sounds better, gives her more.

ODALISQUE

*a painting representing a fantasy or a mixture of real and imaginary features;
a kind of free composition, not keeping to the rules of any particular form.*

That night, I dreamed vividly, it was the end of the world.
I was crossing a field at night, scurrying with a group of people
through the California foothills. It felt like we were fugitives
rushing through a wild place, a sliver of moon casting its
extraterrestrial light on our path. The dark swam with trees
and the air seemed to hiss and gurgle, but when I turned
around, I saw that it was everyone giggling, and the sounds
were shaping the air with metallic colors. When I tried to
rush forward, I was stopped, as though I had hit an invisible
wall. The invisible wall seemed to have a face in it, a body,
but it appeared only as a presence I couldn't see. It pressed
itself against me like an image in a mirror, though it was made
entirely of shadow. I felt it enter me and I squirmed. Then
I realized that it was squirming, and now I was, too, because
it had taken over. I started to run. The washing machine-sized
pot of dirt appeared in my path, and I reached my hand in
and grabbed dirt and threw it behind me onto the presence
in the wall. It made a hard, sad sound that felt disrespectful,

and then there was racket of applause from everyone who was watching me. I threw more and more dirt in fistfuls. I had the feeling I was throwing it at someone. Then came a great friction and a warm feeling of love and trouble, and I started to laugh and sing.

FACTURE

anybody or anything venerated or uncritically admired.

Butterflies with their wings pulled off. That's what I'd show. My renunciation. I ordered them online from a taxidermy specialist whose website announced, "Our company only buys the finest quality butterflies. Naturally, every butterfly we sell has had a different lifetime and is unique. Because of this, they may vary slightly from the photo on the site."

Papilio blumei, Anteos menippe, Papilio aristeus, Eurytides serville, Idea leuconoe, Urania ripheus: exquisite, velvety wings with iridescent blues and shimmering greens and fuzzy blacks and moon yellows. I'd open the frames they arrived in, wearing cloth gloves so as not to smudge the glass, and slice off the wings with an X-Acto knife. It was like slicing through air. Without their glorious wings, they were bugs, creepy little bodies of head, thorax, and abdomen.

The question became what to do with the wings. I wanted to include the gesture of throwing them away, but I wanted to be sure the metaphor was right. If I had a small trash can of wings in the gallery, shoved into a corner, perhaps, beneath the straight rows of frames on the walls, it would make clear, concise sense. There would be one way to read the work, like a crisp sound that rang through the room. Also, it would echo Iris's dead balloons, which I liked. I was, after all, making this show for her, in a way.

But putting the wings in the gallery, even in a trash can, still put them in the gallery. By not actually throwing them away but only throwing them away symbolically, I could be read as sentimentalizing them, making them yet more precious. Thinking through the conceptual implications of this was mine to work on, to luxuriate on in my inner world, which is the actual joy of being an artist, getting to spend countless hours doing nothing else but trying to solve the puzzle of your own work, which is to say, of yourself.

On good days, this centripetal little world of mine eclipsed the larger world around me with its strain and need and problems, the one where Silke was mad at me, where Alexandra was mad at me, the person who I was to them bound to promises I could no longer keep. I could feel it, my disobedience, it was growing well. It wasn't as willful as I would have expected such a revolt to be. It was a simple refusal. I didn't even have to get to my safe word. It was only, I don't want to do that—not that—not anymore.

When I spread the butterflies out on her desk, Silke did her best.

"So, *is* this painting?" she said, "It *is* a kind of a painting, isn't it?"

"No," I said.

"I think an argument could be made that it is," she tried. "They *are* images, of course, and—"

"No. They're not paintings. And paintings are not images."

I watched her thoughts trying to turn over. I had pushed far past the deadline she'd given me, causing the publicity people to scramble with vague press releases, which they kept sending to me for approval, and instead of rewriting 80 percent of them like I usually did, like all artists did, I didn't reply at all. I now definitively occupied the territory of being a bit too eccentric and difficult to work with, and I was glad for it.

"You are saying that all paintings are not images, or just the way that you are perceiving yours?"

"What's the difference?" I snapped.

"But if not images—"

"Listen. When I was in the first year of my MFA, I had an epiphany about beauty," I spoke grandly to the empty room of the gallery. "The stairwell in my apartment was sort of outdoors, with a two-story window instead of a wall. There were always a bunch of bugs trapped against the glass, making noise and trying to get free. But they were bugs—they could never figure out that there was a wall between them and the sky because it was the same color as the air. So they all died there. The landing of the stairs was constantly dirty with dead flies, bees, gnats, mosquitoes. It was gross. One day, when I came home, there was a big tiger swallowtail butterfly trapped in there. It was so beautiful. These huge, gorgeous wings. It looked like it was having a hard time, like it was ready to give up. I said *aww* out loud and moved to save it. Then I realized that I only wanted to save it because it was beautiful. I'd never felt the need to save any of the countless flies or bees or gnats or mosquitoes that had been trapped there before. I passed them several times a day, and I'd never given a shit—but now I did. Why? Because this one was beautiful? That's the reason a thing should live or die? No. So—I let it die."

"Very well," Silke said. "But you must be aware that it will be difficult to sell these for the prices of *Eliza Battle*. And it is not possible to lower your prices. I would not advise this."

"Yes, I'm aware." I appreciated Silke's forthrightness. It was rare in the art world for someone to speak so baldly about how much something was worth. "Oh, and there's one more thing," I said. "Anything purchased from this exhibition must be given, as a gift, to the mother of the buyer. Write that into a contract."

"The mother of the buyer?"

"Yes, the mother. Mothers are never given enough credit. I owe my entire career to my mother. This exhibition especially."

"You want this in a contract."

"Yes. This is my response to Iris," I said, and it was final.

Silke sighed and looked at my butterflies. "Did you see the latest from Iris Wells?" she said.

"No—what now?"

"Iris will open a show of her own, here in Berlin," Silke said. "At a squat that was a factory. It has a troubled history. It is opening the same day as yours."

"Oh. Huh."

"I assumed you'd be interested."

"But what should I do?" My face opened and closed, not knowing which was safest.

I wondered if intimacy was what I had with Silke. I looked at her, her faint mustache on her upper lip, she was doing something with her eyes, they had gone from black to gray to blue, maybe she had a sister from whom she was waiting to hear, maybe she checked her phone anxiously every night, maybe her daughter had stopped speaking to her.

"So—you are not painting because this is your response, to withhold yourself," Silke tried. It was a question asked in the form of a statement, which is the art world's favorite way of asking a question. The word *beauty* kept turning over in me. Love, art. I walked out of the room.

TENEBRISM

a distorted projection or drawing which appears normal only when
viewed from a particular point or with the right mirror or lens.

Toward the end of May, Yves called me abruptly to announce
that he and Theo were going on a holiday to Greece.

"I just have to get out of here. I will lose my mind!" he said.
"It's been years since I've been to Greece, and you know, fuck
it—other people go on holidays with their lovers, why can't I?"
Without stopping, he said, "Let's go see the queen. I should
bring her an offering. She's in prison. I haven't been to see
her in ages."

"Who's in prison?" I said.

"The queen! And she will be there for all eternity."

He took me to the museum of antiquities at the center of
Berlin. He linked his arm in mine, and we went up a few floors.
He directed us, ignoring the vast hallways and rooms full of
vitrines that contained coins, combs, lumps of stone, sacred
and mundane objects made by ancient people, dug from their
graves and brought here. We came to a room at the end.

It was Nefertiti. Without a glass box, the air on her, her
proud head mounted on a plinth. She had her own room, the

walls painted rich phthalo green. The dusty color of her skin was deathlike. Her crown was faded, too, and the guard in the room was as dry and hard as the bust itself.

"But why is she here?" I asked in shock. "Why isn't she at home?"

Yves arced his arm up and around his head, balletic, then brought it down to point at the floor in the corner. There was a little contraption mounted there, slender and silver. I bent toward it and saw that it was a tiny seismograph. Its needle traced a delicate black line on a miniature scroll of paper. A small plaque above it, the size of a square slice of bread, declared that the reason Nefertiti was in Berlin and not her homeland of Egypt was because Germany and its museums were safer and more technologically advanced, so they would do a better job at preserving her beauty than the wretched ones in Egypt. The word "wretched" wasn't there, but it was. I thought of WE.

Above the small plaque was a plaque ten times the size, with several long paragraphs in German and English about the nature of beauty and how Nefertiti was a symbol of universal beauty that withstood the test of time and transcended national and ethnic boundaries.

Yves pronounced, "The colonial imaginary!" as if it were a life sentence, which it is.

The guard twitched at this expressiveness and cleared his throat in warning. We stepped back.

"These Germans, I swear, they will kill me one of these days," Yves whispered to me, one of his favorite things to say. Nefertiti stared out with her one eye, the other blank eye doing its own kind of staring.

Yves looked at Nefertiti.

"Goodbye for now, Queen," he said softly to her. "What a long way we've come to be destroyed." I recognized the quote from *Giovanni's Room*, another of his favorite things to say. As he pulled me out of the room, I saw him vault his eyebrows toward the crown of his head and lift his chin up at the guard, and I remembered a party we'd been at together some years ago, when a white man had approached us and said to Yves, "Don't I know you?" Yves had responded first with his James Baldwin eyebrows. "No, darling. Maybe you're mistaking me for the other mystical Black man you once met at another party."

We walked slowly toward the café, agreeing to get a cake, though neither of us wanted one.

"Have you ever been religious?" I asked him. As I said it, I realized that I didn't know, despite our having known each other a decade.

"Of course," he said immediately. "Of course, of course. But don't tell." He smirked. "To the white European art world, nothing is worse than a religious artist, except—ha—a religious *Black* artist. Talk about the magical Negro!"

I squeezed his hand. We sat at a small table tucked behind a column, hidden from the rest of the café. The waitress brought our cake, a geometric brown wedge, with two tiny forks with three tines each, a very German kind of prettiness, I thought.

Yves stared at the floor for a long time, as though waiting for a song to finish. Finally, he looked up at me and said, "I have always loved the Virgin Mary."

I laughed. "What! Are you Catholic?"

"Being raised in France, it's a kind of atmosphere. It's the whole vibe." He smiled. "One night, I remember, I was a boy—I was maybe twelve or thirteen—and I had left the flat because my parents were fighting again, and everyone was home, no place to sit, and I had to get out of there, so I walked around the streets, not really going anywhere, just away. We lived in a banlieue, though of course we didn't call it that then. To us, it was just where we lived. I knew it very well—I could walk without thinking, without noticing where I was going. I walked and walked. I remember"—he stopped to chuckle and place a hand on mine—"I was thinking about a boy in my class I was in love with. He was so"—he lifted his other hand toward the sky—"so gorgeous! I don't remember his name now. But I was lost in this desire. I was just swimming in it. And then suddenly, I turned a corner, and there was a Virgin Mary shrine. In a little alcove, there in the street. She was so clean and white and small, less than a meter high. She stood there with her hands turned out, you know"—he faced his palms out—"in that lovely gesture of hers. It's a promise and also a plea. It says, *Come here, you are safe with me*, and, *Please don't fuck up anymore! Please stop fucking up!* I stood in front of her for a long time. I felt very loved, I remember, like she was watching me, looking right at me. What's strange is, many times I tried to find her again, the little Mary. I tried to find the shrine. But I never did."

"You never found it?"

"Never," he said.

"Did someone take it down?"

"Who knows."

"But maybe you'd walked really far. Maybe you missed a turn?"

"No, darling, I searched."

"And you never saw her again?"

"Darling, no. I never did." He patted his coat pocket and took out a cigarette. He didn't light it, just held it between his fingers. "You used to be able to smoke in Germany, like in a proper civilization," he grumbled. "Now it's back to fascism. Rules, rules, rules."

I caught myself noticing that he'd smoked the entire time I'd been with him today, stopping only when we went inside the museum, and I saw him, suddenly, as middle-aged. I'd never thought of him like that, half his life gone. Beneath his coat, which was smartly cut and slate-blue, he was wearing a sweater I'd seen him wear for years, dark midnight-blue with flecks of green, with a torn elbow and slumping neckhole. It was not a garment he usually wore in public. I'd sometimes seen dried smears of white at the wrists of the sleeves, where Yves had wiped his nose or his tears. It made me feel close to him in a way that felt painful and protective, Yves in his knobby, smelly sweater that had collected his DNA, the hours he'd spent in it, the hours he'd already used up of his life, doing nothing in particular, washing dishes, sitting at home, falling asleep in the afternoon on the couch, being alone in the wintertime.

Yves said, "Don't worry, I promise to be back for your show. How is it going?"

I was a little taken aback that I hadn't felt anxiety at his leaving until he'd said it. "Silke is shitting her pants," I said finally. "I can't blame her. I'm a painter who's decided to stop making paintings."

"I think of you as someone who makes portraits of female pain, no matter the medium. These new pieces do that."

"You know I hate the word *female* when it's used to describe anything but a chromosome."

Yves rolled the cigarette between his forefinger and thumb and looked very tired.

"But, mermaid, why do you seem so determined to fuck yourself up this time?" he said. "It's been like watching a train crash these last months."

"Why are you getting parental in your old age?" I snapped.

His eyes got dark with hurt. "Only when my friends act like children," he said.

An instinctive laugh fell out of my mouth, and I felt for words but only found teeth.

"I won't ask you why you're making the choices you're making," he said. "I understand that you feel you *have* no choice. I only hope you get what you need."

I was quiet. What I need.

"I've been wondering if art isn't always evil." My voice came, but it sounded as though it were coming from behind me, from the far corner of the room, from three floors up, slipping out of Nefertiti's limestone. "It has no ethics. It salvages whatever meaning it needs to reconcile itself, mutilating the thing it stole it from. In grad school, for this kid's thesis show, he invited his entire family. Grandparents still alive, they hobbled in together, looking confused. The gallery just had a chair in it, in the center. No work on the walls, nothing. We all waited. The kid came in, sat down, and sliced both his wrists open with a razor. That was his 'performance.' We all watched the blood spurt out of him. Then his father stood up and started yelling at the kid for being an idiot, and they took him to the hospital and we never saw him again."

"Did he pass the class?" Yves said.

I shut my eyes. My voice came again, as if from beneath us, deep underground. "And there was a girl with scars on her arms from cutting. Anorexic skinny. She looked so haunted, bags under her eyes. She'd stare and stare at this one guy, the hot white guy who was already showing a lot in Europe—such a nightmare, this dude, always pontificating about Agamben. But she could not stop staring at him. Her face was so hungry. She'd chew her mouth while she stared. When he spoke in class, she took notes. She fucking took notes. For her thesis show, she put a bed in the gallery and invited people to lie in it with her. She said it was about intimacy. It was called something terrible, like, *For You*, and we all knew who the you was. She stayed in this bed in the gallery for the whole month of the show. Only a few people got in with her, and they all got out really fast. Apparently she'd just stare and reach for you with her sweaty hands. She lay there all day in her little bed with her sad art. And he never even went in the gallery, this guy she'd made it for. I'm sure he didn't even know her name."

I opened my eyes and looked at Yves's mute resignation.

"You could always just leave, mermaid. You don't have to make such a destruction," he said. "Why not do what Laurie Parsons did and exit with quiet dignity?"

"Who?"

"Laurie Parsons. She left at the height of her career. Became a social worker for the mentally ill. And she didn't declare her exit or make it into a piece like Lee Lozano. She just stopped and left and found another way." He smiled weakly at me.

"It's not a question of which career I should do," I said. "It's who and what I come from—who I am." I paused, undone.

Van Gogh had shot himself in the stomach, which is the least efficient way to kill oneself. It took him two days to die. At some point, he regretted it, but it was too late.

"I thought Hanne and I looked the same. I thought we could be the same—"

"You did?"

"—if I just wanted it bad enough."

"Why would you want that?" Yves said, but his question seemed from another time.

I saw a large, swollen blackhead near the bottom corner of his eye, like a pinhead was caught under the skin, perfectly round and hardened with age. The moment narrowed onto the blackhead. I thought of how Yves had told me that, every few weeks, Theo would say he felt trapped and wanted to see other people. I thought of how Yves had been born without anything dirty or aged or used about him, how his skin had been new and immaculate once, no bumps or sags or lines or scars or tunnels or wounds, just clean, elastic holes and taut, soft stretches of skin. I thought of how teeth get chipped doing what they were made to do, how eyes get tired from seeing, how knees and backs become pained from bending and walking and sitting and standing, how lungs constrict when they breathe too fast, how nipples crack from being sucked on, how hearts exhaust themselves from their simple, innocent task of beating. There is a fundamental paradox to life, I've always felt infested with it, the fact that life feels most itself, most incorrigibly awake, when it's closest, right up and pushing against the skin of death, this is where I've lived, recidivous, falling back and again and back some more into it, perhaps it's only that I've tried to make a kind of meaning out of this relapse, this lacuna, and it's not about dying, this is the puzzle, but about how to live.

"My mother," I found the beneath-voice saying. "She used to say she was going to kill herself almost every day. As I left to get the bus to school, she'd threaten it. I may not be here when you get back. I have a dream that she finally did kill herself. She did it by slicing the back of her head open, punching a hole through her own skull, and folding the flaps of skin around the showerhead. She hangs there, attached. The blood drips down her body, washing her off. When I told her about the dream, she just peered at me from across the table of her studio and said, 'When I kill myself, buy roses.'

"There is another dream, much more real. When I woke up from it, I was convinced it had happened, that it is still happening. She wants me to help kill her but, more specifically, she needs me to help her get rid of the body, erase every trace of her. She tells me to put her body into the washing machine, coiling it to fit in a ring. Then I boil the limbs. The grease of the fat evaporates onto the ceiling, and I have to scrub it off. Little chunks stick on the stove. The dream is urgent, full of panic. We work fast because she keeps telling me that my father cannot know. I can't lie to my father, though, and I start crying, I feel like I will break with this burden. He'll come home and Marina will be gone and I'll have to tell him that she's gone, and it was me who did it. When I tell Marina this, she explodes. She shouts that I have to keep it a secret. I cry out that I can't. Marina is furious. She calls me selfish, that I didn't really want to help her die. That I'm only doing it to get rid of her for myself.

"It was because she was so determined to make beauty in the world. She wanted to find where it was hiding. But real beauty is only ever solitary—when it stands on its own, it exists for one person at a time. So she locked it up inside herself, afraid it would get stolen. She found the thing we're all searching for. And she had to protect it. She could only ever give me the desire to search for it myself."

I didn't know how long I'd been talking or if I had been talking at all.

Yves stood and started buttoning his coat. He said, "Wasn't she the one who let a dog die in a pool of shit for four years?"

I stood and reached for him.

"I love you, Yves," I said. "We have each other. We have each other."

"Yes, mermaid, I love you too." It sounded tolerant, disappointed, as though he were acknowledging that I'd brought a single hammer to demolish a city.

PAREIDOLIA

a portrait that the artist makes of themselves.

The last time I spoke to my mother was Christmas Day, sixteen years ago. At the time, I had been seventeen years old for almost two months. In March of the next year, I would learn I had been accepted to art school and would start in the fall, but it was still the winter before, so I had nothing in the future that might take away the pain of my present. I hadn't seen my father for years, Marina had told me only that he had a new family, and we weren't allowed to see or talk to them. It was just us. She came into my room in the morning, waking me up by kicking the bed. A dead cigarette was bent in her shaking hand. "I need help," she said. "It's overflowing. It's coming out—it won't go down. It was all over the floor in one second." I sat up, disoriented. "What?" I said. She shook my shoulders and her voice thundered: "The shit in the toilet, idiot, the shit! The shit!" In the bathroom, I found the floor glossy with a thin layer of pale brown water. It looked like the mud of a riverbed. Pieces of shit, gray and yellow and round, gleaming, almost fondant, lay like dead things on the tile. After I had cleaned it up, I threw a roll of toilet paper at her.

I watched it sail past her head and she calmly watched it, too, then her frame blew up, filled my vision, her eyes sharp red, and she reared back her fist, but I felt nothing when it landed on my face, there was only a flash of white. I fell sideways to the floor, and when I came to a couple minutes later, I left.

It wasn't until I had to assemble my portfolio to apply to art school that I began to divorce my painting from Marina's. It had to be done delicately. It was a kind of surgery. Cutting the tumor out. I needed a hard light to be cast onto the work I was doing, like television shows of open-heart surgeries, where the heart under the lamps looks like the most compli-cated piece of meat you've ever seen. Vividly red and beating, thaumaturgical, the body of an animal that somehow is alive and knowing, despite being flayed.

She'd found the work I'd submitted in my art school applica-tion on Christmas Eve. The next day, she punched me in the head for the last time, and I left forever. That was why she'd done it, and I am grateful for this rare, causal clarity, how simple and easy it made things.

I had stretched canvases that were three or four times as large as the ones that had won the blue ribbons, the ones she'd painted for me, and then I cut holes in the big ones and fit her small ones into mine, bracing them at the back with extra stretcher bars like scaffolding, binding them to each other with many layers of duct tape on the back in a grotesque suture that reminded me of horror-movie monsters. From the front, hers sat snug at the centers of mine, engulfed by the wide borders of the whole. There were seven of them for the seven years we'd won the contests each year, her original painting and my new one containing it. On each of her canvases, going from the newest to the oldest, I poured a mixture of mineral spirit and glue, more and more concentrated, so that they blurred chronologically, going from smeared to inchoate, and then froze like that, entrails dragged out and hardened. When I rubbed the mixture into her paintings, there was the stink of mildew and old dirt, the smell of her studio, her work. The rags I used to erase her paintings had to be furtively thrown out. So she wouldn't notice the smell, I took them into the shower with me, rinsing each by my feet and washing them with soap, then I wrapped them in plastic bags and stuffed them deep into the neighbor's trash bin. I had to push my arm to the bottom of the bin, through the garbage, to cover them enough. Then, because the garbage smell had gotten on me, I had to shower again. I'd repeat this procedure for each painting, and it felt necessary, appropriate, that the task should require so much washing.

For the statement I had to write for the application, I wrote something about matricide, necessary for my own survival. I remember I was very honest because I told myself that honesty could be deliverance, that owning my rage could shrive the part of me that needed it. I still believed in miracles then, though I know now that a miracle is another word for a lie.

CAPRICCIO

the class of pictures representing inanimate objects.

I'd been lying to and using Hanne and tonight she would find out, although I knew she already knew, it was a kind of gnostic knowledge that bound us together. But I still wanted to have her, for myself and for us, one last time. I'd get her back into the basement, it would be a performance, a cathartic finale, I had to invite back in between us that odd voice she'd used the first time we'd gone down there. I'd record the audio and play it in the gallery on repeat. I wondered if she'd say she needed me, why she had used me too. But I doubted it.

"Fuck no, I'm not going back down there," she said when I suggested it, but I kept pressing her. "But isn't it too late?" she said. "The show opens tonight, it's already hung and installed. And it's not about me, anyway."

"But it is! And this will be easy to add," I said.

She kept refusing through the early afternoon, and I kept glancing at the time. It was kind of thrilling to race against the clock.

I still don't know exactly which part of my argument worked, but I do feel confident enough in my appraisal of Hanne to know that she liked to consider herself whole and unbroken, so eventually, she found her arrogance again, and I could tell she wanted to prove me wrong.

"It's important that it feels like hell," I said. We were standing at the doorway. Both of us were a foot taller than the little rectangle of black. "Don't be afraid," I said.

"I'm not afraid."

"I'm going to stay up here," I said. I started to take out my laptop and the microphone.

"What? Why?"

"Because I don't want the light of the laptop to fuck up your scene. It has to be totally black down there."

"So I'll be alone?" Her voice was nervous.

"Why are you so afraid?"

I looked at her face. Several emotions passed over it, but I couldn't discern any of them. She looked up, directly above her, as if to the sky, but we were underneath the staircase. She inhaled slowly and made a noise on the exhale.

"Okay, how do I do it," she said, not a question.

I handed her the microphone and its long cable. "Take this down with you. Put it on the floor. Tap it a few times, and I'll get the levels right. I'm going to close the door behind you to make sure it's dark."

"I assumed," she said.

"And, you know, it's a performance—it's performance art—so try to go as long as you can. You'll think it's been an hour, but in reality, it'll have been ten minutes. Performance time always feels longer than it is. Go as long as you can."

"I know," she said, but about what, I didn't know.

She started down the stairs. I sat on the floor and pulled up the recording program on my laptop. I could hear her breathing wetly through my headphones.

"Okay, how's this?" she said. Her voice sounded faraway.

The red bars in the recording jumped and flicked. "Good!" I shouted. I clicked RECORD. "Ready! Start whenever. I'm going to close the door now."

The door was surprisingly heavy, its corners deteriorated and its paint flaking. It had a lock on the outside, black with rust and enormous. That the decrepit little door would have such an excessive and resolute lock—*enough!* I wanted to shout. I don't need any more metaphors for my life!

"Okay, okay," I heard Hanne saying through my headphones.

I sat back down and looked at the screen. Her voice was in my head, so close. Her breathing sounded huge.

"I don't think this is like hell," she said. "Hell is probably a pretty cool place, if we take the Bible's word for it, that all the sinners go there."

Again she inhaled and exhaled loudly, with a measured control. It was the kind of breath that must be taught, practiced, used to dispel panic attacks. She'd learned it from someone who knew.

"The underworld—that's a different place, I guess," she was saying. "So I'm supposed to talk without stopping? Jesus, it is fucking dark down here. I don't know how long I can do this."

She was quiet. The microphone recorded the hiss of the silence. I imagined her resolving to be strong, meeting me on my turf and still winning. I was next to her, lying on the warm, hard ground in the black.

"I'm an only child—that's what I tell people." Her voice seeped into me. "I didn't like it down here when you first brought me because it reminded me of my sister. I felt my sister could be in a place like this. She's dead, but she's not all the way gone. I don't believe in hell or heaven or anything. But I do believe in ghosts. I"—her voice wobbled—"sorry, I'm trying not to stop. Keep talking. Okay. I guess this is how I feel down here and in any darkness, really. I feel like my sister gets close to me. Or—I get closer to her. I've just always been too dark for people. My parents, too, especially my mother, after what happened. Even if people don't know the story, they can smell it, some kind of tragedy. Tragedy has a smell. I can smell it on you, obviously—that's what pulled me in, I guess. I like it best when it's fucked-up. But most artists stink of tragedy. And all women do, which sucks. I hate that. I've never wanted to be one of those chicks with a fucking disorder. Trauma, trauma, trauma. Ugh. Boring. It's hard to notice my body down here, like where its edges are. This darkness feels like a person to me. She didn't even get a name. They didn't get that far yet. They were going to wait until both of us were born—like, breathed our first breath. But then we came out, and one of us never got that far. Once I googled what stillborn babies look like. There's a term for it—there are, like, support groups for people like me. *Twinless twins*, we're called. Always feel like something's missing. Elvis was one. They look plastic. Shiny little dolls. Like perfect dolls with pearly skin, the color of baby pink but then they turn purple, more and more purple, because they are dead but they look flawless, and being in the world and getting hit by this air speeds up the decay process. Everything I read talked about the smell—not just the intense birth smell, which makes all the men faint in the delivery rooms. That has its own special smell, the smell of life, but then it's laced with rotting. My dad told me he threw up as soon as she slipped out, like an old tomb had been opened with a puff of wet dust. All the nurses made a fuss over me, the one who wasn't dead, but my mom said she couldn't look at me for a whole day. She refused to let them take my sister away, she wanted to hold her, and I think she did for a while, if that's possible, if they would let her do that. In my head, there are huge stains of black blood on my mother's hospital gown, and she's growling at anyone who tries to take her dead baby away. My dad was trying to talk with the doctor, trying to deal with everything, but he kept throwing up, he said, and then he shit his pants. So there was that to clean up. He told me he drove home to get clean clothes and decided to just stay there, alone in the house. He couldn't make himself go back to the hospital, to this wreck that was his new family. He told me a few years ago that the next morning, he packed a bag and started driving away. He didn't decide to—it was just a reflex. He sort of woke up on the freeway, driving through the desert. He'd been driving a few hours already. He pulled over, and he told me he had a simple thought then. That the saddest thing is that we are all children. That's all. That's fucking it. A nurse held me all night, if that could be true—I doubt it, I mean, wouldn't she have had to do her job? I wasn't put into my mom's arms until I'd already lived my first twenty-four—in some stories, it's forty-eight—hours without her. They told her the umbilical cord had strangled my sister, and when I was a kid, they sent me to therapy to tell me it wasn't my fault, that I hadn't murdered my own twin in the womb, because there were a few years there where I thought I did. But the official story was that I'd just grown normally and she hadn't. She died and I kept living, right next to her, and we were in there together, side-by-side, one dead and one alive, and my life is this huge gloating that I made it and she didn't. It was meant to be—but also, it doesn't mean anything. If I had to make a choice between which of my children I had to kill to save the world, like in those philosophical thought experiments, I wouldn't hesitate. I'd test them with one question. I'd ask them if they would kill me to save their own life. I'd ask if, in order for them to live, they had to kill me with their bare hands—would they do it? The one who answered yes, I'd let live. Obviously. They gave her a name, but they kept it secret. They never told me. For me, she doesn't have a name. Which feels right. Just a hole where a person should have been. The most fucked-up thing about it is that my mother's aunt—who was really rich, the only person in our family with any money—she'd left a trust fund for both of us because my parents knew they were having twins. So I got it all. The money for my sister too. I inherited it from her, even though she came out first. When I turned twenty-one, two million dollars. For nothing. For killing my twin sister. It's just, like, fuck, it's all so fucking arbitrary. Life. Family. Money especially. The only way is to insist on what you want. If I hadn't been born beautiful, this would all be so fucking different. But obviously, *that* didn't happen. So."

Then came Hanne's regular, unrestricted laugh, the cackle, the satisfaction, but it felt sloppy, for once.

A new score wormed through me, free of something, free, and I reached up and pushed the rusted lock on the door into place. My hand felt hot where it had touched the black metal, and now my freedom was beating in my ears.

She kept laughing until she was done, diminishing into sighs of pleasure.

"All right, that's it for me down here," she said. "There's gotta be something you can use. I tried to make it as dramatic as possible." I heard scraping and thunks in the microphone as she picked it up and started up the stairs.

I stood and pressed my back into the wall, staring at the door with its big lock. As if I were standing in front of a painting, I appreciated the texture of its wood, the flaking paint, the colors of it, the grays and whites.

It twitched when she pushed against it.

"Hey, wait," she said.

She pounded twice on the door.

"What the fuck?" she shouted and pounded again. "What the fuck!"

My eyes snapped to the lock on the door and saw that it was wriggling with hatred. I tried to send hatred back at it through my stare.

The pounding on the door boomed through the courtyard.

I could hear her voice beyond the headphones, so I took them off and put them by my laptop. I didn't need more than one of her anymore.

"What the fuck is this?" she was shouting. "Is this some bullshit, like, *piece*? Fucking bullshit *art*? Fuck you!"

She started to say my name, spitting it out in anger, but also, desperately, she needed me.

"Let me out! Please! Please let me out!"

A cloud moved in the sky, and the courtyard flooded with light. I had to squint. I felt in my head for its pain and found none. I walked into the courtyard and through the hallway and pushed open the huge door of the front of the building, and now I was on the street. The door closed behind me, and the sounds of the street presented themselves, and Hanne's went away.

The sun was out. Winter was over. I looked at the trees. As if overnight, they had grown leaves.

FÊTE CHAMPÊTRE

unaccompanied or with minimal accompaniment.

I spent the rest of the afternoon in the bath, feeling edgeless, but I needed my edges if I were to get through the night, to make the image of someone who feels she deserves to exist. It shook through me, that I'd never believed it. And now—did I? This was what I'd hoped to learn from Hanne, from Zinat, from Marina, from Yves. They each had their existences fixed immovable at their cores, entitled to it, by right, through whiteness, money, purpose, belonging—I would be indebted to them all always. Perhaps my insolvency was the thing that was mine.

Yves came back in time to see the show. While I was dressing, he texted to say he would meet me there. He'd also organized a party at his to celebrate. Theo had ended it in Greece, so the party was also for Yves.

And shall we see what Iris has cooked up? he texted.

I replied with the vomiting emoji, followed by sparkles.

I'd titled our show—my show—*Your Love Is Not Good.* I put the wings in a small metal trash can beneath the long, framed rows of bodies on the walls. Above the trash, I'd made a replica of the large plaque next to Nefertiti, the one about her beauty transcending everything.

A few weeks before, Silke had informed me that this would be my only show with her. She was glad we'd been able to work together, but the fit was not right, our visions did not align. It wrenched that the gallery I was supposed to boycott had dropped *me*.

"This is not what we discussed," she said, conclusive.

I unblocked Alexandra, expecting to receive a deluge of old messages, but my phone only dinged once, a text from today. There was no congratulations or endearment about the opening, just, "Fine, I can take a hint." A clear, solid drop down a well.

The evening light was blue, and the air was warm and still. I could not handle seeing my mother passed out on the train, so I hailed a cab. Taxis in Berlin are Mercedes-Benzes, all of them, and I sank into the wide, black leather seats and kept the tinted windows rolled up. The gallery wasn't far.

I realized suddenly that I'd left my laptop there, outside the locked basement door. The driver turned at the big intersection near the neighborhood of the gallery. We'd be there in six minutes, his GPS said. Or—maybe it had been purposeful, my subconscious insisting on a gesture of generosity to Hanne. She could take it, sell it, as if she needed any money from me. Or she could search it, use it, see all of me, all the photos of my cunt and work and face, my grant applications, my CVs, my emails. She could have it all. Now we were even.

We turned onto the street of the gallery. I sat up. It was a hundred yards ahead, on the right. I peered out the dark glass of the window. Fifty yards. The driver slowed down. The lights were on in the space, and I could see the squares of my butterflies on the white walls. There was no one outside or inside, no group of people standing around holding plastic cups of wine. The driver pulled to a stop. I saw Silke dart across a back hallway with a phone in her hand. Otherwise, the space was empty. The little trash can was the only thing standing on the floor, this was my WE.

"Enough with the metaphors!" I shouted.

"Was?" the driver said at me, *vos* in baffled German.

"Keep going!" I shouted. "Drive!"

The driver blinked at me in the rearview mirror.

"Bitte!" I cried. "Danke!"

He raised his eyebrows and wrinkled his mouth and chin, an expression men often wear when they see a woman doing something they don't understand, but he drove.

"I need to go somewhere else," I said. "I made a mistake." I pulled out my phone and checked for Iris's show. My stomach was pushing against my face. I found the address and shouted it twice at the driver.

He held up a hand, a little flag of surrender, then punched the new coordinates into the phone that was guiding us.

The show was in the East in an old brick factory, huge and long with very high ceilings and broken windows, empty for decades, probably. It was in an industrial park with dirt paths snaking between the buildings. To guide you, there were signs posted, designed in a sleek sans-serif font, with a stark image of a large, empty, white-walled gallery room and printed on AO, the largest format of poster paper, which betrayed the punkness of the show. The show was in a squat, but Iris had still hired a graphic designer. Its title, *An Artist's Apology*, occupied the center of the posters in all-capital letters.

I walked into the gallery to, of course, find nothing in it except lots of art-opening attendees in their various costumes. I saw many who had joined the boycott and many faces that I knew. Here they all were, I thought, the WE. My mistake was clear, a totalizing cut in half, so perfect I was barely bleeding. No one allowed themselves to look at me for very long. Everyone, it seemed, had made an agreement not to give me too much attention, but whether it was out of charity or malice or indifference, I didn't know. Meaning is slippery, and yet it keeps slicing into you.

I started toward the booze. A young Black man was dressed regally in a white suit behind the bar with a white linen napkin draped over his arm.

"Welcome, ma'am, good evening," he said and bowed deeply. "How can I be of service to you this evening?"

"You don't have a martini, do you?"

"As a matter of fact, we do," he said. Wow, Iris had pulled it out. He started pouring expensive liquors into a shining tumbler.

"I'll have one too." Her voice was next to me.

I turned and it was her, her big bun done perfectly, like when I'd first seen her. She was dressed in a gray suit like a Hitchcock hero. Her lips were painted a serpentine emerald.

How did she get out of the basement?

She smiled at the bar man, and when he set the two drinks

down, she handed me mine graciously, with a little smirk on her face. I took it dumbly.

She clinked her glass against mine—they were real glasses, Iris really had gone overboard—and made the shrewd grin I'd seen on her face before.

"And what do we say?" she said in a singsong voice.

I didn't, then did, remember.

"Sisters," I said.

Hanne nodded, sipped her drink, and then hooked her arm in mine, leading me into the great, crowded room.

We had not been there long when I recognized Iris Wells, dressed in an old-fashioned tuxedo, also with a white linen napkin draped over one arm.

Ah, I get it. She's dressed like the house butler.

I saw her look at me and then at Hanne, and I understood something about where exactly I was located. I was the background, not the foreground. No one looked at me outright, and I knew that in the days that followed, my name wouldn't pass through mouths or brains, my execution was not important. I was like any other artist that had had a brief moment and was then forgotten.

Iris came close to us with an exaggerated, syrupy passivity, then made a flourish of a bow and, while bowing, spoke toward the floor in a raised voice that put pressure on each word and made it go very slowly.

"I'm afraid I must apologize," she said.

"I'm so,

so very

sorry.

I am *deeply,*
        terribly sorry.
                I *do apologize.*"

People near us glanced over, and their glances got caught.
Some of them looked me in the eye as if they were staring into
bottomless water. I felt my frail smile slide away. I started to
grip Hanne's elbow, but she tugged her arm free, of course she
wasn't with me. Iris kept speaking toward the floor, bending
over at the waist, and her voice was getting louder. I saw her
knees starting to bend.

Now more people were looking over.

"I'm horribly sorry,
        so *deeply,*
                appallingly,
                        pathetically,
                                very, so very
                                        sorry."

The voice was of a pretend child, an adult flapping the head
of its ventriloquist dummy, but stuck in a nightmare where
time is huge with punishment.

I tried to breathe. I had the vengeful thought that one *can*
exist without belonging anywhere, but my collapse into this
was pathetic and I knew it. My arms hung at my sides. Hanne
stood with the trust in herself that I'd never had. It was trust-
ing gravity to never fail, it was deciding who of your children
deserved to live because of their capacity to murder you.

The force of Iris's voice was rising, and I knew that in a few
moments, she'd be screaming. I could see her intended affect,
the repetition of the words turned them into nonsense: *sorry
sorry sorry sorrysorrysorry.* Soon, everyone in the room would

be running it through their minds just what exactly it meant to say sorry, how the sincerity smears into irony, spite, the emptiness of apology, how it means nothing, does nothing, but how we want so many times to hear someone say it to us. I got it, I saw what she was doing, directed at me, the hostility the back of her head was shoving at me, and how by saying it to me as a gesture of aggression, she was attaching me to it, I'm so sorry to ruin you this way, or am I?, and also as a suggestion she was offering for me to say, I was the artist of the title, here are the words you might be looking for. Here is what you might like to try on. This would look good on you, Master. Thank you, Master. You're welcome, Master.

Her knees were bending so much that she was now squatting, curled over with her head between them. I wanted desperately for her to stop. The room was understanding that the show had started, this was the work, like it was picking up a scent. I was aware that people were looking at me and Iris and then back at me and my white girlfriend and that this arrangement of different colors was evidence of my trespass and what I deserved because of it. I tried to shape my face so that it would appear that I understood my complicity but was not obliterated by it, even that I'd wanted it, but what kind of face can mean that?

In the doorway, across the room, I saw Yves appear. He caught my eye but frowned, seeing the people gathering around me, hearing Iris's shouts but not seeing her. He didn't move toward me. A version of myself that I'd been trying to make huge now shrank. It started saying *no, no, no* in a tiny voice, hiding somewhere inside me.

Now she was on her hands and knees.

"I'm so very *sorry*!
    I *do apologize*!
        Please *forgive* me!
            I am *begging* you!"

Her back was flat and parallel with the floor. Her mouth released the words, but since we couldn't see her mouth, it seemed that the words were products of the quivering her body was doing.

"*I'm sooo sorry!*" She was really wailing now.

How long would this last? Shining coins of sweat accumulated on the floor beneath her face. I thought of the payment for the ferryman that must be included with your corpse.

The boundary of my skin felt sentient, it was adjudicating me without my consent, I should stop it, I was inflicting pain on Iris, I had to do something. *I'm sorry, I'm sorry.*

Then there was a quick movement to my left, and I turned to see Hanne moving toward Iris. All the heads near us turned, too, and then the heads behind those started to turn. I could see a few noses from rows back being poked into the air for a better view. My heart started to strike against my ribs. Hanne's face wore the expression that I hoped my face was making, but she was genuinely in herself: innocent, guilty.

She took two steps and was upon the artist on her hands and knees. Finally, she'd seen me, seen how I needed to be rescued, and this was how she would do it.

She bent her knees, lowering herself to what was almost a squat, and put her ass on Iris's back so that she was sitting on her as if Iris were a chair.

I saw phones being raised.

Hanne drew up one of her legs to cross it with the other, clasping her hands around her knee so her posture was dignified. Iris paused her screaming, and I think she was baffled, which was an evil bliss, the room seemed to devour this fact like it was an addict waiting for its fix. Iris tried to adjust her hands and knees on the floor, but Hanne's weight seemed too much, so there was only some twitching.

Then Iris started to try to shout again, but her lungs were squashed, so the sound was overpowered. I felt something huge and simple, a sting and an itch, fill up the space, and then the lewd catharsis that we all felt crash on us when Hanne said, almost levitating as Iris twitched beneath her, in a poised, perfect voice, "Good doggy! Good doggy, that-a-girl!"

"Now,

who's a *good dog*?

Who's a good *dog*?"

ANAMORPHOSIS

the quality of the execution of a painting; an artist's
characteristic handling of the paint.

Yves was waiting on the street. He glanced up from his phone when he saw me, and his expression was empty, then he turned away. I staggered toward him. My face was numb, but it somehow hurt. I'd insisted that she was art—I'd made her art. Mother of the monster. I stopped and clutched my stomach, and the pavement got close to my face with a suddenness that felt sorcerous, violating the laws of physics.

I saw Yves's shoes start to walk away.

"Wait," I grunted. "I think I'm gonna throw up."

His footsteps stopped, and the silence they made conveyed his annoyance.

I squatted and kept my head close to the ground, staring at Yves's shoes.

He said my name. His tone was neutral.

I tilted my chin up to see. A halo of soft blue light had appeared around his head, his hair, and I felt hot water come to my eyes. My throat contracted and I tried to speak, but my mouth just hung there. I thought of him impersonating the Virgin Mary: You are safe with me, but please don't fuck up anymore. Please stop fucking up. I wanted him to speak, to say perfect words that would fix me.

"Come on," he said, putting his phone in his pocket and starting to walk away. "We'll miss our bus."

People were already there, in the flat. Yves held my hand and pulled me up the stairs. I could hear music coming from behind the door, I envisioned the vases of flowers and bottles of alcohol that Yves had prepared to celebrate. I felt vacant, skinned, I was scared of the ablation of myself. We stood outside the door. He turned to me and pushed his fingers into my mouth. I sputtered.

"Take it," he said. "It's Klonopin."

I crushed it between my teeth and stared into his black eyes.

He stared back. He was dressed in blue.

"Someone once told me that no one you look at is worth it," Yves said, what is unsayable in the other person is what resounds in you. Then he said, "I'm so mad about it."

I pitched forward to throw up again, but nothing came out, and instead I just hung my head there. "I'm so sorry, Yves, I'm so sorry."

"Jesus, let's not start that again." He pulled me upright. "It was probably for the best, anyway."

"What?"

"Obviously it wasn't going to work out."

"What do you mean? Why didn't you tell me?"

"Huh?" He frowned with confusion and blinked a few

times, then smirked. "No, babe, *Theo*. Theo and me. I should have known better. It would always only be a fling."

"Oh," I said. "Right."

"Is it working yet?" he asked me.

"What?"

"The pill," he said and tapped the scar on my forehead.

"Oh, uh—"

"God, that show was blunt, too blunt—what was Iris thinking? Too much fame, I guess. The pressure got to her. And why would she care so much about *you*?" The way he said *you*, like he was speaking about a bit of dirt on his shoe. "Though I heard someone say that the performance would happen around the first scab that arrived, didn't matter who. Tough luck, mermaid."

"Yves—I can't—I just—Hanne—what Hanne did—" I felt my mouth wiggle without me.

Yves held up his hand to silence me.

"Listen now. I need to say something. You need to sort yourself out. And I don't think I can be around you anymore while you're doing it. You *know* this already. I'm also pissed that you're making me say it like this. If I were younger, I'd eviscerate you right now, then walk away and never talk to you again. But I'm so tired. I'm just—*tired*. I can't fight anymore—about anything, least of all this shit. A fucking white girl being a white girl?" He looked up at the ceiling, shaking his head and closing his eyes. I thought of how he had never found the little Mary.

He sank into some deep place in himself for a minute and then finally opened his eyes and saw me.

"I love you." He said my name. "I do." His face released us. "But—damn." He fixed the cuffs of his shirt and placed his hand on the front door. "Now, come on, I want to find some-one to carry my sorrow, if only for tonight."

He smiled at me, a broken, automatic reflex, and led me through the door.

BLEEDING

also known as "wet-on-wet."

It was the after-party, so people, now on their third or fourth or fifth drink and released from the script of public appearance, allowed themselves to look at me with full-faced stares. One man, wearing drag makeup but dressed in jeans and a baggy T-shirt, pushed out his bottom lip in a performance of pity when I walked by. A woman I didn't know came up beside me and patted my shoulder. "It will get better. Just give it a few years so everyone forgets you," she said.

I went into the kitchen, away from the crowd, I couldn't bear to see the care Yves had gone to decorating for the party. Behind me, there was a small group huddled around the table being told a story by someone I didn't see. A smooth, masculine voice flowed out from the center of the group. He kept his voice at a volume like he was speaking into one person's ear, his mouth close enough to their head that his breath fell on the innocent skin of their neck, and it recalled a sensation I'd had before. The air in the room was sincere, all the attention on him. No one noticed me, so I faced the sink, my back to them, and listened.

"I'd just moved out of the house with my soulmate—or who I thought had been my soulmate before she left me for her rich boss—and back into the tiny, rat-infested cabin where I'd lived before I met her. I was reading—ah, what was it?—I think *Infinite Jest*—by a torch lantern, of all things, that, of course, attracted mosquitoes. And I had to wear socks all the time to keep off the ticks."

"Wait, I'm sorry," someone interrupted him. "Where was this again?"

"In LA—Altadena. It's sort of in the hills behind LA."

My thoughts wrinkled into my hometown.

"The cabin," the voice kept going, smoothing me out, "was near a little creek that was mostly dry, but it had just rained— this was in the winter, the only time it rains in LA—so it was muddy and there was some water in it. We were on a pretty steep hill with trees all around. My roommate worked nights, and he had this really old dog. She had been a great dog—smart, calm, the perfect size, kind of, like, footrest-sized"—people laughed—"and her name was Lolita after his favorite novel. She really was special. But she was fucking old at that point, I mean, totally deaf, blind, had trouble walking, and had these disgusting little tumors, like, bulging out of her fur, with, like, a crust on them—you know, an *old* dog. I kept asking my roommate what he was gonna do with her, but he just couldn't, you know, couldn't put her down. She was like his wife. That's what he'd say. 'You can't kill your own wife!' Which gives you a sense of what kind of weak-hearted romantic he was, but never mind." More laughing. "So there I am, reading fucking *Infinite Jest* by fucking candlelight to keep from crying about my dumb breakup, it's almost midnight, the frogs in the creek are croaking this seamless buzz, like"—he stopped to hum—"and then comes this tiny cry of an animal. It sounded like a thought in the back of my own head. It came again. I sat up. Again, this hollow, small yip"—he made his voice squeak—"and I called for her, 'Lolita!' even though she couldn't hear me. So I stumbled out the back, down toward the creek. I'm out there in the dark, and I just, I just"—he paused—"hated everything—the entire world, everyone in it, God, or whoever the fuck. Hated it all. And I'm calling her name, and it's just going from my mouth into the trees. I start to cry out, 'Talk to me! Tell me where you are!' to a deaf, blind dog in the fucking dark. Talk to me, talk to me? Like I'm one of those people trying to get God to listen to them. And then I fell into a fucking patch of poison oak and then into some mud near the creek, and one of my knees hit me in the throat, so I'm just, like, *so* miserable—hitting myself in the throat with my own knee?—Jesus!—but then . . . I saw her. The cataracts in her eyes caught my flashlight. They were these glowing, milky orbs. I scrambled down to her and blurted out, 'I've got you, baby,' but I don't know, when I said it, it was a lie. Like, what am I saying? What if I can't save her? What then? She was so terrified—I could feel her heart beating inside her—I mean, she's blind and deaf. She's squirming and terrified. I pull harder, and she makes her little noise again, and then, I don't know—I got her free. Her body went limp, like, with total trust in me. I carried her up the hill, and then we collapsed, both of us, on her disgusting, crusty cushion in the living room. Her front paws and my hands were all bloody, and we were both covered in mud. My wet pants turned warm under her body like she'd peed on me, or maybe I'd pissed myself, I don't know. I wrapped her in a towel and we sat there together, both shaking for I don't know how long. When I woke up the next morning and went in to check on her, she was still alive, and—and—I don't know—I don't how to describe it to you, but—it felt like a miracle."

The people around the voice collectively exhaled. There was clapping and a few cheers. I turned around in a trance, the voice running through me, and found my eyes on Jonah. Everyone else was staring at him too. My high pooled in my head, and I felt soft waves of surrender shiver down my body. He turned his head and spotted me. Something scattered his expression, both graceless and discerning. He turned and addressed the group abruptly—"I think I need a cigarette now, you'll have to excuse me"—then he grazed me again with his eyes and, hooked, I followed him to the balcony.

The air outside was strangely cold. Jonah looked me up and down flagrantly, one side of his mouth slyly pulled up, as though I were a work of art he'd just bought. My world shrank to the pinpoint of his eyes, they were small and black and hard, little hawk's eyes on me. He drew them up from my tits to my face, cocked his head, and said, "Well, now, there you are."

His voice was still at the level it had been during the story, like his mouth was very close, pouring through me with an easy intent, hunting for something it could already see. What was his real name again?

Suddenly, his body was against mine. "Congratulations," he said. "You have been very brave."

"Brave?" I said.

"You have been very brave," he repeated, and I felt a burning thread between us snap awake.

"But I think I was the opposite," I said.

"And the title is wonderful," he said. "Very clever. I love that it means more than one thing."

I put both hands on his chest and then on his face. It had turned warm somehow. I must have been distracted.

"A psychic said it to me." I heard my voice coming softly out of me, as if on furred paws. "On the street. She hit me. She was my mother."

I touched his earlobes, his neck, and he turned his head a little, slowly, from side to side, to give more of himself to my fingers.

"I get it, I get it," he was saying. "I get you. I'm someone who gets you."

"You don't even know me," I said.

"But you attracted me," he said, and his face was open and forgiving. "We are what we desire."

I tried to see if he had pores in the crack of his nostrils, but his skin was smooth and perfect.

"Why are you talking to me?" I said, but it only made him laugh without a sound.

"Because I understand you better than you understand yourself."

"But how?" I was saying. "Tell me how."

"You wanted to prove something, to stand outside of it and point it out." He made one of his fingers long and caressed my nose. "You said, 'Here, look at this, everyone, look here.'"

Now he pushed the finger into my ear, and his thumb held my jaw. I started to say no. No.

"But you forgot that the best way to get someone to look at something is to tell them *not* to look at it."

"But I don't want to look at it!"

"You're lying. You lied to yourself, and you kept on believing the lie. You thought you had no power, that the powerful are the only ones who can give it to you. But that's the trick. That was your mistake. Power is not an object you can take or give."

"But I *am* an object. And I only made a world of more objects. I failed."

"Power is in the space *between* objects," he went on. "It's the thing that *makes us* objects." His face made a smile, and then, finally, he was ugly. "It's everywhere, and it's free. It just shape-shifts. The kind I have is different than the kind you have, but it's still power."

"But I like giving mine away." I let myself become small.

"I know, babe." And then he was touching my mouth. "Remember what I told you about meaning." And he was lifting strands of his own hair away from my eyes, my scar, I could smell his mouth, its stench of cigarette and alcohol, and then his chest pressed into mine. He changed the smile, becoming even more gentle, fatal.

"You do know you deserve to exist, right?" he probably said.

"Wait," I said. "Wait!" I was startled to hear my own voice. "Let me show you something. I've found the place."

"You found it?" he said, like he'd already been there.

"Yes, let me show you," I said again. "I want you to see it—it could be for you too. We can share it. It could be for both of us."

I wanted to rest my face in his palm. My head felt weighed down. I bent it forward. I kept saying, "I want you to see," sometimes ending the sentence with *it* and sometimes with *me.* He tenderly turned my head in his hand, from side to side, and spoke to me, asked me things, I don't remember what exactly, but his soft coat was around my shoulders and he was pawing playfully at my head, and then we were in a cab, sailing through the city as the lights streaked into lines of gold and his sibilant voice breathed into my ear, falling on my innocent neck.

SOTTO IN SU

there is an adage that all portraits are self-portraits.

We arrived at the building of my studio, though it seemed to be standing on its own. It was dark, and the taxi was gone. We pushed into the courtyard. I held Jonah's hand and skipped, pulling him along.

"We have the same shoes!" one of us said, but that couldn't have been true.

"You look like someone from one of my paintings," the other said. This was true.

I turned back and saw him smiling at me and, when I remember it now, I'm sure we both giggled because I remember the sound ringing up the walls of the building and into the sky. I saw there was a great moon above us. I tried to point it out, but now the little door was open, and he was pulling me inside, so I left it out there, the ball of light, like a present I'd brought but forgotten to give him.

We tumbled down the stairs together, a couple just married, entering our good, new home.

Inside, it was warm and black and fleshy as always, and I lay down, spread out my limbs, and sighed, gratified, belonging here. I heard Jonah's shoes scraping the concrete, coming close to my body and then going away, the noises leaving imprints on my skin that glowed.

Then there was a clicking sound and sharp, searing light flooded the room. The light chafed me, burning away my safety. I opened my eyes, squinting. The cashmere scarf had been unwound from his neck, had he been wearing it tonight? I saw that he had an exquisitely thin, breakable neck, like a girl's. For the first time, I noticed that he had sea-green eyes like me. Not hard little black ones. Jonah. What was his real name again?

"Am I saying your name right?" I asked. "Jonah?"

"Tsk, tsk," he said.

"It's Jonah, right?"

"It's not." His voice was hard.

"I'm sorry," I said. "Jonah."

"It's not my fucking name," he said. His voice rattled through the room. The space was irradiated, the light bulb bare and buzzing above us. I could see the wood beams and hollowed-out walls and crooked ceiling and it was small, the room, very small and cramped and dirty. I longed for him to turn off the light. He had taken my magnificent place away with one flick. But I liked that he could do that, change everything, change what I wanted.

"I want what you want," I said.

"I know," he said. When his bare shoulders touched the insides of my thighs, I felt that my skin was clammy, and it reminded me of who I was, making me tractable as he spread me apart. He used his middle finger in time with his tongue, someone gracious had taught him that, I thought, and my head skimmed along with the stirs and waves and fell away.

"Um." His face was in front of mine, yanking me out of my swim. "Um, I think you—you have an infection." He touched his tongue against the roof of his mouth, tasting me.

My hands shot down to cover myself. "I'm sorry," I said. "I thought it was gone by now. I thought I was cured."

"You thought you were what now?"

"I'm"—I felt myself move beneath him—"I'm sorry, Jonah— uh. Sorry."

"Oh." He clucked his tongue. "But I can't hear you. *What* are you?"

Something flitted across his eyes, a magnanimity that was all for me.

"You're sorry?" he said with a simpering command at the end. "Hmm?"

I wanted to play this game, my voice was pure when I sang, like a lullaby, "I'm sorry I'm so sorry Jonah Jonah Jonah."

Yes. I did. I want to. You are not afraid. But it's okay if you are afraid. That's how you know.

He pulled at my wrists and pressed them into the floor. His body pushed mine into the concrete, not brutally but with certainty, because he knew me. I was completely naked somehow, clothes blinked on, then off, he was a magician. In the light from the one bare bulb, his face transformed to the ugly man's eating his birthday cake, the cake that Hanne had fed herself, profane, yes, but the opposite and a murk of both. I reached for him.

"That's right," he said.

"What are you?" he said.

301

"This is what you need," he said.

"Yes," I said. "Yes, I am."

He put his fingers in my mouth, pressing down the rows of my bottom teeth, opening my mouth too far, it felt good, all that mouth with something in it. My jaw cracked as he stretched it open, there was the elemental desire to be torn apart. There was the crushing smell of my antifungal cream, though I hadn't been using it for months, maybe it was in me now forever, it had become my smell.

"I want you to sing for me." His voice was majestic in its roughness. "Come on and sing for me."

I did, and he sang too.

I was on my hands and knees, and he wore a suit with a black jacket and pants, his cock rising out of the opened fly. Had I told him to wear that? "Keep singing, dove," he said as he hooked two fingers into the flesh of my face, like the bit of a bridle. He started to ride me from behind, my knees rubbing on the ground, the skin breaking, not quickly but slow and thick, my skin was not thin, I was not so easily torn, which made me want to be even more. There was a blow with each word, I felt it deep in my belly, my liver, a prayer, thud, thud, thud. "Come on, now. Coo for me. Coo like a bird. You're not a dog, are you?" "No, you are," I said, and the sounds coming out of me deepened into guttural moans. At these, he moaned, too, like I'd called him the right name, finally. He slapped me, my ass, my face: "Don't you like me like that? Isn't that what you want?" The slaps stung with reward. "Yes," I said, yes, yes, yes, I have never said no to anyone I've loved. "What do you want?" he asked me again, but he knew, and soon he stopped asking it with words. "I'm in charge," I told him. "Of course," he said, and the mocking was sweet. He'd stop every few moments to kiss my nose, my eyebrow, and he'd make that commanding but patient noise, "Hmm?" as though he were speaking to a small child. His eyes became drenched with plain, eager need, I'd never seen anyone so happy. He bent his face toward me and bit my shoulder with an insistent, grateful mouth. He said my name in a tiny voice, then said it again to my neck, and again in my ear, do you see me, do you see me, too, and at the sound of it, my name making him so pliant, so poor, I came. My face filled with heat, and then there was a lot of wetness on it, wetness everywhere, it dripped down my neck. I reached up to touch my forehead, my hand hopping because of his thrusts, and when I felt my scar covered in slime, I pulled my hand away, sure to see it glazed with red. But my scar was still sealed. My hand was covered in water, my own ordinary, sacred water. I opened my mouth to wail a big, ecstatic cry of come and absolution, Jonah! A name liberated that belonged to neither of us. But I didn't have enough breath, and only a little moan of awe seeped out. Seeing this small struggle of mine got him to his end. He rolled off in his suit jacket and pants, cock withered and harmless. The ground was cold as a tomb, but he lay sprawled in comfort.

He reached for me. "Mmm," he sighed. "You were great."

I snorted through my nose.

He opened his eyes and became serious. "No, really. Take the compliment. I'm giving you a compliment."

I let myself look deeply into his eyes, into where they began, and I thought I saw a sort of road tunneling into him, to the originary place of his trust in himself, a trust he extended to the world, and, I saw now, he was giving that inceptive trust to me too.

"Thank you," I said.

"You're welcome," he said. He closed his eyes. "Come here," he said and held his arm out, offering his armpit as a pillow.

He was asleep in moments. I sat up and looked around the room, then back at him. He looked aimless, beyond innocence or guilt. I kissed his forehead. I could've killed him by pushing my thumb through his fontanel.

On my way out, I climbed the stairs carefully, hoping not to wake him, and, as I closed the door, I wondered at its big lock, the one I'd needed earlier today, what had still been today, but I didn't need it anymore. I saw a line of silver gleam by my feet. It was my laptop and the microphone with its cord coiled around it. She had left it there, tucked inside the door, so as not to get stolen. She hadn't wanted it, hadn't wanted me. I laid my hand on the laptop's cold metal. It was inert under my palm, but it was still mine. I picked it up, walked out into the street, and hailed a cab. The sky was getting light.

STILL LIFE

if it seems that one has to fight to obscure the underpainting,
it is a sign that it was not done properly.

I woke up alone. My bed and bedroom and flat were entirely mine and empty of Hanne, as though she'd never been there. It was late afternoon, and I stood at my stove, making coffee, feeling mute and clean. My hands and knees and shoulders and hips were scraped raw and skinless and red, and they felt washed in vacancy, a kind of grace.

It took me a little while to decide what to say to Hanne. Finally, I texted: *Well that was a good night wasn't it? Sorry for leaving you there. I showed up and I thought I deserved a treat.*

Several days passed before she replied: *I didn't notice you leave with anyone. Think I'm done. Take care.*

Soon after, I got a text from my bank, alerting me that my balance was below the limit.

TROMPE L'ŒIL

the management of light and shade in a picture.

My truck was where I'd left it, but I couldn't get used to the light. It had me from every angle and also from inside, like oppression. On my first day home, standing in my studio, surrounded by my work, I pushed the power button on my phone—the little phone icon had a bright red 42 above it of missed calls, the message icon with 103 unread messages, and the email icon a swollen 2,789 unread emails—until the screen went black, and then I opened the lid of the trash can under the sink and dropped it in.

I bought a cheap, dumb phone and gave the number to no one. I added Marina's number and Yves's. Just in case.

I took the contents of my studio, armful by armful, out back to the dumpster. I dropped them all in, paints, brushes, some that Marina had given me long ago, pushing at the expensive paper of my drawings, shoving in paintings, rolls of linen, stretcher bars, all of it, all of me. I set the furniture out front on the sidewalk, and it was gone in an hour. I did the same to my apartment, taking truckfuls of stuff to the thrift store, my fancy designer coffee table, the one I'd spent so much on in the wake of my first show, got scratched as I took it out of the truck. I left the keys in the mailbox and didn't say goodbye to anyone. There would be trouble, thirty-day notices, but I wouldn't be around to know them.

I'd heard some years ago that Joan Raíz had left her post at the museum. I'd not known why, we were not friends enough for me to know the details, but the story that went around was that she'd renounced the art world completely and made her exit to the mountains somewhere. I emailed her, asking if I could call her. I said it was urgent, that I needed to escape and I needed her help to do so. A few days passed, and then she wrote to say she'd drive into town the next day and would call me from a pay phone. I gave her my new number.

Joan now lived at a place called Old Rosa, which had been a commune until the 1980s, called Rio Rosa in its heyday. Old Rosa is wedged between two hills behind Santa Cruz, which is on the coast in the middle of California, though the forest from the north has crept down, its redwood trees crowding toward the beach, making the air cool and damp. As I drove north, I thought of Santa Cruz, a small university town that doesn't have the heat or dirt or scale of LA and has always felt to me like a quaint, forgotten village stuck in a fairy tale, where women live in cottages swarming with cats and men wear necklaces made of garbage they've found on the beach.

The stars streaked my vision on the drive, but as I pulled onto the dirt road toward her cabin, my aura became merciful and dimmed. Stepping out of my truck, there was a big, wet smell of ocean and stale sand, but after a few moments, I could detect the scent of cool air trapped in the shade of mountains. It reminded me, startlingly, of the smell of tears.

"So, well, hello there!" she was saying, trudging up the dirt driveway. Her body was smaller, thinner, and more skeletal than I remembered and dressed not in red but in brown. Her head was smooth, save for a thin layer of fine hair, like the down of a baby, and small and round, the color of a bright cloud, and the skin on her face had drooped into jowls. She opened her bony arms to hug me, and I saw that her fingers were hooked with arthritis. When I put my hand on her back, she was skin and bones, frail but alive. There was nothing about her that I recognized, except for the expression on her face, that fist-like smirk, and then she said, "Well, fuck, you look completely different, dearie!" Joan rubbed both of her crooked hands on my head. "Bald like me!" I'd shaved it before leaving Berlin. She saw me frowning at her and said, "I died of cancer, dearie, didn't you know?"

"I'm sorry, I didn't."

"Oh, sure, I may be a feisty dead woman, but let me tell you, there are four thousand ways to die and still be alive. The doctors—those fuckers—they *gave* me six months to live, although it seems like they did the fucking opposite! But then, lo, since I'm a tough little bitch, I just kept on being alive, I'm doing a very long dying, you see. And it all changed, all of it—see, dearie, it was like a ball of candy that tastes different on the inside than on the outside. You try to suck on it, but all that happens is you drool on yourself. You drool on yourself, with your jaw aching, for fucking ever. See, I'm talking about *life*, dearie. You flick your tongue at the big ball that's been shoved in your mouth, you lick it little by little. Then, when you finally lick through the sweet outer skin, there's a blast of sour that stains your tongue. And that's your reward, dearie. That's your fucking reward!" She spat a sound at me that I realized was laughter only after she started slapping her thighs as though she were playing bongo drums.

Now I saw that this was Joan Raíz, the Joan Raíz I'd known, and it wasn't shocking but somehow more correct, that she would come to be drawn like this.

She pointed at my bags. "You're going to have to carry those yourself, missy. Even though I've still got all my teeth, I *am* pretty dead."

I followed her down the little hill. There were heaps of seashells everywhere amid many plants growing in cracked pots and little sections of garden fenced off with sagging chicken wire. Her cabin slumped to one side, half-hidden by a bougainvillea bush twice as tall as a man. The front door was not so much a door as half a piece of plywood with some window screen stapled around a flimsy frame. Joan opened the door, which let out a screech, and disappeared into the cabin.

I reached for the door, which screeched again, and stepped inside. It was dark and cool, and I couldn't see anything except decisive squares of windows letting in green light that had the effect of shadows. The darkness in front of me moved, and then Joan was standing there with smoke coming from her fists. "Close your eyes, palms out," she said. "I need to cleanse whoever's gotten stuck to you." I tried to demure, but: "Palms out," she insisted, digging at me with her elbows. "Like the Virgin Mary, come on!"

I stood as she told me. She waved her hands around and blew the smoke in my direction. It smelled clean, like the bars of wood soap that had been in my Berlin flat. "In the name of the great mother, Isis," she said, and then a bundle of words about protection, guidance, and service rumbled around me. It didn't smell like the sage my mother used to burn, and for that I was grateful, I didn't want to be reminded of my mother now. I opened my eyes to see Joan swishing both arms through the air, holding little sticks on fire in her bent hands.

It was shaded in the cabin, almost chilly, and without the fizz of stars, I felt a mild ache in my eyes as they worked to adjust to the shadow. All the windows were crowded with leaves from the trees outside, like we were inside a dirty aquarium, but the interior of the cabin felt austere, a convent or prison cell. It was one long room about the size and shape of a school bus, with a kitchen on one end that consisted of a crooked stove, a countertop, and a short box of a refrigerator, and on the other end of the room was a loft with a mattress on top of it. In the middle was a table and two mismatched chairs, a black iron potbelly stove, a large stack of what looked like old newspapers, and—I counted—seven piles of seashells that came up past my knees.

"Now, don't be alarmed, dearie, I'm crazy, but I'm not that crazy," she said. "My shaman told me to make a shelter for good spirits, and when you're practically dead, you find that your openness to weird shit is quite . . . well, yes. Keeps the place protected. Right! So—toilets!"

She pushed open the screen door, which screeched louder than the last two times, and went outside. "Up here, we water the earth, so pick a place, any place, and pop a squat."

"Okay."

"Not what you were expecting from the former queen of the castle, is it? Well, let me tell you, art won't save you from dying, no, no, it won't, no, no, no." She thwacked her lumpy hand on my shoulder in quick, hard Morse code with the no's. "So, for shitting, you use the bathhouse up the road, past Old Bob's place, but remember: you bring your own paper and you take it away. The plumbing is kaput"—she spit on the dirt to punctuate—"so no flushy nothing but poop. Got it?"

I nodded and she patted my shoulder again, yes yes yes.

"Okey dokey, now, for the bed where *you're* going to die." She laughed and turned to go behind the cabin, following a meager dirt path around the side. In the back was a claw-foot bathtub tucked into a tiny glen of bay and datura trees, perched at an angle, and surrounded by more patches of garden and heaps of seashells. "Wash yourself here. You're welcome to my soaps, homemade and homeopathic, obviously, I can't be using any chemical shit because death, death, death!" She punched the air in Morse code with the deaths and kept walking, disappearing into a crowd of trees. I followed her, and we came upon what looked like a readymade shed that you could buy at a home improvement store. I peeked inside to see a cot the size of a child wedged into the structure. There was no room for anything else, when the door was shut the walls closed in around the cot. In one corner was a small triangular shelf, and I saw that she had put a branch of datura in a jar of water on it. The jar had a ruined sticker for pickles.

"You can fling your stuff up there"—she pointed to the hammock hung across the ceiling—"and good thing it's summertime, missy, so you'll have a little light at night. It's just too complicated to run electricity out here, and anyway, I never have visitors. This isn't really meant to be a guest room, obviously. Old Bob was throwing her away, so I took it. You never know who might show up needing a bed for a night, especially when you live in the land of the dead."

Again she tapped my shoulder, but I couldn't tell if it was for no, no, no, yes, yes, yes, or death, death, death.

IMPASTO

*for centuries, the pigment that was the most coveted and
expensive was used in depictions of the Virgin Mary
because it was the most coveted and expensive.*

The next day, I slept very late, rolling in my cot under a heavy
film of dreams. The sunlight baked the sides of my shed, and
the air inside was stifling. I finally woke up, mouth dry and
spluttering, like I'd been tossed ashore after a shipwreck.

I came into the cabin and sat at the table. Joan must have
heard me because she soon entered. "Morning, dearie! Or
should I say, good afternoon!" She started making breakfast
for me.

"Joan, you don't have to do that," I said.

"Nonsense!" She started slicing tomatoes from the garden
and cracking eggs into a skillet. "We've gotta stick together, us
gals. Ain't no one else gonna be there for you or for me." She
brandished her big kitchen knife above her head. "Take this
knife: it's been through *two* husbands!" She started cackling.
"Ha, ha, ha! I do love a double meaning."

The trees outside breathed with the soft wind, their leaves
whispering against the windows of the cabin. It was August,

and the light was golden. It had been just over a year since Hanne appeared in my life. I touched my face, trying to concatenate what was living in me now with myself.

Joan put one plate in front of me and one for herself. We ate together while she talked about astrology, how the Saturn–Pluto conjunction wouldn't be pretty.

There were faint shouts of someone calling from outside. "Hello? Hello!"

"Who could that be?" Joan muttered. "You invite someone?"

"I don't have anyone," I said.

Joan got up and went through the door. I heard her footsteps crunch up the driveway. A few minutes later, they returned, and I heard someone with her. She came into the cabin. A young man with black hair in a ponytail followed her. He was tall and svelte and wore an expensive-looking garment, white and crisp and folded, like a piece of origami. He had high cheekbones and curved eyes, and I knew he was half Asian, like me.

"Dearie, it isn't for me," Joan said. "And it isn't for you. It's for that person who uses your name." She was holding a business card and squinting at it. "This is Danh."

"It's pronounced Yan," Danh said.

"Ah, of course! Yan," Joan was nodding. "Yan, Yan, Yan."

"Hello," I said. I stretched out my hand and realized I was still wearing my sleeping T-shirt and nothing else, and I hadn't brushed my teeth.

"Hello," he said, taking my hand. His wrist was slender and delicate. "I'm here on behalf of Colomba Espinosa."

"Who?" I said.

317

Joan swatted my shoulder. "The art collector, dearie."

Colomba's cage of birds and room of fish aquariums and four black dogs flared in my memory.

"Oh, Colomba," I said. Then I remembered how she'd grabbed my arms, attacking me for looking like her mother. "How—how is she?"

"She sends her regards," the man said. "She has purchased your show." He reached into the folds of his garment and pulled out an envelope, handing it to me.

"How about that!" Joan swatted me again.

"She what?"

"She has purchased your show." He pointed to the envelope. "*Your Love Is Not Good.*"

"Colomba always did have the best taste." Joan nodded.

I opened the envelope and saw a check for the total amount, minus Silke's cut. There was also a copy of the contract, stating that each piece in the exhibition must be given to the mother of the buyer. Colomba's grand signature was scrawled at the bottom. I wondered how they—Silke, Alexandra—had found me. I'd told no one where I was going.

"And I am supposed to give you this." Danh now pulled another smaller envelope from his clothes.

Inside was a small piece of rectangular paper the color of dark honey, the same color Colomba was wearing when I met her, the color of her skin and hair. On the card, she'd written, *She could be you.*

There was the photograph, small, old, black-and-white, the same one she'd dug out of her desk and thrust at me last summer. It was of a woman with a round, moonlike face with small eyes. She looked at the camera with an awake, guarded expression, bearing it. I turned the photograph over. Someone had written on the back in pencil, *Mama*.

Danh leaned forward slightly, a bow, and said, "Good day." He turned and went out of the cabin, though the door didn't shriek this time, and we listened to his footsteps disappear into the mountain air.

I knew, then, that Hanne was wrong. It's not that we are all of us children. It's that none of us are mothers.

SILHOUETTE

the outline of someone or something.

"Why don't you come on a walk with me today, dearie," Joan says. "You should get to know the land if you're going to be staying, which I'm assuming you are." She clears our plates and does not leave room for me to respond. "The monastery burned down in the 1980s, and the ruins are still up there. The trees were so motivated after the burn, they went a little hog-wild. It's all uphill one way, which makes the walk back down a dream. We can just sail down it, it'll feel like the wind is helping us. Ha, for once! Always makes me think of Sisyphus. I tell you, dearie, once you've died and come back to life, his repetitive ass gets even more profound."

She pushes through the door, and it makes its screech. I can hear her talking as she walks up the driveway.

When I catch up to her, she is still talking.

"Ah, there you are, dearie—well, as I was saying, I knew what was coming, I knew it. Yesterday, an hour before you were to arrive, I saw a dead baby bird in the road." She reaches out and yanks a piece of yarrow off its bush and flails it around like a severed limb. "Very puffy, very dead, dearie. Takes one to know one." She stops walking and raises her arm to point the twig at my center. "Bad omens," she says. "I hate to be so blunt, dearie, but you know me, I'm all-knowing, I'm from the beyond, and I can see it floating behind you. It's stuck to you like a color, like you're dragging your own universe behind you instead of living in this one."

My black cube distends.

"You're wrong, Joan. It's not behind me," I say.

"Bad omens," Joan says and keeps walking, as though she hasn't heard me.

"Joan!" I shout, my voice big with the blackness.

She stops and spins around. "Jesus, dearie, what?"

"My mother. I need her. I need her with me. I want to invite my mother here. To live with us. I called her last night and invited her here."

"How did you get cell service?"

"I sent a message through the air. I'll keep calling until she hears me."

"So, you didn't call her?" Joan says.

"I did! Just not with the *phone*. I need her! She's wise—she's so brave! She's the one who is free."

"Okay, dearie, okay."

"We haven't spoken in years," I say. "I—I abandoned her."

"Well." Joan clucks her tongue. "It was probably a mutual abandonment. You abandoned each other."

"I don't think it works like that with family," I say.

Joan makes a beastly noise that is a laugh. "Family is the *only* thing that works like that. If you can't abandon your family, then who?"

"Are we a family?"

"Yes, dearie, we are. But this will change," she says with joy, "and it will be scary."

"I don't know if my mother is dead. I mean, she is. I never saw her actually die, but I watched it happen my whole life. Her death was my life. She loved me more than anything. I was her life!"

"Of course you were, dearie."

"She gave me her entire life. And I did nothing but lie with it!"

"Oh, dearie—"

"The biggest lie I've ever told—the biggest lie I've ever told was—"

"—there, there, honey, it's okay—"

I crumple over, as if trying to hide from the sky. I can't breathe.

"Just breathe, honey," Joan says.

"The biggest lie—" The heaves start. "The biggest lie I've ever told"—I see Marina, old, bloated, yellow from her desecrated liver, her desecrated life, on the floor, alone in a murked room with a broken mattress, she is dying alone, she is calling my name, and I hear it, me, I hear *her*—"was that I told my mother I loved her."

My forehead touches the dirt.

It was a lie. It was a miracle. It was a lie.

Joan walks toward me and kneels, puts her arm around my shoulders.

"Mothers are hard to love, dearie, it's true. It'll be okay. We'll be together, all of us, like a family. You, me, and your mother, who's welcome to come in whatever form she wants to take."

"I've never said no to anyone I loved, Joan. I've never said no!"

"But dearie, it seems to me like you *did* say no to her."

I look at Joan through my tears.

"It sounds like you *did* love her, dearie, *because* you said no."

A horizon detonates, a hole that makes the world different.

"Because," I murmur. "Because."

"Yes, dearie, because."

"But will she come now?"

"It may take some time. The dead have their own work to do."

"I can't feel her anymore. She's not close to me anymore."

"That means she's finally in you, dearie. She's *finally, really* in you."

"I told her no." I laugh. I feel warm all over. "Joan, I told her no!"

"Yes, you did, dearie. It's how mothers and daughters love each other. They tell and tell and tell each other no. Didn't you know that?"

"No," I say, but as I say it, I realize that I also know it. "Yes," I say.

Joan nods and helps me stand and pushes us forward on the path. I follow her, climbing up.

The ruins of the old monastery are tucked into a dark glen. The trees fold over the site, masking all the light. Charred walls of brick are overgrown with moss and vines, and the air smells worn with time and earth. It feels as if no living thing has been present here for thousands of years, but there are tags of graffiti and the ashy graves of campfires, dotted with cigarette butts, beer cans, used condoms.

Joan disappears into the maze of ruins and trees, and I stand still. The truth is alive in me like a skeleton wet in its marrow. The walls of my body have thickened and closed around me, sacred and complete, and I am protected, like a worm that's been touched and recoils its whole body, it is tiny, just a little thing, and the lightless, miracleless universe is all around us now, it says my name, which is its own name but also my mother's name, they link themselves together, a kind of braid attaching itself to itself in pairs, circling in loops, holding each other, which means that it also carries itself, ouroboros, a bite, a hunger, a need, a mirror, who we are for each other, to each other, about, and because of.

I feel my black cavity behind my head, my own universe, my very own, I feel it move, and now I am staring at it, face-to-face, it reaches into me and sees me, and I see it back, I am looking right back.

And then I forgive my mother everything.

A NOTE ON SOURCES

The information about ultramarine blue and Isabelline white is from *The Secret Lives of Color* by Kassia St. Clair.

Several of the painting and visual art terms are taken from the "Painting Glossary" on the "Encyclopedia of Art" website at www.visual-arts-cork.com.

The essay that Silke quotes about art world boycotts is "Are Boycotts the New 'Collective Curating'?" by Sergio Edelsztein, published online in *On Curating*, Issue 26, October 2015.

I must credit Hannah Black, Ciarán Finlayson, and Tobi Haslett, the writers of "The Teargas Biennial," published in *Artforum* on July 17, 2019, as well as the interview with Forensic Architecture, published in *Artforum* on May 13, 2019. I began writing this novel in 2014 and finished the first draft in 2017; in that draft and many after it, until mid-2019, my character Iris's statement was framed as a callout on social media. When the momentum of protest started to ignite around the 2019 Whitney Biennial, I was moved to reframe Iris's statement as a boycott because of the powerful eloquence and articulation in these pieces.

ACKNOWLEDGMENTS

Much of this book was written on unceded Chumash, Tongva, Kizh, and Tataviam territories. I also want to acknowledge that a land acknowledgment is not the same as land.

Thank you to all the friends who read or heard about scraps of this thing before it was anything and told me it might be something. I especially could not have made it without Willem Henri Lucas, Silvia Rigon, Lauralee Pope, Millie Wilson, AM Kanngieser, Ken Baumann, P. Staff, and Christopher Weickenmeier. The Sagittarian armchair bombast in my chart is especially grateful to Jordan Lord and Hana Noorali, who gave me their most critical Virgoan minds to enumerate all the ways I was speaking nonsense. To Seren Sensei: thank you for the time and feedback you gave to this book, and thank you for your friendship over the years; I've learned so much from you and your work and I can't wait for that to keep being true for the rest of our lives (Buffy forever!). Thank you to Josephine Shokrian for the critical feedback on Zinat. Thank you to Joey Cannizzaro, who read and thought about this with me for years, who pointed out that the basement was very important, and whose cackling way with words is what I want to be close to all the time. Thank you to Mark Allen for that conversation all those years ago, where I said I might try to write a "real novel" and you said that sounded like an interesting idea. Of course, these acknowledgments would not be complete without a nod to the enemies and exes—lotta important instigation, them.

In 2016, Emma Borges-Scott emailed to ask if I might be working on a book and this changed everything because I wrote back to say . . . yes? Emma, I am grateful to you always for the hours and years of care that you put into this with and for me. Thank you to the editors of *The White Review* and *Black Warrior Review* for publishing early excerpts. Thank you to Suzy, Sho, and Anthony, for letting me read some new and naked nervous pages in *xii–xix, a talk series, An Invitation of Sorts*. Thank you to Caroline Sydney for the notes that made the book so much better. Thanking my agent Clare Mao would not be complete without mentioning that she is a superhero who keeps saving the world, and, when I say the world, I mean me. Clare, I cannot believe my good fortune that you're on my side—best email- and life-wingwoman ever. Thank you to Anne Boyer, who responded to my whining about the publishing world with the simple "have courage," something I look to her again and again to learn how to do. Then she said, "send it to Jeremy," and, well, that was that. I will never forget the feeling after that first meeting with Jeremy M. Davies and Stefan Tobler because it felt like meeting old friends. Oh, hey, there you are. Thank you to Jeremy, for being guilty of gnostic turpitude and always commenting in the margins the very motivating "meh." Thank you to everyone at And Other Stories for bringing this into the world, and for your commitment to practicing an ethics toward a better one. Thank you to Whitney Hubbs for being so damn cool. Thank you to Ian Byers-Gamber for that author photo. I mean . . . Thank you to all the brilliant colleagues—Caren Beilin, Mattilda Bernstein

Sycamore, Harry Dodge, Lucy Ives, Legacy Russell, and Bryan Washington—and to the booksellers who gave their endorsements to the book.

I am blessed and amazed to count among my friends some of the most fearless, talented, cute as hell, visionary, and fiercely kind people on earth—I wouldn't have made it without any of you: Vivian Ia, Henri, Chandler, Silvia, Sarah, P., Lauralee, Joey, TT, Jordan and Shoumik, Amalle, Park, Carolyn, Ame, Ken, Isabelle and Jon, Christopher, Sam and Tega, Matt and Cindy, Seren, Nora, Pamila, Neve and Tony, Alexandra, Charlotte, Hana and Lynton, Lara, Jessa, Janice, Henry and Merkel, Mark and Emily, Asher, Nick and Dez, Hannah, Vivian and Three, Uma, Megan, Jessika, and N. My sixth-house sun would suggest that the most important one of all is my cat, Penelope Schwarzweißer Flausch. The Taurus in my chart requires me to give all the credit to my hair. And the stellium in Scorpio holds that it is my death who deserves the most attention.

The dedication of this book is about chosen family as much as blood family and those who've joined the ancestors; but my Cancerian moon, which I inherited from my mother and her sister and their mother, and my Capricorn which I inherited from my father and his mother, would not let me sleep without saying again that this, and me, would not be if not for the ones I come from. They taught me almost everything, and what they didn't was just as important, because it's what I had to teach them. To Mom, Dad, Auntie, Grandma Genny and Grandpa Bud, Grandma Connie, and Rhi—this, the whole enchilada.

And then there's Johannes, without whom none of it, and definitely not all the good stuff.

THIS BOOK WAS MADE POSSIBLE
THANKS TO THE SUPPORT OF

Aaron Bogner
Aaron McEnery
Aaron Schneider
Abbie Bambridge
Abigail Gambrill
Abigail Walton
Ada Gokay
Adam Lenson
Adrian Kowalsky
Ajay Sharma
Al Ullman
Alan Hunter
Alan McMonagle
Alasdair Cross
Alastair Gillespie
Albert Puente
Alec Logan
Alex Pearce
Alex Pheby
Alex Ramsey
Alex von Feldmann
Alexandra Kay-Wallace
Alexandra Stewart
Alexandra Tammaro
Alexandra Webb
Ali Riley
Ali Smith
Ali Usman
Alia Carter
Alice Wilkinson
Aliya Rashid
Alyssa Rinaldi
Alyssa Tauber
Amado Floresca
Amaia Gabantxo
Amanda
Amanda Astley
Amanda Dalton

Amanda Fisher
Amanda Geenen
Amanda Read
Amber Da
Amelia Dowe
Amine Hamadache
Amitav Hajra
Amy and Jamie
Amy Bojang
Amy Hatch
Amy Tabb
Ana Novak
Andra Dusu
Andrea Barlien
Andrea Oyarzabal
   Koppes
Andreas Zbinden
Andrew Kerr-Jarrett
Andrew Lahy
Andrew Marston
Andrew McCallum
Andrew Place
Andrew Rego
Andrew Wright
Andy Corsham
Andy Marshall
Angela Joyce
Angelina Izzo
Anita Starosta
Ann Morgan
Ann Rees
Anna-Maria Aurich
Anna Finneran
Anna French
Anna Gibson
Anna Hawthorne
Anna Milsom
Anna Zaranko

Anne Edyvean
Anne Frost
Anne Germanacos
Anne-Marie Renshaw
Anne Withane
Annette Volger
Anonymous
Anthony Cotton
Anthony Fortenberry
Anthony Quinn
Antonia Lloyd-Jones
Antonia Saske
Antony Pearce
Aoibheann McCann
April Hernandez
Arathi Devandran
Archie Davies
Aron Trauring
Asako Serizawa
Ashleigh Phillips
Ashleigh Sutton
Ashley Marshall
Audrey Holmes
Audrey Mash
Audrey Small
Aurelia Wills
Barbara Mellor
Barbara Spicer
Barry John Fletcher
Barry Norton
Beatrice Taylor
Becky Matthewson
Ben Buchwald
Ben Schofield
Ben Walter
Benjamin Judge
Benjamin Pester
Beth Heim de Bera

Betty Roberts
Beverley Thomas
Bianca Jackson
Bianca Winter
Bill Fletcher
Birgitta Karlén
Bjørnar Djupevik Hagen
Blazej Jedras
Brendan Dunne
Briallen Hopper
Brian Anderson
Brian Byrne
Brian Callaghan
Brian Isabelle
Brian Smith
Brianna Soloski
Bridget Prentice
Brooke Williams
Buck Johnston & Camp
    Bosworth
Burkhard Fehsenfeld
Caitlin Halpern
Caitriona Lally
Callie Steven
Cam Scott
Cameron Adams
Camilla Imperiali
Campbell McEwan
Carl Emery
Carla Castanos
Carole Burns
Carole Hardy
Carole Parkhouse
Carolina Pineiro
Caroline Kim
Caroline West
Carolyn A Schroeder
Catharine Braithwaite
Catherine Campbell
Catherine Cleary
Catherine Lambert
Catherine Tandy

Catherine Williamson
Cathryn Siegal-
    Bergman
Cathy Sowell
Catie Kosinski
Cecilia Rossi
Cecilia Uribe
Chantal Wright
Charlene Huggins
Charles Fernyhough
Charles Kovach
Charles Dee Mitchell
Charles Rowe
Charles Wats
Charlie Levin
Charlie Small
Charlotte Furness
Charlotte Middleton
Charlotte Ryland
Charlotte Whittle
Chenxin Jiang
China Miéville
Chris Gribble
Chris Johnstone
Chris McCann
Chris Potts
Chris Senior
Chris Stergalas
Chris Stevenson
Chris Thornton
Christian Schuhmann
Christiana Spens
Christine Bartels
Christine Elliott
Christopher Fox
Christopher Stout
Chuck Woodman
Ciarán Schütte
Claire Mackintosh
Claire Riley
Clare Wilkins
Clifford Wright

Cliona Quigley
Colin Denyer
Colin Hewlett
Colin Matthews
Collin Brooke
Conor McMeel
Courtney Lilly
Craig Kennedy
Cynthia De La Torre
Cyrus Massoudi
Daisy Savage
Dale Wisely
Dan Vigliano
Daniel Axelbaum
Daniel Coxon
Daniel Gillespie
Daniel Hahn
Daniel Hayes
Daniel Jones
Daniel Oudshoorn
Daniel Sanford
Daniel Smith
Daniel Stewart
Daniel Syrovy
Daniela Steierberg
Darcie Vigliano
Darren Davies
Darren Wapplington
Darryll Rogers
Dave Lander
David Anderson
David Cowan
David Greenlaw
David Gunnarsson
David Hebblethwaite
David Higgins
David Johnson-Davies
David F Long
David Miller
David Richardson
David Shriver
David Smith

David Smith
David Thornton
Davis MacMillan
Dawn Bass
Dean Taucher
Debbie Pinfold
Deborah Green
Deborah McLean
Declan O'Driscoll
Denis Larose
Denis Stillewagt &
  Anca Fronescu
Derek Sims
Derek Taylor-Vrsalovich
Devin Day
Dietrich Menzel
Dinesh Prasad
Dirk Hanson
Domenica Devine
Dominic Bailey
Dominic Nolan
Dominick Santa
  Cattarina
Dominique Brocard
Dominique Hudson
Dornith Doherty
Dugald Mackie
Duncan Chambers
Duncan Clubb
Duncan Macgregor
Dustin Haviv
Dyanne Prinsen
E Rodgers
Earl James
Ebba Tornérhielm
Ed Smith
Edward Champion
Ekaterina Beliakova
Elaine Juzl
Elaine Rodrigues
Eleanor Maier
Elena Esparza

Elif Aganoglu
Elina Zicmane
Elizabeth Braswell
Elizabeth Cochrane
Elizabeth Coombes
Elizabeth Draper
Elizabeth Franz
Elizabeth Leach
Elizabeth Seals
Elizabeth Sieminski
Elizabeth Wood
Ellen Beardsworth
Emiliano Gomez
Emily Walker
Emma Barraclough
Emma Bielecki
Emma Coulson
Emma Louise Grove
Emma Post
Emma Teale
Eric Anderson
Eric Weinstock
Erin Cameron Allen
Ethan Madarieta
Ethan White
Evelyn Eldridge
Evelyn Reis
Ewan Tant
Fay Barrett
Faye Williams
Felicia Williams
Felicity Le Quesne
Felix Valdivieso
Finbarr Farragher
Finn Brocklesby
Fiona Liddle
Fiona Quinn
Fiona Wilson
Fran Sanderson
Frances Dinger
Frances Harvey
Frances Thiessen

Frances Winfield
Francesca Brooks
Francesca Hemery
Francesca Rhydderch
Frank Curtis
Frank Rodrigues
Frank van Orsouw
Freddie Radford
Gail Marten
Gala Copley
Gavin Aitchison
Gawain Espley
Gemma Bird
Genaro Palomo Jr
Geoff Thrower
Geoffrey Cohen
Geoffrey Urland
George McCaig
George Stanbury
George Wilkinson
Georgia Panteli
Georgia Shomidie
Georgina Hildick-Smith
Georgina Norton
Gerry Craddock
Gill Boag-Munroe
Gillian Grant
Gillian Stern
Gina Filo
Gina Heathcote
Glenn Russell
Gloria Gunn
Gordon Cameron
Gosia Pennar
Grace Payne
Graham Blenkinsop
Graham R Foster
Grant Ray-Howett
Gregor von dem
  Knesebeck
Hadil Balzan
Hannah Freeman

Hannah Jane
  Lownsbrough
Hannah Rapley
Hannah Vidmark
Hans Lazda
Harriet Stiles
Harry Plant
Haydon Spenceley
Hazel Smoczynska
Heidi Gilhooly
Helen Berry
Henrike Laehnemann
Hilary Munro
Holly Down
Howard Robinson
Hyoung-Won Park
Ian McMillan
Ian Mond
Ida Grochowska
Ines Alfano
Ingrid Peterson
Irene Mansfield
Irina Tzanova
Isabella Livorni
Isabella Weibrecht
Ivy Lin
J Drew Hancock-Teed
JE Crispin
Jack Brown
Jacqueline Lademann
Jacqueline Vint
Jacquelynn Williams
Jake Baldwinson
Jake Newby
James Avery
James Beck
James Crossley
James Cubbon
James Elkins
James Higgs
James Kinsley
James Leonard

James Lesniak
James Portlock
James Ruland
James Scudamore
James Ward
Jamie Mollart
Jamie Veitch
Jan Hicks
Jane Anderton
Jane Bryce
Jane Dolman
Jane Leuchter
Jane Roberts
Jane Roberts
Jane Willborn
Jane Woollard
Janet Digby
Janis Carpenter
Janna Eastwood
Jasmine Gideon
Jason Lever
Jason Montano
Jason Timermanis
Jason Whalley
Jayne Watson
Jeff Collins
Jeff Fesperman
Jeffrey Davies
Jen Hardwicke
Jenifer Logie
Jennie Goloboy
Jennifer Fain
Jennifer Fosket
Jennifer Harvey
Jennifer Higgins
Jennifer Mills
Jennifer Watts
Jennifer Yanoschak
Jenny Huth
Jenny McNally
Jeremy Koenig
Jeremy Morton

Jerome Mersky
Jerry Simcock
Jess Wood
Jesse Coleman
Jessica Kibler
Jessica Laine
Jessica Mello
Jessica Queree
Jessica Weetch
Jethro Soutar
Jill Harrison
Jo Keyes
Joan Dowgin
Joanna Luloff
Joao Pedro Bragatti
  Winckler
JoDee Brandon
Jodie Adams
Joe Huggins
Joel Swerdlow
Johannes Holmqvist
Johannes Menzel
John Bennett
John Berube
John Bogg
John Carnahan
John Conway
John Gent
John Hodgson
John Kelly
John McWhirter
John Purser
John Reid
John Shadduck
John Shaw
John Steigerwald
John Walsh
John Whiteside
John Winkelman
Jolene Smith
Jon Riches
Jon Talbot

Jonas House
Jonathan Blaney
Jonathan Fiedler
Jonathan Gharraie
Jonathan Harris
Jonathan Huston
Jonathan Ruppin
Joni Chan
Jonny Kiehlmann
Jordana Carlin
Joseph Darlington
Josh Sumner
Joshua Briggs
Joshua Davis
Joy Paul
Judith Gruet-Kaye
Judy Davies
Judy Rich
Julia Foden
Julia Von Dem
  Knesebeck
Julian Hemming
Julie Greenwalt
Juliet Swann
Jupiter Jones
Juraj Janik
Justine Sherwood
KL Ee
Kaarina Hollo
Kaelyn Davis
Kaja R Anker-Rasch
Kalina Rose
Karen Gilbert
Karin Mckercher
Katarina Dzurekova
Katarzyna Bartoszynska
Kate Beswick
Kate Carlton-Reditt
Kate Shires
Kate Stein
Katharine Robbins
Katherine McLaughlin

Kathleen McLean
Kathrin Zander
Kathryn Burruss
Kathryn Edwards
Kathryn Hemmann
Kathryn Williams
Katia Wengraf
Katie Brown
Katie Cooke
Katie Freeman
Katie Grant
Katy Robinson
Kay Cunningham
Keith Walker
Kelly Hydrick
Ken Geniza
Kenneth Blythe
Kenneth Masloski
Kenneth Peabody
Kent Curry
Kent McKernan
Kerry Parke
Kevin Winter
Kieran Rollin
Kieron James
Kim Streets
Kirsten Hey
Kris Ann Trimis
Kristen Tcherneshoff
Kristen Tracey
Kristin Djuve
Krystale Tremblay-Moll
Krystine Phelps
Kurt Navratil
Kyle Pienaar
Kyra Wilder
Lacy Wolfe
Lana Selby
Lara Vergnaud
Laura Ling
Laura Murphy
Laura Pugh

Laura Rangeley
Lauren Pout
Lauren Rosenfield
Lauren Schluneger
Laurence Laluyaux
Lee Harbour
Leeanne Parker
Leelynn Brady
Leona Iosifidou
Liliana Lobato
Lily Blacksell
Lily Robert-Foley
Linda Jones
Linda Lewis
Linda Milam
Linda Whittle
Lindsay Attree
Lindsay Brammer
Lindsey Ford
Lisa Dillman
Lisa Leahigh
Lisa Simpson
Lisa Tomlinson
Liz Clifford
Liz Ketch
Lorna Bleach
Lottie Smith
Louise Evans
Louise Greenberg
Louise Jolliffe
Louise Smith
Lucie Taylor
Lucinda Smith
Lucy Moffatt
Luiz Cesar Peres
Luke Murphy
Lynda Graham
Lyndia Thomas
Lynn Fung
Lynn Grant
Lynn Martin
Madden Aleia

Madison Taylor-Hayden
Maeve Lambe
Maggie Redway
Malgorzata Rokicka
Mandy Wight
Marco Medjimorec
Margaret Jull Costa
Margaret Wood
Mari-Liis Calloway
Maria Ahnhem Farrar
Maria Lomunno
Maria Losada
Marie Cloutier
Marijana Rimac
Marina Castledine
Marina Jones
Marion Pennicuik
Mark Bridgman
Mark Reynolds
Mark Sargent
Mark Sheets
Mark Sztyber
Mark Tronco
Mark Waters
Martha W Hood
Martin Brown
Martin Nathan
Mary Addonizio
Mary Angela Brevidoro
Mary Clarke
Mary Heiss
Mary Wang
Maryse Meijer
Mathias Ruthner
Mathilde Pascal
Matt Carruthers
Matt Davies
Matt Greene
Matthew Black
Matthew Cooke
Matthew Crossan
Matthew Eatough

Matthew Francis
Matthew Gill
Matthew Lowe
Matthew Scott
Matthew Woodman
Matthias Rosenberg
Maureen and Bill
   Wright
Max Cairnduff
Max Longman
Max McCabe
Maxwell Mankoff
Meaghan Delahunt
Meg Lovelock
Megan Wittling
Mei-Ting Belle Huang
Mel Pryor
Melanie Stray
Melissa Beck
Melissa Stogsdill
Meredith Martin
Michael Bichko
Michael Boog
Michael Dodd
Michael James
   Eastwood
Michael Floyd
Michael Gavin
Michael Schneiderman
Michelle Mercaldo
Michelle Mirabella
Michelle Perkins
Miguel Head
Mike Abram
Mike Schneider
Mike Turner
Miles Smith-Morris
Miranda Gold
Mme Vita Osborne
Molly Foster
Morayma Jimenez
Morgan Lyons

Moriah Haefner
Nancy Garruba
Nancy Jacobson
Nancy Langfeldt
Nancy Oakes
Nancy Peters
Naomi Morauf
Nargis McCarthy
Nasiera Foflonker
Natalie Ricks
Nathalie Teitler
Nathan McNamara
Nathan Weida
Niamh Thompson
Nichola Smalley
Nicholas Brown
Nicholas Rutherford
Nick Chapman
Nick James
Nick Marshall
Nick Nelson & Rachel
   Eley
Nick Sidwell
Nick Twemlow
Nicola Cook
Nicola Hart
Nicola Mira
Nicola Sandiford
Nicolas Sampson
Nicole Matteini
Nicoletta Asciuto
Nigel Fishburn
Niki Sammut
Nina Nickerson
Nina Todorova
Niven Kumar
Norman Batchelor
Norman Carter
Norman Nehmetallah
   Invisible Publishing
Odilia Corneth
Olga Zilberbourg

Olivia Clarke	Phoebe Millerwhite	Robert Sliman
Olivia Powers	Pia Figge	Robert Weeks
Olivia Spring	Piet Van Bockstal	Robert Wolff
Paavan Buddhdev	Prakash Nayak	Roberto Hull
Pamela Ritchie	Priya Sharma	Robin McLean
Pamela Tao	Rachel Adducci	Robin Taylor
Pankaj Mishra	Rachael de Moravia	Rodrigo Alvarez
Pat Winslow	Rachael Williams	Roger Newton
Patrick Hawley	Rachel Beddow	Roger Ramsden
Patrick Hoare	Rachel Belt	Ronan O'Shea
Patrick McGuinness	Rachel Carter	Rory Williamson
Paul Bangert	Rachel Van Riel	Rosalind May
Paul Cray	Ralph Jacobowitz	Rosalind Ramsay
Paul Ewing	Raminta Uselytė	Rosanna Foster
Paul Jones	Ramona Pulsford	Rose Crichton
Paul Munday	Rebecca Carter	Rosemary Horsewood
Paul Myatt	Rebecca Michel	Rosie Ernst Trustram
Paul Nightingale	Rebecca Moss	Royston Tester
Paul Scott	Rebecca O'Reilly	Roz Simpson
Paul Segal	Rebecca Parry	Rupert Ziziros
Paul Stallard	Rebecca Rosenthal	Ruth Edgar
Pavlos Stavropoulos	Rebecca Shaak	Ryan Day
Pearse Devlin	Rebecca Starks	Ryan Oliver
Penelope Hewett Brown	Rebecca Surin	SK Grout
Perlita Payne	Renee Otmar	ST Dabbagh
Peter Aiau	Renee Thomas	Sally Baker
Peter and Nancy Ffitch	Rhiannon Armstrong	Sally Warner
Peter Gaukrodger	Rich Sutherland	Sam Gordon
Peter Griffin	Richard Dew	Samuel Crosby
Peter Hayden	Richard Ellis	Samuel Stolton
Peter McBain	Richard Gwyn	Sara Bea
Peter McCambridge	Richard Harrison	Sara Kittleson
Peter Rowland	Richard Mansell	Sara Unwin
Peter Wells	Richard Shea	Sarah Arboleda
Petra Stapp	Richard Soundy	Sarah Brewer
Phil Bartlett	Richard Village	Sarah Lucas
Phil Curry	Rita Kaar	Sarah Manvel
Philip Herbert	Rita Marrinson	Sarah Pybus
Philip Warren	Rita O'Brien	Sarah Stevns
Philip Williams	Robert Gillett	Scott Chiddister
Philipp Jarke	Robert Hamilton	Scott Henkle
Phillipa Clements	Robert Hannah	Scott Russell

Sean Johnston
Sean Kottke
Sean Myers
Selina Guinness
Serena Brett
Severijn Hagemeijer
Shannon Knapp
Sharon Dilworth
Sharon McCammon
Shaun Whiteside
Shauna Gilligan
Sian Hannah
Sienna Kang
Simak Ali
Simon Malcolm
Simon Pitney
Simon Robertson
Sophie Rees
Stacy Rodgers
Stefano Mula
Stephan Eggum
Stephanie De Los Santos
Stephanie Miller
Stephen Cowley
Stephen Eisenhammer
Stephen Pearsall
Stephen Yates
Steve Chapman
Steve Clough
Steve Dearden
Steve Tuffnell
Steven Norton
Stewart Eastham
Stu Hennigan
Stuart Grey
Stuart & Sarah Quinn
Stuart Wilkinson

Sue Davies
Sunny Payson
Susan Edsall
Susan Jaken
Susan Wachowski
Susan Winter
Suzanne Kirkham
Sylvie Zannier-Betts
Tallulah Fairfax
Tara Roman
Tatiana Griffin
Taylor Ffitch
Teresa Werner
Tess Lewis
Tessa Lang
The Mighty Douche
   Softball Team
Theo Voortman
Therese Oulton
Thom Keep
Thomas Alt
Thomas Campbell
Thomas Fritz
Thomas van den Bout
Tiffany Lehr
Tim Kelly
Tim Nicholls
Tim Scott
Timothy Moffatt
Tina Rotherham-
   Winqvist
Tina Juul Møller
Toby Halsey
Toby Ryan
Tom Darby
Tom Doyle
Tom Franklin

Tom Gray
Tom Stafford
Tom Whatmore
Tracy Bauld
Tracy Birch
Tracy Lee-Newman
Tracy Northup
Trent Leleu
Trevor Latimer
Trevor Wald
Turner Docherty
Val Challen
Valerie O'Riordan
Vanessa Dodd
Vanessa Fernandez
   Greene
Vanessa Heggie
Vanessa Nolan
Vanessa Rush
Veronica Barnsley
Veronika Haacker
   Lukacs
Victor Meadowcroft
Victoria Goodbody
Victoria Huggins
Vijay Pattisapu
Vikki O'Neill
Wendy Call
Wendy Langridge
Will Weir
William
   Brockenborough
William Orton
William Schwaber
William Schwartz
Zachary Maricondia
Zoe Thomas